14,000 Reasons to be Happy

and

Other Stories

by Luann Krull

Copyright © 2014 by Luann Krull
All rights reserved. No part of this book may be used or reproduced in any manner without the written permission of the author except for brief quotations.

Contents

Running 5
Silent Night 25
Nightshift 38
Wondrous 59
Woodworking 76
Genomes, Quarks and Brahms 100
You Be You 123
The Neighbor Who Gave Me Flowers 144
The Ride 158
This Good Life 170
14,000 Reasons to be Happy 202
The Family of Camden High 226
The Big Burp 284

Running

First published in "Oasis" 1995

Most mornings Denise gets up in the dark, and puts on shorts and a T-shirt. Sitting at her small kitchen table, with all apartment windows open, she listens to the hum of traffic from Highway 59. She drinks a glass of water and wipes the sweat from her forehead. Summer is just starting, but Houston has been hot for months. When the sky begins to change from black to violet blue, she puts on socks and sneakers and goes out and runs. While running, she knows where she is and who she is. She thinks about her life, and about Tony.

Denise met Tony Levanti last spring in Johnson's hydrology course. In a rare burst of friendliness and goodwill (Tony looked dismal, burdened by the mountainous reading list) Denise showed him where Johnson kept the reading material, and where the secretary hid the duplicating machine counter. Then

She took him to her office, in the basement, where the walls are shelves of dusty rocks, and where half-hearted theses projects—ideas at one time destined to augment the eminent theories—sit abandoned and neglected, like toys a week after Christmas.

"Neat," Tony said, looking around enviously. "In the midst so much important activity."

"You think so?" Denise said with surprise. "You really think so?"

Denise admires Tony's new car and his superbly pressed jeans, and when they went to happy hour, in his part of town, he treated. The free tacos and fried potato skins rated as one of her better meals of the year.

But the basis of their relationship, Denise believes, is competition. At Secal Geophysical, where they work for the summer, Denise and Tony compete to see who can process the most seismic lines without dropping any traces. At the university, they compete for grades, and in private, they compete for who can be cruelest. A love-hate relationship, Denise admits, but a relationship nevertheless. Still, she misses her old boyfriend, Louis. She wonders what he's up to.

Having been brought up on fairy tales: "The Three Bears," "Hansel and Gretel," "Dumbo," Denise has undying faith that people ultimately do good, although their procedures may vary. Thus she believes that if she gets to know Tony better, his more elusive and nobler qualities will emerge. It's like cutting a rock, knowing how to angle the rock to enhance mineral presentation.

Later that summer Tony has Denise over for dinner. No sooner does Tony fling open his apartment door, than an odor of garlic wafts out into the hallway. The table is craftily set for two: china plates, real silver, red candles. A premeditated effort to bestow an aura of intimacy and romance, despite the neighbor's booming stereo.

The apartments may be new, but the walls are still cardboard. Tony's apartment is in the swinging singles part of town, Southwest Houston where the complexes are massive behemoths of two or three hundred units. They come with blue pools, central air-conditioners, and wrought-iron banisters that guard each private balcony.

The trees were demolished en masse in favor of expedient construction. Every few blocks stands a bar with blinking neon lights that advertises dancing and two-for-one drinks. The sweet alcoholic drinks give Denise terrible hangovers. Tony has wisely reserved judgment on her part of town.

Tony pulls out her chair, and pours the wine. With both hands, he lifts a heavy Corelleware dish out of the oven.

"It's good, Tony," Denise tells him as she flips another meat and cheese filled shell smothered in tomato sauce onto her plate. She doesn't know its name, although she's aware the food has a name, and that it required substantial work: all those shells to stuff. He watches her closely, as if each jaw movement contains a hidden message for him, as if her pupils expand for some reason other than food. Denise eats and eats, more than she should, as if she has been fasting, which is partially true: for the past year, except for the happy hour and a professor's retirement party, she's been living on tuna, peanut butter and apples.

"You look so thin, so pale, Denise. I figured I'd make something hearty."

Denise stops her full fork midair. "I haven't been eating meat because of the heat." The fork completes its journey, and Denise chews and swallows. "It's impossible to eat meat in Houston in July, especially if you're running. May I?" She indicates across the table with her fork.

"I know you hunger for me."

Tony's had two glasses of wine, which Denise decides is his excuse for silliness.

"Another shell, Tony. Do you mind if I take another shell?"

After dinner they sit on his couch, which matches his plaid chairs. It's modest, but solid. It's been a long time since Denise had sat on anything that smelled so fresh.

"You know Sally?" Tony says. "She wears the peasant dresses? I used to go out with her." He slyly moves his arm, so she can feel the heat of it on the back of her neck. He has the longest arms and the longest legs of anyone she's ever known.

Denise nods. The peasant dresses are long and dark and they make Sally appear flatter than she really is. But what is most striking about Sally is her persistent smile. Even if Secal Geophysical's computer crashes and she has lost a day's worth of data, she smiles: a huge, so-what smile. She draws smiley faces or she plasters yellow smiley stickers on her keypunch sheets and seismic sections. A message to the geophysicists, Denise initially thought, to enable them to better find oil in Prudhoe, and therefore justify their salaries, which is triple of the technicians'.

"I was going out with her when I met you."

"Great." Denise scans the neat and orderly apartment for evidence of smiley faces. Maybe they are hidden beneath the coffee table. Surreptitiously her hand investigates. Nothing, not even any gum, but that's because Tony is such a meticulous housekeeper. Feeling none, and seeing none, she doubts any significant amour between Tony and Sally. She imagines that for her romantic dinner for two, Tony made thin noodles; spinach noodles in a delicate sauce that they washed down with Kool-aid.

"When I told her it was all over, she grabbed my arm, and pleaded: 'Don't leave me!'"

Tony demonstrates with Denise's arm, squeezing hard, as if he's getting back at her for her earlier lack of enthusiasm. Denise shows no alarm, refusing to be hostage to this. She realizes this may absolve her from something more strenuous later on. And this may be his only chance: the arm-wrenching is about as intimate as they've gotten in the past month. Denise isn't complaining.

"But you did," Denise says, grimacing in pain. "You left her. Sally. Poor Sally." Denise attempts one of the Sally smiles, but it doesn't come out because her teeth are clenched together.

"She wanted to marry me!" Tony suddenly releases her arm. He shrugs as if to say Sally were one of many, a discard, reject, relegated to the accumulating pile of scrap girlfriends. He is Tony Levanti: Mr. Stud of the Gulf Coast. He closes his dark eyes, perhaps, Denise thinks, savoring the memory of smiley Sally.

Denise imagines the furtive groping as the strings on Sally's dark peasant dress are unlaced, or perhaps, in a fit of uncontrollable fervor, broken, and her airy voice repeating: "I'm okay; You're okay." She imagines the smile Sally willing gives as they Become One.

Denise rubs her injured arm and is about to grill him about the smiley faces when he says: "I went out with a divorcee once."

Denise nods and inches away from Tony. Her arm still hurts. She's not sure why he's confessing, or if the confessions will get more interesting as he drinks more wine, or if he will indeed say what he really wants to say. Usually he does most of the talking, and she does most of the drinking. Then he sulks. Denise never went out with a divorced man, at least not that she's aware of. Denise can count her romantic liaisons on one hand.

"Divorcees know what men like."

"Is that supposed to make me feel insecure?" Denise says contemptuously.

He gives her a sardonic smile.

"Okay, what do men like?" Denise decides the wine is too sweet. She wishes she had a cold beer, like a Lone Star. She wonders briefly, what Louis is up to. It is her fault, she decides; she told Louis he needed to get a job.

"Come on, Hoffman."

She looks at Tony as if he is an adolescent on his first date. Even through his glasses, which are a little thick, his eyes protrude.

"They have experience. You don't have to tell them every move."

"I guess it must get pretty exhausting," Denise says, "giving instructions all the time. Do this, don't do that. A little more here."

Tony gives her some room and says: "Aren't you drunk yet?"

"No," Denise says with perfect sanguinity. Apparently he's watched her at the department parties.

Tony sighs with defeat, goes into the kitchen to uncork another bottle. Denise appraises his few books: undergrad geology texts and "The One-Hour Orgasm."

On the back cover of "The One Hour Orgasm" is a color photograph of the authors, a middle aged couple. Denise imagines Tony and she as middle-aged couple: unkempt hair, flowing clothes to hide the bodies bloated by extravagant pasta and sweet wine. The woman, wearing something black and lacy and see-through says: "It's a matter of good communication." Denise fans the pages looking for smiley faces or other inviolable signs (like yellow magic marker in his hydrology text) that the book has been thoroughly studied. Only the pages with diagrams are worn, but this gives Denise the evidence she needs: "The One Hour Orgasm" is his Bible. She slips the book back before Tony returns.

He's clearly exasperated. His face puffs out, his eyes are a little mean, and protrude a little more, as if harboring poison darts. Denise knows he doesn't know this, about the eyes.

The alleged seduction is costing too much, and taking too much time. Tony, an orderly and organized person, would be in bed right now if it weren't for Denise's antics. The original idea, as Denise imagined it, was to have dinner then watch "Saturday Night Live." As the elaborate Italian shells settle in Denise's stomach, she feels less right about being here. The two red candles which Tony has moved to the coffee table, burn with reverence, as if anxious to witness something important. Denise watches the candle flames lick Tony's eyes, even through the glasses. He's waiting too, unsure how to proceed. Once he'd told her he'd never met anyone like her before, but he had not meant it as a compliment. Yet Denise likes "Saturday Night Live." It's a highpoint of her week. When Louis left, she gave him the TV. Louis still calls. He calls when she least expects it and usually when he's drunk. She asked him for his number, but he couldn't give her one: he joined the Marines. He's still in town, somewhere. Denise can sense it, and is waiting for him to suddenly appear.

"You like this wine?" Tony says, as he fills her glass.

"Sure."

"Okay, now." Tony gulps half the glass down, which Denise recognizes as courage garnering. "Would you like to go to a wedding?"

"Keeping things from me, huh?" Denise feels both relief and disappointment. "When are you getting married?"

"Come on, Hoffman. This woman I used to go out with."

"Usually that's how it works."

Tony gives her a disparaging look, empties his wine. He goes into the kitchen. Bottles clink erratically for several moments, then Tony returns with a bottle of rum. "She told me to bring a date. The reception's going to be first class. Champagne fountains, fresh shrimp, live lobster." He stands there, holding the liquor and gives her a cocky look. "She invited me specially, because of this special service I gave her."

Denise half believes that Tony, the Gulf Coast Stud, will start rattling off facts, like they've been trained to do in hydrology. "You don't have to tell me." Denise really means it; she doesn't want to hear about it.

"Did you ever hear of recreational underwear?" Tony's eyes grow. Denise detects unmistakable malice in his voice, something bred into a person without them even knowing it.

"No." Denise finds his cuckoo clock. A half hour to "Saturday Night Live."

Tony's hand shakes as he brings the rum to his mouth. He drinks, amazingly, without coughing or gagging. Then he slithers down into the couch, as if to enhance the rum's effect. It puts him closer to Denise. "Ahh," he says, exhaling tomato sauce and sweet wine.

"Another?" She pours a shot in the wine glass for him, and one for herself. She enjoys watching Tony throw down the shots, which he doesn't do quite gracefully: the rum dribbles down his chin. While he gazes around in admiration at his apartment, she pours her shots into his palm tree.

When half the bottle is empty, and Tony is slightly moaning, but not in ecstasy, or even in anticipation of ecstasy, Denise pours him one last shot and says: "I need to go. Okay?" Missing "Saturday Night Live" won't kill her.

Tony vaguely waves his hand, mumbles something that sounds like "Volvo." It's either take it or don't take it, but Denise decides to take it because Tony can't possibly drive her home, not the shape he's in. By the time she puts away the food, and clears off the kitchen table, he is snoring. She blows out the candles, and leaves.

The next morning Denise gets up in the dark. Already her face is coated with a veneer of sweat, a fine mist mixed in with the dust and debris from Highway 59.

Outside her ramshackle building, she ties a red bandana around her forehead. Sunday mornings Denise does a 12-mile run, the object being to get from A to B. When she gets to the bad part of the city it will be light enough, or there will be cars out. Now the streets are dark and empty, so she runs with a light step, soundlessly, so as to pick up any threatening noises. Someone once sprung out at her from the shrubbery around Rice University. She easily broke away from his hold; it only worried her when the man started running after her.

What few trees the city has not cut down become silhouetted by the rising sun: black branches, stark and thin against the paling blue. There are no people, no cars, only a muted highway hum, a backdrop for the quick soft movement of sneakers on asphalt. She runs in the streets, beneath street lights avoiding the concrete which has little give. The city is flat, except where a street arches over Highway 59. She finds an arching street as the sun rises, and above eight lanes of thruway, of vehicles in constant motion, she calmly, purposefully, runs into the rising sun.

By the time the sun has become round, she is at the Medical Center. Once when she was there, a woman in a sari began screaming she'd been robbed. Denise picked up her pace and pursued the thief. She was in his shadow, unsure of what to do — grab his leg, pull his hair? — when he jumped a fence and threw the purse. Denise retrieved it and gave it back to the woman. The purse was empty.

Denise keeps running because running helps her think. After the first few miles, her body finds a rhythm, and along with achieving a rhythm, her mind begins sliding from consciousness to semi-consciousness. It's almost no effort to run. Her body works independently, taking her mind along for the journey. She's aware only that she's moving forward, and she moves through entire neighborhoods, rich and poor, and back again, crisscrossing the city.

Denise has several routes: some long, some short; routes through Rice University and Herman Park, and routes around the zoo. She prefers the circular routes; they're sensual, graceful. Routes signify where a person is, how far they've gone, and how much further they need to go. They stabilize a person and give them clues as to who they are.

Still Denise wonders what she would do about Tony. Maybe she shouldn't do anything except continue provoking him until he explodes and chucks her on the heap with smiley Sally the bride-to-be with recreational underwear.

She wonders who she will be. Denise the graduate student, who lives in a slum? The sky lightens further. She's at the zoo, circling. The lions roar ahead of her, they roar behind her.

It occurs to Denise that after the instability of Louis, she's on the rebound. Tony's conventional Volvo and pressed jeans seem not only attractive, but necessary. She's been alone too much. The endless monologues about old girlfriends and Italian food save her from something potentially more dangerous. By seven she finds her reflection in the glass walls of the Art Museum. The person staring back at her is at first a surprise. The legs are strong and the arms are pumping furiously, as if they will never stop. The back is straight. She stares at the woman and can not believe this is her.

Next Saturday they go to an out-of-town party thrown by Tony's friends. Tony, who is six-foot-five and slender, has a cadre of basketball friends, more basketball friends, Denise thinks, than anybody in the world. It doesn't end there, because after basketball season, there's softball. Then there's football. In the interim, while the athletes regroup and form their constantly-shifting alliances, there are girlfriends. Once, Tony invited Denise to a basketball game. Denise sat in the stands with all the other gushing girlfriends, but rather than obediently admiring the biceps and hamstrings, the jaws clenched in anger, she worked on a paper. Afterward, when they went out with the gang to a bar, he kept pulling the basket of peanuts out of her reach. "Why didn't you talk to any of those girls?" he said, perplexed and annoyed.

Denise likes traveling away from the hot city, leaving behind the concrete and the crime. She realizes the necessity to get out of her running routes, with their interlocking circles that curve back upon themselves. The routes start to repeat, like the compound eyes of insects.

Tony is wearing his red and white basketball shirt and his pressed jeans. He has a long back, so the shirt's a little short. She senses Tony has plans for her, but she doesn't know what. Something unpredictable will happen, and this will absolve her of further responsibility, and clarify their relationship once and for all.

The lit-up farmhouse is isolated, surrounded by fields of wheat and weeds. Numerous cars — but none nearly as nice as the Volvo — zigzag along the dirt road leading up to the old farmhouse. The music blares, pulling at the ear drums, not letting go without acknowledgement. The atmosphere is holiday-like, even though it is July. To Denise, it's promising; maybe she didn't make a mistake this time.

Once inside Denise quickly realizes she doesn't know anyone except Tony, but she recognizes faces. She looks for Tony's best friend and his girlfriend, who Denise and Tony sometimes double with. Tony, the best friend and girlfriend are from the Bronx and have known each other since high school.

They laugh and tease each other in mutually gratifying ways, and compare how many times they or their relatives have been pistol-whipped and mugged. They make faces and gesticulate as they jab and hit each other on the back of the neck. The three have told their jokes and stories so many times, and Denise brings something new into the circle, even if most of the time, it is simply being the new observer. And she completes the second couple. When she gets drunk she entertains them, which Tony usually appreciates. But the other couple isn't here, which means Denise need not talk. Furthermore, she can be whomever she wants. She can do whatever she wants, within limits. So she decides to drink, just enough to find the pleasure of silence in the crowd. Being silent alone is something altogether different.

Tony rounds his shoulders. "Hey Bean Head!" he says, effusively, eager to discuss strategy for the next game. His legs cover the room's diagonal in ten steps. He joins a group of teammates wearing identical red and white shirts.

Only the numbers have changed. In fact most of the assembled crowd — which includes several shapely women — wear the shirts, along with the bright white socks and white sneakers.

Denise finds an inconspicuous wall to lean against. It's far enough from the speakers so she won't go deaf. Someone has put on a tape of <u>The Cars.</u> The diffuse red lighting makes Denise feel as if she's seeing everything through watered-down tomato sauce. The red shirts with their glowing white numbers move in and move out, forming patterns that Denise believes have some meaning, although she isn't sure what.

"What's the matter?" Tony says, returning to Denise. He hunkers down and accidentally spills some beer on the wood floor.

"Nothing," Denise says, "except that you're making a mess."

He ignores her comment. "What are you looking at?"

"Shirts." She wonders what they can talk about for so long. Another basketball game? Basketball sneakers? Basketballs, period? "I'm just not in a talkative mood."

"Why do you always have to be so belligerent?"

"Big word, Tony." She figures he got it from "The One Hour Orgasm."

Denise stares at the red and white shirts. Tony sighs, shifts his size thirteen feet, and says, "Say something, Hoffman."

"I don't have anything to say."

"Don't be weird," he says. His eyes are starting to protrude. Tony sucks in his thin chest. He stands up straight, looking around anxiously, trying to figure out what to do so he won't look like a fool. Some girlfriends are already hanging on to their boyfriends.

Denise knows then that whatever she says, he won't understand. Maybe he'll never understand. Her heart sinks momentarily, but the thought of another beer buoys it. It shouldn't be like this: she always working against him, Tony always trying to pull her some place, jam her into a puzzle, as if she is a wooden block. But the alternative as she sees it, is total isolation.

"Don't you like my friends?" he says.

"Sure. I like your friends."

"Don't you think they're great guys?" Tony beams in their direction, holds up a hand in one of their secret salutes. As usual they're hitting each other on the back of the neck and making faces, although they are not all from the Bronx. They spit out words at each other and scream over the music. They haven't had a game in a week and they need some way to funnel their unfathomable energy. They pretend they have bats in their hands, or they pretend they're throwing balls. Their girlfriends, who wear too much makeup and keep their fingernails honed for a killing, clump together like barnacles on an ocean breakwall, as if they fear the imaginary hardballs and basketballs could actually harm them. Their blue lidded eyes ineffectively suppress a mixture of longing and despair, although they appear to have accepted their dilemma without significant protest.

"They're loads of fun, Tony. I've never had so much fun in my life."

"Don't be so sarcastic, Hoffman."

"You don't mind if I just stand here and think, do you?" Denise is sincere, but the words come out sounding mean.

Tony takes three steps before he's with some blonde who has a fluid Texan accent. She's not wearing one of the red and white shirts. Tony stands there, talking into her chest.

Denise gets another beer, nurses it, promises herself that this is the last one. She goes outside, sits on a fence, and watches a breeze move through flat fields of weeds and wheat. This way, that way, and back again. She is so far away from the city lights that she can see stars. On the full moon she sees the marias. She wishes Louis was here. She would tell him how the moon's craters form, and he would say: "Is that so?" He'd want to know more, always more.

Back inside the air is again red and diffuse. The music seems thinner and less profound. A woman in one of the red shirts is crying in a corner, her arms around her knees. A couple is arguing at the keg.

Tony, a cigarette stuck between his teeth like some kind of weapon, apprehends Denise. "Hoffman, you just can't run off like that." He blows smoke in her face, a warning, or remonstrance, but it's unclear which.

She's never seen him smoke before. He's lectured to her about how athletes shouldn't smoke or drink. It took them a half hour to get here, so Denise doesn't say anything, instead, she dances with Tony. She drinks too much. Like the blue-lidded girlfriends huddled together earlier, she accepts destiny. Going home, she hangs her head outside the Volvo's window. The air, cooling and refreshing, rushes against her, making her forget about the disturbance in her stomach until she vomits.

When they get to her apartment she sits down, in the parking lot, on the still-warm, broken concrete. She watches Tony throw bucket after bucket of water on the Volvo's passenger door. That she tastes vomit in her mouth doesn't bother her: she made it this far.

It's her job to guard the Volvo while Tony clambers inside up two flights of rickety stairs to fill the bucket again. A carload of drunk men with weekend beards pass by slowly, so slowly it seems impossible that the car is moving; it's powered, Denise decides, by a primitive force, like Fred Flintstone feet. The men leer at Denise, but she's used to it. They say something rude in another language to Tony, but Tony just throws on the water with more vigor.

"Good exercise for the basketball arms," Denise says.

With the bucket poised, he looks back at her. But it's empty: worry supersedes the anger. The gawking men with the stubble chins look longingly at the new white Volvo. Maybe they'll slash its tires, which are not inexpensive.

"This isn't the Bronx, Tony," Denise says, picking up on his concern.

"They're all desperate," Tony says. Big sweat marks are on his cherished red and white shirt. His protruding eyes have receded. "We're all desperate."

"I didn't mean to do it." Denise looks up at the sky. It's a seamy black. The stars have been milked out and she can't find the moon. She puts her head in her lap and crosses her arms over it. She wants to go to sleep. "I'm sorry, Tony. I screwed up again." She needs to go to sleep and forget this happened as soon as possible.

Tony frantically throws another bucket of water on the Volvo. He runs inside for one last bucket. Denise uncovers her head and dutifully watches the car.

Finished, Tony moves the Volvo beneath the only street light on the block. "I'll kill anybody who touches my car," he says.

Inside her apartment Denise slumps down on the couch. The couch is second-hand, and greasy along the arms. It sits directly on the floor, without legs, as if in acceptance of its final resting place. In spite of his excitement—his face is red, his hands shake—Tony lights a candle and has the presence of mind to station it on a plate. He turns off the lights that Denise turned on. He just about has Denise's shirt off when the phone rings.

"No," he murmurs. "No." His eyes are closed for once.

The phone keeps ringing. Instinctively, Denise picks it up, ready to slam it back down when she hears his voice. It's rich, and gentle. Her eyes jerk open. The voice makes every cell in her body listen. He says, "Hi, Babe," and Denise looks at Tony.

"It's—" she says, pointing at the phone.

"You're cold," Tony says.

He jumps up and grabs his wallet and keys. "Cold," he repeats as he does a little hop, then thumps down the stairs, out onto the concrete to the reliable Volvo. "Cold," he shouts, as he accelerates the Volvo past the second story window with its stubby, flickering candle.

Denise's inclination to defend herself is usurped by an intense feeling of relief. When she puts her ear back up to the phone, Louis is gone.

The next morning Denise runs. A hard fast run that puts her in the inner zone, at the twilight of sunsets and sunrises. Body and mind separate, freeing her. The city's glare and harshness have been transcended. The air becomes still, a primordial still, and it resuscitates something in her core of being.

The way Denise sees it, the city doesn't exist. There's no concrete, no cars, no noise. It doesn't always happen when she runs, but this time it does. It's as if someone else is running, and she's there for the pure experience. She's going somewhere, getting from A to B. For however long she can hold out, she is a person. She is Denise Hoffman, a person who feels and thinks. She can do anything, as long as she is running.

Silent Night

She agreed to see him, although she knew it would cost her in some way; the experience of being with him would return to her again and again, in subtle and unsubtle ways over the next several weeks, and she would be powerless to stop it. That was the kind of effect he had on her and the kind of idiocy that she played into. If she could just let it go and be done with it: forever, finite, the end, but she couldn't; she might as well stop drinking coffee in the morning and watching the bare trees take form and the sky bleed into existence.

He wasn't any good for her, and she knew it and he told her as much. And not just once. No commitment and that too, was what she wanted. Honesty. No lies: not to her, not to him, not to herself.

He'd set her on edge, then he'd send her back, again and again and he'd make her lose her focus and pose a question that she wasn't prepared for. *That* would make her reel.

He sent the e-mail at two in the morning and there was an urgency to it and that was what she responded to, or that was what she told herself, and she was trying to be honest although she knew one's true motives were more often than not deeply buried, and to unearth them required not only courage and persistence, but a tightly-centered obsession, and a person had only so much of those qualities and hers were nearly exhausted because of what had happened last year. It was never simple.

She was seeing someone else and she was perfectly happy with this relationship (smart guy, regular phone calls, regular visits, his head together), and why did she have to mess everything up by responding to the e-mail? Dammit.

There was something about him: like a spirit from the sky talking to her in ways that were clairvoyant and that not even he was aware of, and when she tried to shake it, it just came back more intensely. Yet if she examined it closely the spell might break, everything would be gone leaving only space, and she wasn't sure she wanted to do that.

Fuck it, she thought. You think too much. Just go.

Rosie had never been to his apartment before. She wasn't the kind of person who felt secure unless she had proper nouns and when he gave her directions, he'd neglected to mention road names, so she took the precaution of MapQuesting his address and found the names and a good thing because his instructions had not been accurate (and later, that seemed to upset him: so what?).

She wondered if he really wanted her to come, but then she was never sure what he wanted, as if that mattered. Funny how you said one thing and you wanted it to mean something, but it didn't: it meant something else entirely.

For her part, she made no wrong turns during the 43-mile drive and arrived at her destination within 5 minutes of her projected time. That wasn't bad. That was something solid.

She parked in the lot he indicated and saw the graveyard.

She hadn't predicted a graveyard. That was a nice touch, a graveyard: one foot here, one foot there.

Not only that, but a graveyard on a hill. How wonderful was that? It cast the visit in that metaphorical glow of tension between what could happen and what would happen. Lurking around the edges of consciousness was the certainty of death. She wondered if he thought about it much.

She went to the door and Jack buzzed her in.

"You're here," he said, as if surprised that she had materialized in the flesh and the blood. Was that good or bad?

She shrugged. Yet she felt reassured because she had predicted the white, pictureless walls, the beige rug, where the kitchen would be and the TV, and the empty space: an immense space where the sound of doors opening and closing echoed, and the labored walk up three flights of the dusty stairs could take forever. The blinds were closed, sealing in whatever was inside letting in nothing from the outside, except Rosie now and the cold air that had stagnated in the hallway leading up to his door.

"Follow me," he said, pulling on his leather jacket. They went out to get wine because he didn't have any.

They drove around the dark city with its houses built up against the narrow road, dun-colored row houses one somehow locked against the other, grime on the windows, no lights, except for the light emitted by the TVs when there was a TV. The two-story houses had no adornments, nothing frivolous as if setting out a strand of white lights was just too much effort. She had passed through another small town on her way over and there had been a celebration: bright lights and music and the smell of freshly-cut evergreens and families in colorful stocking caps singing Christmas carols. *Silent Night* seeped in through the closed car windows.

"Hold on," he said, and they went over a pot-hole and bounced and the car jerked to the right and he expertly re-adjusted the car's course. On they went.

They passed more houses where the workers from the shoe factories had happily lived and from which they had sent their children to school, good schools with teachers who never heard of a discipline plan.

The city had been a shoe factory hub in the 30s and 40s. Now the shoes were made in China or India, and all the factories were gone, most of the workers too except those who were too old and tired and poor but for some reason they were able to hold on by their fingertips.

It was hard to imagine such people living in the houses that they passed, and harder still to imagine them at one time going out on dates and getting laid and then getting bouquets of red roses on their birthdays, and later, holding onto second-hand bikes as their kids balanced on two wheels. The houses were mostly empty. But there were a few with TVs.

She imagined people mesmerized by the rich and the famous, watching them through a haze of cigarette smoke and a liquid cloud of alcohol dripping into in their veins.

And their kids: rather than riding bikes, well, they ran wild and smoked pot and dared each other to do things that were stupid and menacing, things that would somehow stop them in their tracks even before they even got started, defining the rest of their sorry lives. *This is how you are going to live.* She could hear the beer bottles thumping on the low-set tables, no books or magazines on the tables. She watched the line of houses, expecting someone to sooner or later open one of the doors. There was no one.

Then she was back, in Buffalo, at her friend's, Mary's, a day after her father's graduation. Mary's father had graduated from high school. In the cramped dining room was a sheet cake with aqua-colored frosting and thick white scrolls and CONGRATUATIONS BOBBY! (Someone left out the "L" she noticed, but she said nothing to Mary.)

That was back when stores first started selling sheet cakes. Aqua-colored frosting — she couldn't believe it. Every time she had the opportunity, Rosie stared at the sheet cake.

Mary kept asking why she was going downstairs. *To use the bathroom*, Rosie told her. *If you have the curse, don't throw anything down the toilet.* Rosie was 12 and hadn't yet had her period.

The O'Brien's had one bathroom for seven people. Mary O'Brien and her stick-like siblings lived in a rundown duplex (no screens, no storm windows, paint, likely lead-based, peeling everywhere) within sight of the steel plant's natural gas torch. The damn thing burned day-and-night. It shrouded the ramshackle neighborhood in a perpetual orange haze and with its constant filtering down of coal dust, made it look like a Dickensian slum and smell like one too, with that hard-boiled egg smell. Mary never brought egg salad sandwiches for lunch. She didn't care for deviled eggs — even if there was paprika on them.

They talked about their parents fucking, although they didn't use that term back then. *It's so embarrassing that Mom's pregnant again,* Mary said.

Do they like doing it? Rosie asked. Her parents didn't, she knew, and she wondered if all parents hated sex. *Why would they do it if they didn't like it?* Mary, the epitome of reason, or at least she was before the hormones overtook her. *Do your parents love one another?* Rosie asked. *They have to — they're married.* Huh.

Still, all Rosie wanted was a piece of that sheet cake with the aqua frosting; instead, she got black feet from the coal dust because she ran around their house without her shoes. She'd heard that Mary had four kids and she lived out in the country in a trailer and the word was that her husband, some rail-thin guy with a handle-bar moustache, sold vacuum cleaners and dealed. He didn't make any money from the vacuum cleaners.

It was a small liquor store that they stopped at, with a red neon sign out front: LIQUOR. Funny word, Rosie thought: it wanted to be an elixir and a liquid at the same time, moreover, a benign and ceremonial liquid, but there was too much history, too much emotion: liquor was not a black-and-white word. Engineers were fond of such words. He was an engineer. Black-and-white words had no room for negotiation, and they might as well have been numbers. Numbers could make you feel good, especially if you got them right. While waiting for the check-out person to scan her food purchases, Rosie would usually estimate her bill. Sometimes she got it right on the dollar, and sometimes, but rarely, only a few cents off.

Inside the liquor store was a group of young black men, discrete but intoxicated, wearing expensive earrings and expensive clothes and it did not seem that they needed any more alcohol, but she saw what they bought: good whiskey and a type of bourbon that she wasn't familiar with. No wine. One of them looked at her, then Jack, then he shook his head; "Shit," he said, and then they were gone.

Rosie and Jack bought a bottle of wine and a corkscrew.

Back at the apartment, Rosie opened the wine and poured herself a glass. She drank it down and poured herself another glass. Then she was okay. She took a seat on his couch and she was ready to talk. There always had to be talk: you just couldn't do what you came for, although sometimes, that was what she wanted. Rosie once had a boyfriend who pushed her in the talk direction. *You have to talk to me, Rosie*, he'd say. *I don't know where you are and I've never been a good mind reader. Tell me what you're thinking. I know you're thinking, because you're always thinking. I want to understand you. Isn't that okay? You think I would use it against you someday? No. You have to trust me. I would never attack you. You believe me, don't you?* Every time they had sex, he'd tell her, *I love*

31

your body. Your breasts, your arms, your legs. And your cunt. She'd smile and he'd go on: *And I love the way you kiss. I love the way you smell. I love...I love...I love.* And then he stopped loving.

Jack turned on the TV and stared at it. That meant something was wrong, and she asked him.

"I usually sit there."

She moved to the other side of the couch.

"Sorry," he said. He sat down and put his arm around her, a proprietary gesture.

They watched TV for a while and she recalled his rule. Whenever two or more were gathered together there were always rules and she accepted the fact and she tried not to judge, because if she started to judge he'd know it. He would pick up on those kinds of things.

There were certain words — emotional words — you had to stay away from, and you weren't even supposed to think them although that part was hard. You had to be vigilant.

For instance, if you forgot about the last piece of bread in the breadbox you'd eventually find it soggy, riddled with mold at the bottom of its plastic bag. If you forgot about the words, you exposed your heart, making it vulnerable to waste and sickness.

There was supposed to be no emotion and she knew that and thought that was right given who he was and where he was; she too, who she was, and that was to her benefit, not his.

They talked a little. She had another glass of wine. He made some comment about the TV show. He said it was a stupid show. She agreed. So that much they agreed on.

"Are you ready?" he finally said, looking at her. She nodded. He peeled her fingers off the glass and set it down on a table. Then he removed her glasses. He took her hands and put them on his shoulders and he looked at her, then he pressed himself against her and she felt him. He kissed her, lightly, then deeper.

Then they were in his bedroom, and he was sitting on his bed, and she was between his knees. He unzipped her jeans and raised her T-shirt just enough so that he could put his head to her stomach and smell her. Then he lifted her arms and took off her T-shirt. Then her bra. There was nothing else to take off.

"You're so small," he said, in wonder. "Fine-boned." It was true. Then as he removed his clothes, his back toward her, he said, "Don't think there's anything built up between us." She knew what he meant. He'd take her there, but that was all the further he'd go. Nothing beyond. Whatever they built up would be dissolved by tomorrow or the next day. That was the rule. If one did not adhere to rules, chaos reigned. Armageddon was always around the corner: you just had to have faith.

He put on a condom, and then they began with him below her, tasting her.

"How does that feel?" he said.

"Fine."

Then he laid on top of her, still at first, seeing how they fit. Then he was inside, moving, both of them moving, her hands touching him. They were kissing, and he stopped and asked again, "How does that feel?"

"Fine," she said.

Then he kissed her breasts, her stomach, the inside of her leg, asking: "How does that feel?"

"It's good," she said.

He kissed more. Then he lifted her and she was on top, and he didn't have to ask how she felt.

"You ready?" he said.

"Sure."

He put her back to his chest, and when he was inside her, she registered his surprise when he said: "You're so fucking wet." Then they were together, rocking, pushing, rocking faster, pushing harder, Rosie holding onto his shins for leverage, then they slowed down and so they could listen to the wind coming from the graveyard, the sound a cry, like a wolf, and it seemed to go on, and then they started again, more impassioned this time, her eyes bouncing in their sockets, and then he came, a convulsive shudder as if every nerve ending exploded not once or twice but five times, and his arms were around her, his body melded to hers so that she felt the electricity outside, and inside it expanded, a wave with an asymptotic amplitude. I want you to feel this, was what he would have said. Don't forget it.

They must have slept. Then they talked. A little, not much. She mentioned the graveyard and he told her something about himself: how he used to cut the grass at one. She imagined him with a pair of shears, trimming leaning limestone headstones, kneeling on top of dead bodies, maybe crossing himself then closing his eyes and sensing the mysticism of being up here, inhaling good air and producing healthy red blood cells so he could run his marathons and calculate the power produced by an electrical circuit. Alive. Now he was restless. He wanted her to go, but he wouldn't say it, so she got out of bed and pulled on her jeans, her T-shirt and she kissed him goodbye.

It was a long drive home along country roads. She put on a CD of Shostakovich, her mind following piano notes up and down the keyboard, faster and faster until it seemed impossible that they could move any faster without losing their integrity.

The notes leaped out at impossible places, surprising her, but they also helped her think. She would listen to a piece of music a hundred times, and each and every time she would think of the piece differently. That was what she liked about him, he did the same thing, maybe for the same reason. She didn't know. If she listened hard enough she thought she'd pick up a clue about who she was. When the music was fast it gave her a foothold and she did not think about other things, such as what she was doing to make a mess of her life. She just couldn't let things be. Could she?

As she drove along the country roads she passed the country houses with their overabundance of reindeer and bloated Santas, their cracked bricks walls and their rusted station wagons with bald tires. The homes were similar to the one she grew up in, and that made her remember her father, and her mother.

Her father rarely talked. He was dominated by his wife, surely, but the problem was that Rosie's mother was not a thinking person.

She got an idea and she never turned it over. For instance, she thought sex was dirty, made for animals, uncultured and degrading especially to women because of all the babies, maybe.

This became her truth. Everything important that could have been beautiful was judged from this truth, and that was how she lived her life, that was the core from which all emanated, and this was how she told her children to live their lives. Rosie, in her infinite desire to understand, to make sense of the insanity of her mother's truth, moved very slowly from the disgust and humiliation and into a world of mysterious and tenuous pleasure. Perhaps love. It had taken her decades to move in this direction, and like a long-time prisoner finally exonerated by DNA evidence, she didn't want to lose what she had worked so hard for. Maybe love, she thought: fleeting moments because once you tried to capture it to expand and enrich, you obliterated it. At least that had been her experience. Its essence eluded her.

Her parents' marriage of 52 years had been all commitment, little love. Love, one of those words. A black-and-white word, although it shouldn't be. Commitment was a black-and-white word. And even that fell apart on them during the last few years. Her father, in his 70s, having affairs because he never got what he needed. Right up until last year, until his death. Imagine.

Rosie knew why she married someone who would stop loving her. And when he stopped, she lied to herself, not just little lies, but big lies, lies that went on for years. Now lying about anything: how many chocolate chips she ate, how often she washed the floor or washed her hair, or how little she gave to the poor: even simple lying made her sick to her stomach.

She thought about Jack as she was driving. It was habit to recreate whatever happened, beginning with him opening the door, driving through his city, buying the wine and drinking the wine, watching TV, being intimate.

Hers was the only car on the road and there were no streetlights. The wind was blowing and she heard that sound again, an animal cry. A deer suddenly leaped out in front of her. They missed colliding by a fraction of a second. That was almost too close. Then she suddenly remembered his fingers, long, delicate fingers passing over her forehead, touching her face, and she heard *Silent Night* —clear as could be— although she had passed through the town with the lights an awfully long time ago.

Nightshift

Joe Emerson found the dirt road and drove along it through a forest of spruce and fir and where the road ended, his headlights picked up the trailer, and the rise of land behind the trailer. It looked very different from what he had remembered, but some things were still the same: the clothesline strung up between two poles, a battered car in back. The trailer, once a brilliant red, had faded to a washed-out pink. Nearby a 55-gallon drum smoldered, wisps of smoke escaping into the frigid January air. His headlights picked up bushes; blueberry bushes he recalled fondly.

Joe turned off the Jeep, the lights, and removed the flask from his leather jacket. He swallowed two aspirin with some schnapps, then screwed the top back on and put the flask beside his briefcase and computer manuals on the Jeep's floor. The moonlight shined on the rearview mirror as he looked at his tired eyes, then his teeth, the bottom ones crooked and tobacco stained.

With his fingertips, he traced the edge of an acne scar on his face. He'd always believed that when he grew up, the scar would disappear, but it hadn't and every time he looked, he wondered who else saw it.

He opened the Jeep door and his snakeskin boots, a birthday present from his wife, crunched on the gravel. Yellowish light poured out through the mobile home's small, filmy windows and fell around the spruce trees. He smelled the pungent odor of pine and thought his brother, Ralph, was lucky; this far out, it seemed unlikely that anyone or anything could bother you. You could be your own person. Walking in closer he smelled the burning garbage and he had to hold his breath until he reached the front door.

He knocked. There was no outside light. He heard the humming of a generator, a TV, the dull clatter of plastic dishes. An owl hooted and he looked at the trees, and feeling a chill, he raised the collar of his leather jacket. Knocking quickly again, he called out, "Hello. Anyone home?"

A light went on above his head. A lock turned and the door opened revealing Ralph's thin pale face. His hairline had receded an inch or two, and what hair he had was sporadic and completely gray.

"Joe, well...I wasn't expecting," Ralph said, his hand still pressed against the screen door. His eyes shifted and settled for a moment on the far end of the trailer, then the eyes came back to Joe, and Ralph grinned. "Come on in." Ralph held out his hand, and it shook a little. Joe took it with his two hands and felt the thin bones beneath Ralph's skin. His right hand was a little sooty and smelled like the burning garbage outside. Joe took two steps inside and looked where Ralph had been looking. Two electric heaters whirled on high and a TV blared. He saw the bottoms of a woman's very large feet. The woman had on a sleeveless, scoop-necked dress of an indeterminable color, its design washed out. She was cracking open peanut shells with her teeth and the floor around her was littered with the empty shells. The woman completely ignored Joe.

Joe looked away and said, "I hope this isn't a bad time, I-"

"Bad time? No time like the present." Ralph stuck his head outside the door and peered about. "Nice Jeep, what I can see of it." He stepped back inside. "No wife?"

"I'm on business."

"Well, have a seat and I'll make you a drink. Vodka?" Ralph backed up into a dish rack and a plastic glass thudded onto the linoleum floor.

Joe pulled out a chair and hung his jacket around the chair's back. When he sat down, he could not see the large woman, instead, he faced a wall that was completely covered with photographs, many of them small prints in black and white. The color in the newer ones was not quite right. They were of Ralph's wife, Marilyn: the brilliant, red ripple hair, the sharp blue eyes, and her father, a successful businessman, his arm around her waist. Joe rolled up the sleeves of his white shirt and loosened his tie because the air inside was warm and stale.

"I was just about to get dinner started. You like macaroni and cheese?"

"Sure," Joe said. He drummed his fingers on the Formica table top. Ralph got out some clear plastic glasses from the aquamarine-colored cupboard and made two drinks. He handed Joe a drink then he set a dented pan of water on a burner, and he lit the burner. Joe was close enough to feel the heat. The flame was too high and it started licking around the pan, so Ralph turned it down.

On another wall, which looked as though it had never been painted, were craft hangings that said: "Home of the Fearless" and "My Other Home is a Mansion."

"Hon," Ralph called to the large woman on the bed. The woman kept her eyes on the television. "Marilyn, I'm home. And guess what? We have a guest." To Joe, he said, "I was out back. Just got home myself."

"Son-of-a-bitch." Marilyn was propped, half-slumped on a bowed king-size bed, her enormous legs slightly spread. Numerous books were scattered on the bed. Marilyn stopped eating peanuts, and opening her eyes slightly, said, "Who's there?" She tried to pull a yellowish comforter over her legs then said, tentatively, "What does he want?"

Joe stood up so she could see him. "Hi, Marilyn," he said, saluting her with his plastic glass. "It's me, Joe. I didn't recognize you at first." He stopped. "What I meant was, see I thought ...well, that. . ." He was about to take a step towards the bedroom, when Joe felt Ralph's hand, the fingertips cold, on his shoulder.

"What are you doing here?" Her legs started to shake and her back arched. Using leverage from an end table that had several dirty glasses on it, she rose. Then she closed her eyes, and breathed deeply. She began, slowly, one leg at a time, walking towards them.

Joe tried to smile. He had a smile for everyone: for his wife, for clients, his boss; drunk smiles and sober smiles; friendly smiles: kind, calm, clever, translucent or opaque: any smile to fit the situation. Smiles that could mask surprise at anything.

The dishes in the rack shook as Marilyn approached them. She sat down at the table in an extra large chair.

"How was your day, Marilyn?" Ralph said.

She squinted at him and replied: "How do you think my day was? It was just like every other day." She put her hands on the small table and closed her eyes and wheezed.

"Just like every other day?" Ralph said. "Nothing new?"

Marilyn just stared at him.

Joe watched her tiny eyes, eyes hidden almost completely by the soft flesh. It was a face that made him think of many people crowded together, people with vastly differing opinions on life, all competing for recognition, with a single solitary person trying to emerge, but unable to.

"My day was like every other day," she said, her voice flat. "It was a day of hell."

Ralph went to the counter and opened a plastic tub and poured macaroni from it into the boiling water. "I was going to fix the place up a little," Ralph told Joe. Ralph opened the freezer and Joe felt a welcome current of cold air. The freezer was stacked with plastic ice-cream tubs.

Ralph made another drink and handed it to Marilyn. "I thought you said you were coming tomorrow, Joe. Your postcard said, in your typical cryptic Joe Emerson style: 'To settle things. Be there on the ninth.'"

"I must have meant *by* the ninth. I don't write much."

"You know how I always do things at the last minute?" Ralph said.

"That's what you always say," Marilyn said. "I'm going to fix the molding, or paint the walls."

"It's true, I just haven't had time. And you have to take down your photographs first," Ralph said, indicating the wall.

Marilyn stared at the photographs. The electric heaters droned on.

Joe shifted in his seat, and asked Ralph, "Still working hard?"

"I sell real estate, work security at the food warehouse and do seasonal accounting at Lamark's Lumber."

"That real estate," Marilyn said.

"I'm getting close, Marilyn."

"You haven't sold a damn thing."

"You're still writing your book?" Joe said.

Ralph looked at Marilyn.

"He's always writing his book," Marilyn said. "Just open any drawer and you'll find a scrap with something on it. The woodshed is full of his files. He thinks he's the next Hemingway."

"I wouldn't go that far, Marilyn. But I take that as a compliment." Ralph smoothed back his short hair. "Actually I prefer to think of myself as the next Dostoevsky."

Marilyn grunted.

"Who's that?" Joe said.

"He wrote Notes From The Underground. He's dead, of course. When you have some time, Joe, take a look at it. And Cervantes', Don Quixote."

43

They drank more while the noodles cooked and talked about how the nearby town, which had never been a Mecca for businesses, was now going through severe belt-tightening times. When the food was ready, Ralph handed everyone a plastic plate, a knife and fork.

Using a rusted ladle he put a huge scoop of macaroni and cheese on Joe's and Marilyn's plate, then he set a two-pound container of garlic powder and one of chili at the table's center. "Don't wait for me," he said, "eat while it's hot."

Marilyn started eating.

Ralph freshened the drinks and he put some white bread on the table. Joe saw mold on the crust and told Ralph he was fine with what he had. Then Ralph sat down with his plate, and grabbed the neck of the chili and sprinkled his food liberally with the red powder. He did the same with the garlic. "After it cools, it loses some of its appeal," he told Joe, holding out the garlic to him. "Have some. They say it's good for bronchitis too. Keeps the mucous flowing."

"Ralph's always been a vast repository of arcane and dubious medicinal advice," Marilyn interjected, then went back to eating.

Joe sprinkled on a little garlic, and they ate and drank and talked about Joe's last visit, twenty years ago when he'd spent the summer in an army tent a hundred yards from the mobile home.

All the driving and talking made Joe feel light headed. He'd been drinking since he left his last client in Ellsworth. The client decided to network his office with the system Joe recommended, and Joe'd felt so good about it, he'd called his wife. She wasn't home. He thought he'd try calling again, and let her know that if he drove all night he could make it home by three or four tomorrow, then he'd take her out to dinner at a place on the lakeshore that had the best fish fry in town. Maybe they'd go dancing.

"That was some summer," Ralph said.

"The event I remember most vividly is the time you quit your job, Ralph," Joe said.

Marilyn looked at Ralph, and Ralph looked at the table and started playing with his glass.

"Twenty-five years ago," Joe said. "Remember, Ralph? Marilyn? We were living like one big happy family. We never had a family life at home, not with the way Mom was." Joe watched his brother's eyes, and he didn't see any reaction, so he continued. "You were working road construction and going to night school. What was it? Trying to get your MBA?"

Ralph nodded.

"Then you quit or got laid off or some shit, I don't know. But you left the house everyday at eight, and came home at seven or eight, depending on if you had class. So one day I came home from work, and I said to Marilyn, 'Did Ralph find anything yet?' and her mouth went taut and her eyes kind of squeezed together, and I told myself: 'I ain't gonna be here when Ralph gets home.' Oh, the screaming, the dishes that flew." He laughed, and looked at Marilyn, then Ralph.

They were both staring at the Formica-topped table.

"You don't think that's funny?" Joe laughed and rocked back in his chair and the front feet lifted off the floor, and for a second he thought he was going to fall, he felt himself falling backward, but Marilyn grabbed the chair and her blue eyes opened. He looked up and caught a glimpse of the shape of her face as it had been, and he saw her blue eyes smiling slightly, and he remembered how the sun had made her red hair shine and how he had almost kissed her at the back door, some twenty-five years ago.

"I think you've had enough vodka," Marilyn said. Then she reached for the pan and scraped the remains of the food onto her plate and started eating it.

"You don't think that's funny?" Joe said, because he had to say something. He looked down at the worn linoleum floor. "I thought it was funny."

"Sure, Joe," Ralph said. Joe looked up and Ralph grinned. "I think it's funny."

"Where'd you go every day?" Joe said.

"I went to the library."

"Ralph," Marilyn said, closing her eyes. "Make me another drink."

"Sure," Ralph said. He made three big drinks and distributed them.

"I'm not trying to make you feel bad," Joe said. "Marilyn, I have to tell you, that was the best summer of my life. I went to work every day. I was doing road construction. It was something I could see, and I didn't have to use my mind or my imagination like I have to now."

"Mind and imagination!" Ralph quipped, then stood up and cleared off the table and put the dishes and silverware in the sink in a tub of hot water.

"I'll tell you what I remember," Marilyn said.

"What?" Joe said.

"Those notes. You always used to leave us notes." Closing her eyes, she almost smiled and the folds that made up her face seemed to melt away. "I can still see your handwriting. Scratchy. Small, and up and down, like a kid's handwriting, like what you had to say wasn't important, because you weren't sure of yourself." She opened her eyes. "Like you didn't want anyone to think too much of you because you didn't want to disappoint them." She closed her eyes again. "The notes said things like, 'I won't be home for dinner.' Or, 'I'm working late. I left some pancakes. Let's go to Gardy's and play pool on Friday.'"

Ralph started washing the dishes and said: "Marilyn's been reading books about the mind and the imagination. Every night we talk about them—the mind and the imagination. The imagination and the mind."

Marilyn looked at Ralph skeptically. "Ralph who was going to own his own lumber business."

"My book is more important," Ralph said, drying his hands on a thin towel that hung on a nail. He sat down opposite Joe, and talked mostly to him. "This is the way I look at it. Everybody's looking inside themselves. They're all going to therapy, reading self-help books, talking group consciousness. I'm not trying to ridicule them, but people are forgetting to look outside themselves. At the larger factors."

"Don't listen to him, Joe; you have to look inside too. It's not all one way or the other."

"Marilyn," Ralph started, "I'm surprised to hear you say that."

"People change," Marilyn said.

"So what's this novel about?" Joe said.

"Ralph's going to solve the world's problems," Marilyn said.

"I am solving the world's problems," Ralph said excitedly.

He looked at Joe. "It's like this, American culture is in serious decline. Serious. Everyone admits that. Values gone to hell. Serial murders, robberies, rapes, terrorist cells: people are out of control. They're unstable and need to have a giant rubber band put around them. My approach is different from everyone else's — and it may not be one hundred percent right, but it's different—"

"He's always been different," Marilyn said leveling her blue eyes at Joe.

"—and different counts. Marilyn's been a big help in that respect. She stays home, because she likes to," he raised his eyebrows at Marilyn. "She reads all the time. Every goddamn minute her nose is in a book. Did you know she has a photographic memory? She sucks it up and spews it out. She's given me lots of great ideas. Most recently about lawyers and unions, and government conspiracies."

"The government is always engaged in conspiracies," Marilyn told Joe evenly, raising an eyebrow.

"I don't know anything about writing," Joe said. "I was never good in school. You were always the smart one, Ralph—you with your merit scholarship."

"Tell him where you're getting your characters from," Marilyn said, looking at Ralph from the corner of her eyes.

"See, all my jobs are solitary. When I do security, I'm the only one. Same with real estate. Once in a while—"

"—a great while—" Marilyn added.

"—I take someone out. So, I start conversations in my mind."

"In your mind?" Joe said, and put down the drink he was about to sip. "With yourself?" Joe suddenly thought of his Mom, and wondered if she was staring comatose at the TV, or if she was hunched over an industrial-sized table, eating mechanically?

"I make up characters. Maybe it starts with something the grocery store clerk said. Or something I see hanging in a car's back window. It's easy."

Ralph smiled.

Marilyn sighed, "The characters argue a lot."

"What are you talking about?" Ralph said.

"I hear you in your sleep, all the way from the other end of the trailer."

Joe looked in the direction of Marilyn's eyes. He saw a plastic recliner, ripped at the arms, and two makeshift bookshelves filled with paperbacks.

"He's obsessed with his book," Marilyn said.

49

"See the protagonist is denied justice as a kid, so as an adult," Ralph said, "he becomes a fighter for justice, but he doesn't know it yet. See, most of your mental activity occurs at the level of the unconscious mind—most people don't recognize their deepest thoughts, eh? Along the way, this individual who lacked self-confidence will test himself and do things he never would have done. He will embrace humanity and thereby find his own humanity."

"How's that going to work?" Marilyn said.

"I'll give you a hint there, Hon: my protagonist will lose everything: Wife. Job. Integrity."

"Gee, not much left, is there?" Joe said.

"There will be betrayal," Ralph added ominously, glancing at Joe, "by the one closest to him." Ralph smiled manically.

"You seem to know this person," Marilyn said.

"Indeed I do. He's a hero, but he doesn't know it."

"We're all just normal people, Ralph," Joe said. "There are no heroes."

An owl hooted.

They each drank some more, then Joe said, "Can I see a few pages?"

Ralph was quiet. Then he said, "Not yet."

"Just the beginning. I don't read much, most books I don't even—"

"He hasn't started writing," Marilyn said.

"You need a computer?" Joe said. He smiled and put his hand on Ralph's thin shoulder. "All the writers use computers now. Computers: that's my business. Mostly I network computers, but when my clients have some out-dated equipment, I take if off their hands. I could get you a computer cheap."

"You give him a computer, he might actually have to write," Marilyn said.

"I don't need a big fancy computer. Real writers use pen and paper. You know me, Joe: I do things my own way. Always have. That makes me me. See Joe, you have to prepare yourself. Writing a novel is a monumental undertaking, and right now, I'm in the process of gathering data."

He slapped his hand on the table. "This novel will leave unturned no stone." Ralph gazed upon Joe and leaned over the table and pointed his finger at him. "The people who read it — and I guarantee many will, many millions — will learn about justice and truth and love. They'll learn about love's strange manifestations." Ralph looked uncertainly at Marilyn. "How love waxes and wanes — like the seasons. Wait a second." Ralph produced a pen from his back pocket and wrote something down on a napkin and stuffed it in a drawer.

"See what I mean?" Marilyn said to Joe.

"Love's many facets," Ralph seemed to say to himself. Then he looked at Joe. "Joe: The Incurable Romantic. Loves everyone. Heart's as soft as a pillow. Maybe you could give me some insights?"

Joe shrugged. "I don't know what you're driving at."

"My novel will explore truth's gray areas and its perturbations. Truth coming from several different and independent directions, and disciplines. A subtheme will be the infidelity of young wives." Ralph paused and glanced at the photographs on the wall. "Young wives whose expectations are too high, who demand a lot of attention. It's a big phenomenon."

"Is it?" Joe said.

Marilyn looked coolly at Ralph.

"Or maybe the wives do other extreme things," Ralph said.

"I don't know anything about that," Joe said.

"I have to rest," Marilyn said. She put her hand on Joe's chair, and he felt her weight, and smelled her warm breath, and for a moment, he thought she was going to bend down and kiss him, and he remembered the sun on her hair, the almost-kiss and the heat rose to his face.

But she turned, and free of the kitchen table, she walked slowly, her large shoulders slumped down into herself, a drink in her hand, toward the bed. Once comfortable, she picked up a book and took the remote control and turned up the TV.

"After her father died," Ralph whispered, nodding toward the photographs on the wall, "she wouldn't get out of bed — only to go to the bathroom. She was gorgeous, wasn't she?"

Joe nodded slowly. "Ralph, I wanted to ask you — "

"Let me finish. Then she started drinking. She wouldn't go to a doctor. AA helped for a few months, but then she stopped going, and she got worst. Drinking all the time. Drinking the hard stuff. She started eating a lot. You want to hear Marilyn's philosophy? 'I'll read enough and figure it out.' She believes it. She also believes now, that a lot of it's genetic predisposition. What can I say? Maybe she's right. It's her life."

They were quietly drinking, and Joe said: "You know why I'm here?"

"You told me, Joe. In your postcard." Ralph got up and started opening drawers. "It's in here somewhere," he mumbled. "I know I put it—"

"Ralph, sit down. Sit down," Joe said, louder. "Forget the damn postcard."

Ralph sat down.

"I put Mom in a home. I couldn't handle her anymore. Especially at night." Joe picked up his cup, and his hand trembled. "She has her own room. It's clean. There's a TV. But you walk in there, and you hear a moan. You hear it all the time—it's constantly there, even when you can't hear it. It's a sound that makes the hair on your head stand up."

"The doctors will put her on something, and she'll be out in the world again," Ralph said confidently. "The drug companies come out with new medications every day. It's amazing—any mood disorder even those not in the DSM IV yet."

Joe leaned over the table and his eyes flashed. "You don't get it. There's nothing more to put her on. Her brain's gone. I don't think she even knew where she was. Thirty-five years of those kinds of drugs—no body's brain can handle it. She's a vegetable."

Joe eased back in his chair and looked out a filmy window. It was black and he couldn't see a thing. "Remember those nights, during the summer, when we used to sleep outside so we

53

wouldn't hear her pacing and talking to herself? Slamming things around? Remember how we used to stare at the sky, looking for falling stars so we could wish she'd get better? She's never going to get better. She can't even get worse."

"Why are you telling me this?"

"You got all that education. You got your degrees and you're sitting here rotting. You're rotting and I can smell it. I can see it and hear it. And Marilyn—I don't know what happened to Marilyn."

Ralph shrugged. "Things are going to change. I can feel it. I have it all figured out. Maybe I'm getting up there in age, Joe, but I'm certainly not old. See, I get my book published, and I get a little fame. I become a minor guru. This of course makes Marilyn very happy—it restores her faith in me, and she stops eating. Then drinking. I have faith in myself—that's what a writer needs to succeed: faith and hard work." Ralph grinned.

"You're doing this weird stuff again, Ralph, and you don't realize it," Joe said, shaking his head. "You don't even fucking realize it. I've come from the outside, and I can see it. You can't."

"There's nothing wrong with me."

"Remember when Mom started getting sicker and you moved down to the basement?"

"You took care of her, Ralph. More than anyone else. You were her guardian angel."

"Let's stick to the topic. You'd come upstairs to get food, then you'd scurry right back down to your basement. You had those strange blue and green posters on your walls, and strange books.

I used to ask myself: 'What's it like being Ralph Emerson? What's it really like?' What the hell did you do down there?"

"Study."

"Study what?"

"Well...see I had my insect collection. I used to take apart the butterflies, the flies and ants, and identify their parts, then shellac them and glue them on posterboard. Take pictures of them."

"You're almost as crazy as she is. Goddamn, Ralph. Look at yourself."

"Hey—I'm a little obsessive, but obsession can be a virtue—if you know how to use it. Almost anything can be used to your advantage."

"Ralph, I'm a salesman. It's my job to look beneath the person's exterior."

"You have absolutely no faith, Joe."

"I'll level with you, Ralph: when you started living in the basement, coming up only for food, I told myself, if I ever had kids, I would never let them live in the basement."

"You have kids?"

Joe shifted in his chair. "My wife can't have them. Anyway, I work too hard. I'm still struggling to make payroll every two weeks. Beth works. She's a nurse."

"A nurse, huh. A pretty nurse?"

"What do you mean by that?"

"Nothing, Joe. Every time I hear something, I think: how can

I use it in my novel? I have lists and lists of potential ideas and potential characters. This novel is going to be an all-encompassing treatise. It will explain everything, or at least make a valiant attempt to."

"I bet." Joe dug out his wallet from his back pocket. "Here," he said, placing a worn photograph on the table.

Ralph picked it up, and studied it, holding it up where the light was better. "Oh. She's pretty. Curly brown hair. Nice green eyes. She looks like she's in love. Did you take the picture?"

"How should I know—does it matter?"

Ralph shrugged.

"I forget who took it. But I love her," Joe said. "I love her more than anyone or anything. More than I thought I'd ever love anyone."

"Yeah?" Ralph said, scratching the side of his face. He put down the picture and looked at Joe. "I think you loved every pretty girl you ever met."

Joe laughed. "Maybe. But not everyone loved me back."

"Why'd she marry you?"

"She loved me," Joe said, his voice trembling a little. "I mean, she loves me." He felt himself starting to sweat.

"She doesn't mind you working so much?"

"Once I get the business rolling, I won't be working so much." Joe looked around the trailer. "See ...Beth.... I don't know. This is just a feeling."

"What?"

"Do you have a phone?"

"You know me, Joe," Ralph said, shaking his head. "I've always been a thrifty guy. There's nothing extraneous about me or my life. I take after Thoreau. I'm fit and compact." He patted his thin chest and grinned. "I'm surprised you don't have a cell."

"I left the damn thing somewhere."

"Go on. Tell me some more about your wife. Beth. Do you call her Bethy?"

"There's nothing to tell." Joe took the photograph back, and straightened the edges and looked at it, wondering if she'd forgotten to tell him she was on the nightshift, imagining her white shoes making a soft patter along the shinning hospital floors.

"She's working now? At night?"

Joe slipped the photograph back in his wallet beneath some plastic then his hand went back to his drink. "Lots of people work at night."

"She shouldn't, Joe."

"Ralph, if you have something to say, say it."

"I don't have anything to say that you don't already know."

"I have to go," Joe said. He rose and put his glass in the sink. He looked toward Marilyn, but she was busy reading and drinking and watching TV.

"You haven't changed much, Ralph. But you need to come down and see Mom sometime. For your own benefit."

"Maybe I will," Ralph said.

"Ralph. . ." Joe gave Ralph a hug. "Take it easy."

"You too, Joe. Don't drive too fast."

Joe opened the door and Ralph stepped out behind him. He got in his Jeep, and turned on the lights, and took one last look at Ralph: a small and frail man, gray against the backdrop of yellow light and faded pink. Joe beeped the horn, turned around, and drove through the blackness. At the first gas station, he called his apartment. He called again, but kept getting his answering machine. He tried at the next gas station, and the next, and after that, he just kept driving.

Wondrous

Esther had been reluctant to sign up for the on-line dating service, and it wasn't just the 40 dollars the service extracted from her, although that was bad enough: it was dangerous to subject your deepest desires to public scrutiny. Yet she hadn't met anyone that she was attracted to in years, and it was time to take a proactive approach. Within an hour, after her profile was posted, a potential suitor asked her out to dinner.

"Go," Sylvia, her good friend, urged her. "What have you got to lose?"

"A night of quiet contemplation."

"When was the last time anyone took you to dinner?"

"Long time ago," Esther said. "Sam and I were still married and I was pregnant and we ate fried fish and I spent the night in the bathroom."

"Sounds romantic. You've been divorced how long?"

"Five years."

"Girl, you got work to do!"

Esther was to meet her date at a ship-themed restaurant on the lake, ship-themed meaning there were buoys, thick ropes, and a humongous smiling shark that one could almost hear growling: *I'm going to eat you right up, honey!* She decided to wear a new white blouse and blue skirt with pale green flowers, a little clingy, but the skirt had been only four dollars at a re-sale store. Looking in the mirror, Esther pronounced herself presentable. She borrowed a pair of matching shoes from Sylvia who also trimmed her hair, and who would have manicured her nails had there been time. As she was driving to her rendezvous, Esther realized that she had no idea beyond the *Hello* as to what she would say to the man; at least with a job interview there's a script and an expectation. She parked her car, exited, and walked toward the restaurant's lights. When she heard faint, polka-like music, she wanted to run back to her car and pretend she never agreed to this, but if she left now, it would be that much easier to leave again, and that much she knew about herself. Taking a deep breath and counting backward from ten, she proceeded toward the giant shark and opened the heavy wooden door of the restaurant. A very tall man with long sideburns, whom she recognized from his photograph, stood before her. This was her date. When he shook her hand, she detected a subtle leer in his smile and she knew she'd made a mistake, yet she wasn't sure how to extricate herself. She would hope for the best—*That's the spirit*, Sylvia would have said. And she was hungry: all day long she had been fantasizing about restaurant food: steak, shrimp, baked potatoes, exotic salads. She sat down with her date at a table with a white linen cloth and ordered salmon and broccoli, and he did the same. The thought of the salmon with a little butter, toasted pecans and lemon juice made her mouth water, and she did not feel so nervous anymore. They began with a conversation about New York City (he had driven some trucks there) and when he mentioned "Blacks and Jews" in an unflattering way, Esther told

Buster ("Buster" was what he told her to call him) that she did not feel well, and she picked up her bag and left just as the salmon and broccoli arrived at the table.

Another man she talked to (kids, jobs, politics, movies) almost every night for a month before she asked to meet him in person—just to assure herself that he wasn't a bigot. Esther was hopeful. A meeting was planned at a nearby coffee shop. Esther waited an hour for the man, and when he did not show, she surmised that he must have seen her through the large, plate glass window and decided that she had not met his standards. She was not an unattractive 48-year-old, yet while waiting, she had folded and refolded 36 (she counted) napkins that she had removed from a napkin dispenser. She had folded them into the tiniest size possible.

There were others she conversed with, but nothing ever came of the conversations. She would share a few observations, a joke, an insight, then the other (and it was always the other) would decide that Esther wasn't worth the time or the effort.

There was something flawed about her, she decided. It quickly became clear to her that one had to make a good impression, and fast. The idea called to mine the 60's television show, *The Dating Game*. Yes, *The Dating Game* with its air of self-promoting arrogance, its attempts at humor, and worst of all, its subtle ways of meting humiliation: this was the model from which she was working.

"I'm not very good at this," Esther told Sylvia. Sylvia had come over for dinner of stir fry: onions, kale, cabbage, patty pan squash: all veggies from her garden. "Especially with first impressions. I'm not an impressive person."

"Give it some time," Sylvia said. "Some effort. Come on, Esther: be brave. Be positive. Don't take it so seriously."

"I don't know if I can do that."

"Esther, and don't be so god-damn obtuse. It's not that hard. You're making it hard. You need to be an example for your own daughter, who is probably already dating."

"You think so?"

They both considered Ally: A student, track runner — third fastest girl on the team. Driven in everything. Nothing scared her.

Sylvia nodded. "Men and women meet every day and connect. That's normal. Ester: that's the real world."

They finished eating and stacked the dishes in the sink, and then went to the corner of the kitchen where Ester had set up the desktop computer and she turned it on.

The idea was to make a package for yourself that potential suitors would find somewhat interesting but not too interesting: you didn't want to intimidate them. First, you were required to answer a fairly extensive checklist, questions ranging from your favorite color to your preference in automobiles: are you a Honda, or a Hummer? The sexual innuendoes were fairly blatant. Esther preferred walking or biking, but there were no walking or biking options.

You were required to invent a tag line, something clever but simple and in some cases, deceptive: "If you like wine, music and boats, I'm the vehicle for you" or "Fun-Loving man desires Fun-loving woman." Or "Buddhist-inclined sustainability deep thinker monogamous looking for similar soul mate." There were questions that one was to answer in paragraph form, and here you styled your words so as to impress readers with your wit and essential talents. *I am the mate for you. The only one.* The idea was to convince the other that you were wondrous, kind, giving, intelligent, patient— a gentle person, but for most people, was this true? How many people, indeed, were wondrous, kind, giving, intelligent, patient—and gentle? A handful? And most of them were in committed relationships. Yet Ester and Sylvie read the testimonies of these men, all in pursuit of that "special lady".

"Another Special Lady!" Sylvia guffawed. They sat side by side, elbows on the kitchen counter, eyes glued to the screen. They were searching the 45 to 55-year-old category.

"Oh right: to cook, to clean, to caress. The Three Cs. Can't they think of anything else? How imaginative is that?"

"What do you think?" Esther said anxiously. Sylvia, who always had a boyfriend trailing her, was a woman of the world. Sylvia understood men. She knew how to talk to them, how to flatter them, and how to get them to pay attention to her. She put on heels and perfume and tight pants and guys went ga-ga. You would think they were 15 again! The blue-black hair and Elizabeth Taylor eyes helped. Why, if Esther were half the woman Sylvia was, Esther would have dates every night of the week.

Sometimes, Sylvia even liked her dates.

"There are too many overweight men," Sylvia said, tsk tsking. "Look at that shirt! Now that's a problem. The first word that comes to mind?"

Ester studied the man: big grin of dubious teeth, plaid shirt with buttons straining and wiry hair pushing out. "Slob?"

"I should say!" Sylvie slapped her hand down on the counter. "So you want to sleep with someone who doesn't brush his teeth?"

"Oh come on!"

"Ester, you don't want to be their mother, and you don't want them to have a heart attack on your watch. And the ones without photos — forget those — they're just playing around. Guaranteed: they don't want their wives or girlfriends to know they are doing this. And the ones without incomes — they're looking for a free ride. Remember Tom?"

"Yes." Tom had been Sylvia's paramour for 2 months – exciting, charming, funny, adaptable, a man who could endlessly recite facts from <u>The Guinness Book of World's Records:</u> largest number of people who dressed as penguins at one event? 325. The number of hula hoops 10 women can keep spinning? 264.

Everything was fine until he asked her to invest $10,000 in a business somewhere in the Bronx. Where did he get the idea that she had such money? He was very vague about the details.

A few months after they separated Sylvia pointed out his name in the paper, associated with unscrupulous activities in New York City.

"You see anyone you know?" Ester said breathlessly. "Any patients?" Sylvia, a dark-haired beauty from Mexico, was an x-ray technician for a medical office. She x-rayed legs, arms, feet, breasts—almost any part of the body. She knew many, many people in town.

"No. I don't see any," she said, her nose to the screen.

"Are they still asking you out?"

"Yes!"

"What nerve! What creeps!" Esther said indignantly.

The two continued to examine the glowing screen, clicking on portraits that offered promise, and reading the details together. "Let me tell you, Esther, about this one patient who needed a hip x-ray. You won't believe this. I gave him a gown to put on and I left the room as I usually do to give the patient privacy. I came back five minutes later and he's standing there completely naked except for his socks. Like he's waiting for something."

"And we know what. Uh-huh."

"Averting my eyes, I tell him, *Sir, you can keep your underwear on*. He looks at me with his big blue eyes, straight-on, a challenge, and says, *Miss, I don't wear underwear*. Okay, I think to myself. Meanwhile, my co-workers are watching all of this, and giggling, and I motion to them to keep it down, but that only seems to increase the laughing. You could hear them in the x-ray room! *How about putting the gown on anyway*, I say. *I don't need it*, he tells me, cocking his head with a smile. Oh boy, I think. It was his hip that needed to be x-rayed, and I had to position him. I had on my latex gloves, still, I used this little cushion, gently redirecting him: *Sir, please move this way. Thank you. Now a little this way.* Meanwhile my co-workers are in hysterics, barely able to contain themselves."

"That's something," Esther said with a smile. Never could she do such a job, and she admired Sylvia's command of the situation.

"One more thing, Esther, about the men. You need to look at their eyes. It's all in their eyes."

After Sylvia left, Esther let the dog out and returned to the computer. It was exhausting reading their stories. There were so many. At first, she felt disingenuous, as if she were spying on them, stealing something. Some, inadvertently, let you into secret corners of their minds. *I want someone to cuddle with. I like hunting, fishing, camping, trapping, skinning and skinny dipping! I don't play golf or wear polo shirts but I do burp, and I try to do it discretely. If you have seen a UFO, had sex with a family member, or believe in global warming, do not reply.* Huh, she thought: and what if the man did find his designer mate: would he be happy? Could you actually portray on paper what was in your heart? Esther did not know. Settle for less, she wanted to tell them, or settle for something else. BMWs? Mansion in the hills? Do you really need that? You think that's going to make you happy? *I want someone to go to museums with. Someone to dine with. I want someone to talk to. When I was a kid, I stayed up all night and saw the most glorious sunrise and I want to do that again ... I remember...*

Search deeper, she wanted to tell them, look for that haunting detail. And as she read more, she began to feel as if she was with them, as if they somehow knew she was there, cheering them on.

Later that night, her ex called to tell her that he'd seen her profile, that he would have guessed it was her even without the photo. There were certain phrases she always used, and a quirkiness that the other profiles lacked.

"Yes, Sam," she said, "I am selling myself."

Sam had tried the service many years ago and met a woman who he had planned to marry. But those plans fell apart, and although he had dates with other women, he never found anyone quite like his first date.

"You're objectifying yourself. Making yourself into an object. You know that, right? You see what you're doing? You think you're one thing, but really, you're another. You see that, Esther? Esther?"

There was long pause.

"Esther. You still there? Are you listening, Esther?"

"Yes."

"It's all about being an object. You understand me?"

"Yes."

"Although I have to say, Esther, your profile is well-written. That's a nice photograph. Who took it?"

"The guys at work who take photos for your badge."

"So they did something right, eh?"

The next morning Esther found an e-mail from a person on the dating service who expressed interest in talking with her. His name was Leo and he was a mechanical engineer. They exchanged a few e-mails, spoke on the phone, and arranged to meet at the Farmers' Market at 10 on Saturday.

The sky was clear and blue and the narrow road nearly empty, so Ester decided to bike into downtown. Biking would give her something to focus on, and it would use up that pent-up energy that threatened to explode and tear her apart. The leaves of maples and oaks shimmered in the sun as she biked down hills, and the air was fragrant with summer daylilies.

At the market she found a "No Parking" sign to lock her bike to, but her hands were shaking so much she could barely work the combination. She felt like a fraud. What was she doing here? She shook out her hands, and then looked behind her to see if anyone had been watching her. No one, but then she saw that she was wearing two different socks. It was all starting out wrong, and she was beginning to regret spending a morning with a stranger. Didn't she have enough to do at home? Yet Sylvia would have told her she was being a baby, so she left the bike and proceeded toward the lake, and the wooden booths where the artists and farmers had set up their goods. .

Everything that you would expect to find at a farmer's market was there: hand-made jewelry, tie-dye T-shirts, honey, wine, pastries, flower bouquets, but most of the booths were filled with bushel baskets of beet greens, tomatoes, potatoes, lettuce, basil, zucchini—lots of zucchini. August was zucchini month. And there were green pints of blueberries, peaches and the apples were just starting to come out.

The farmers with their tanned, earnest faces stood behind the bushels of food. They came to the market in battered trucks, and rubber boots up to their knees, their uncut hair tied back with whatever they found lying around. You passed by their booths and smelled rich, dark earth and the fragrance of fresh food.

She met Leo by calling him on his cell and they exchanged descriptions of their clothes. When she found him, he was standing alone, looking lost, wearing what every other man his age was wearing — beige shorts and a black T-shirt. Just like everyone else, and the thought vexed her. Why was she doing this? She must be mad.

"Hello, Leo," she said, extending her hand, attempting a smile.

They shook hands.

Behind them, on the lake, the HV Haendal (*Lake Tours and Floating Classroom*) was just leaving the dock. The tourists sat obediently beneath the red tarp, their backs straight, their eyes alert as if they knew they would see sights this morning that were not only extraordinary, but sights that they would never see again. They were all going out on a wondrous adventure.

"Something to eat?" she said. A man with a rack of hot barbequed meat passed right between them as Esther asked the question.

"Excuse me?"

"I said," she sighed, "something to eat?"

"No thanks," he said almost gaily.

"Coffee?'

"No thanks."

Esther groaned. They walked along the rough-hewn floorboards, glancing at the booths on each side. She was waiting for him to say something — anything — and when he didn't, she made her second assessment: he wasn't a talker.

It was going to be work being with this person, but if she was working, then she wasn't so nervous. Esther noticed her hands were no longer shaking.

"How about some juice? Genuine organic juice. Have you ever had genuine organic juice?"

He smiled but said nothing.

"It's so hot out. That drive here must have parched your throat. Sure you don't want something to drink?"

"Okay."

She found the organic juice stand: "Carrot juice. Prune juice. Special Blend" — whatever that was. She sized up Leo as being an orange juice person.

"We don't have orange juice," a young woman with blonde spiky dreadlocks said. "We haven't been buying oranges. They're too expensive."

"I'll take a Special Blend," Leo said.

The young woman took his money then poured a purplish liquid into a paper cup. No sooner had he been given the juice than Leo held it out to Esther. She didn't understand at first until he said, "Here. Try it."

She did. "It's good," she said, lying. She hoped he didn't pay a lot for it.

They continued on through the crowd, which had gotten thicker, dodging mothers with strollers, dads with babies in backpacks and front packs, kids with dogs, college kids with freckles across their noses who were just hanging out, swimming during the day and listening to music at night, enjoying a lazy summer day on the lake. What a way to spend your summer! They passed the gyro stand with its sizzle and aroma of lamb and its owner's refrain: "Cucumbers on that? Tomatoes? Onions? You absolutely have to have the special sauce and feta cheese. The special sauce is not an option: it's what makes the gyro. It's what makes it special."

Esther bought a cup of coffee, and then they sat at a bench in the shade, facing the lake. Nearby was a hollowed out tree with an interior staircase, and an opening at the top that children periodically peeked out of, the scurried back down inside. Near the dock a thin young man with uncut hair, sandals, and a loose T-shirt strummed his guitar and sang an anti-war ballad.

Esther and Leo talked. What did they talk about? The things you always talk about with someone you've just met: their work, where they lived, their favorite movies and books—and Ester got a little excited because they'd both read Louise Erdrich's The Round House. She suddenly found that it was easy to talk to him, and she had not anticipated that.

"Look," he said, indicating the lake. There was a blue kayak, a man with a bright green life jacket on, paddling: to the right, then to the left, gracefully, musically, barely breaking the lake's soft green surface. There was a sense about him that he was alone but not alone, out on a mission to discover truths of other worlds.

Nearby a woman with gray hair was describing how bread was baked on a stone was superior to that baked conventionally, on a metal sheet. "Of course it's unusual, a little quirky sounding at first, but it's better than the other way. There's nothing like it. I can't describe it, you have to try it."

They continued to talk. Leo did not look her in the eye; it seemed that his eyes were darting back and forth, as if he wanted to say something but was unable to.

A band started playing. There was a banjo player, a violinist, a flautist. Another musician rose up from the crowd and, harmonica in hand, joined in, and in front of them, on a red brick patio near the dock, children and mothers began to dance.

The H.V. Haendal was carefully making its way back to land. It had been gone nearly two hours. When it finally docked, its covey of travelers, all with tired, but radiant smiles of contentment, exited the boat, and the captain shook each person's hand, one-by-one, as they walked off and thanked him.

"I guess it's time to go," he said softly. "You've probably had enough of me."

She nodded. It was time, and she was glad he'd said so. Hoisting up her backpack, she led him to where she had locked her bike.

Her hands were a little damp, not yet shaking, but she was having difficulty with the lock and she felt him standing there, right beside her, and thought for a second that he was going to miraculously reach out and unlock the lock—for some inexplicable reason he just knew the combination—when the lock suddenly snapped open. He hadn't said a word. He just stood there in the sun, waiting. She moved the bike away from the metal post and she sensed again, that he was very close to her, and at any moment he was going to reach out take the bike, and ride off, down the gravel road.

As they walked, they talked about the city, the lake, then they were at his car. He mentioned the fragrance of the water lilies, and then she thought he was going to shake her hand, but instead, he very gently brought her close to him, and she smelled the heat of his skin. The intensity of the experience surprised her.

She snapped on her helmet and her foot was on the pedal when he said: "Send me an e-mail if you'd like to go out again."

"Sure." She looked off in the distance to where she was going.

"And if you don't, that's okay too."

"Sure, Leo."

"Esther, whatever you want to do."

"Hmm."

"Just let me know. Okay?"

She nodded.

As she biked alongside the lake, then through the back lots, she replayed images of Leo, smiling, tilting his head as he listened and she recalled walking among the bushels of greens, flowers, the honey, and looking up when he wasn't looking, and seeing his intense green eyes.

Woodworking

First published in <u>Barkeater: The Adirondack Review</u>, Summer 1998

Fran had put on her rayon blouse with the scoop neck and aqua polyester pants because her in-laws were coming to visit. She'd never met people quite like the Krulls, and doubted she ever would again. She was propped up on Walter's very first project, which was a wood couch. There was a romance novel from the library on her lap. Beside her, Walter rocked on his favorite chair, back and forth, back and forth. Every room of the decrepit farmhouse had a rocking chair, though not much other furniture. Fran shifted her legs — one of the couch's boards was not aligned quite right — and her romance novel fell to the floor.

Still rocking, Walter glanced at Fran. The looser floorboards groaned.

Walter had light blonde hair to his shoulders and a beard that was reddish and pointed, like a leprechaun's. When Walter got excited about a project (he was involved in several projects) his gray eyes became animated and he seemed to leap all over the farmhouse, and that made Fran, at least momentarily, forget the illness that incapacitated her two years ago.

Their Adirondack farmhouse had been a real steal, although Walter's mother, Mrs. Krull, who helped them find it, hadn't recommended it. She told them it was isolated and cheap: way too cheap. But Walter insisted, and Fran: she never argued with Walter.

"When are your parents coming?" Fran said. She shivered and pulled her pink comforter up around her thin shoulders.

"Who knows?" Walter said. He looked at Fran, and rocked a little faster. He was a little frightened, she knew; her dark eyes and the purple hollows beneath them, which made up most of her face, sometimes frightened even her. She didn't look in mirrors anymore.

"You know what they say, Fran," Walter said whimsically, looking out the bay window at their pines and the cherrywood trees. "They're unencumbered." Walter laughed, and Fran laughed. Then Walter rocked, and Fran, too exhausted to do anything else, stared out the window at the trees and tried not to think about her nightmares. They started with her falling into something black. The latest one had a damp, musty smell to it, and she didn't enjoy it; no, not at all.

A few minutes later they heard pounding footsteps and knuckle rapping at the door. "Hello-oo! Anybody home? Here we are! Hello-oo!"

"Stay just where you are," Walter told Fran, but before he could reach the door it flung open and Mrs. Krull appeared, her solid body poised for action. She was a plump woman, shaped like a gumdrop.

Mrs. Krull's inquisitive eyes darted past Walter to Fran, and then sliding her heavy pot of food onto the kitchen cupboard, she advanced with determination toward the couch.

'Fran," she said, her freckled hands reaching out. "How are you?"

"Okay," Fran said, her voice high and slightly irritable. In Mrs. Krull's eyes she saw shock and disbelief and thus Fran made a valiant attempt to raise herself, but the blood rushed from her head and she felt faint. The very next second, however, Walter was beside her, taking her elbow. He had her sitting up.

Fran heard shuffling in the kitchen. Glancing behind the couch, Fran saw Mr. Krull in his red lumberjack coat. His shoulders were slightly hunched and his expression, as usual, was impassive. In one arm he carried a full grocery bag, in the other, a stack of newspapers.

"How do you like the couch, Mom? Dad?" Walter said.

Mrs. Krull took two steps back from the couch. She frowned. "It's very. . ."

"Rustic," Mr. Krull said, from the kitchen. He set down his items and walked pensively into the front room. "You built it yourself?" He pushed his glasses up on his nose and bent down to examine the couch. Light-weight wood.

Fran felt the couch shake and she heard him sniffing.

"Pine." Mr. Krull sniffed again. "But pine doesn't smell like that. What's that smell? Something smells funny." He sniffer more, peering around the room.

"George," Mrs. Krull said, flinging out her hands. "See what happens when you marry a farmer?"

"I haven't farmed in forty years."

"Once a farmer, always a farmer."

"It's like a coffin," Mr. Krull said.

"Don't be so morbid." Mrs. Krull slapped Mr. Krull sharply on his back. She gave him a look, and then said to Fran: "Is that comfortable? You don't have any cushions."

"It's just a tiny, tiny bit hard," Fran said. But her in-laws gave her such an odd look that Fran tried to smile. "I'm going to make cushions, but I haven't been out to buy the material."

"Reading another romance, I see," Mr. Krull said. He picked up Fran's book from the floor and handed it to her and she thanked him.

"She reads them all the time, Dad," Walter said.

"I enjoy them," Fran said. "These days the heroines are strong. Most people don't buy the passive woman myth anymore." She held up her book. On the cover was a clever-looking woman in a tight emerald green suit; her hair, a mass of brilliant auburn waves, seemed like it could propel her forward into unspecified adventures. "These women are liberated."

"I've always been liberated," Mrs. Krull cried out. She put her hands on her wide hips and laughed.

"You have to be careful," Mrs. Krull said quietly to Fran, so quietly she thought at first he was talking to himself. "You don't want to confuse reality with fantasy."

"Oh, I never do that," Fran said, blinking rapidly. "I know the difference."

"Dad," Walter said, "let me tell you, we're not going to live here the rest of our lives."

"Praise the Lord," Mrs. Krull said with a laugh. Then, regarding Walter closely, she said, "You're T-shirt's getting a little tight."

"Must be those delicious dinners Fran's cooking." Walter rubbed his protruding stomach and winked at Fran.

Fran winked back. Fran was still adjusting to Mrs. Krull, whom she'd inherited three years ago when she married Walter. Mrs. Krull sold real estate. After finalizing a deal, she'd show up in her gaudy makeup and neon-flowered pantsuit, her brown hair in short tight curls, and offer to take Fran and Walter out to dinner, which Walter always accepted. She'd return with them and lounge around like she owned the farmhouse and tell them they needed a new stove, or a dishwasher, or curtains instead of towels on the windows. What really annoyed Fran, however, was when Mrs. Krull joked about Walter being cheap. She didn't understand, Fran believed, the subtleties of frugality.

Walter was explaining how it was more efficient for him to cut down the trees for the cabin and plane the wood himself. "Bypassing the middlemen will save us at least fifty percent. Then we'll sell the by-products."

"By-products?" Mr., Krull said skeptically.

"The chips. The sawdust. Farmers feed it to the pigs." Walter pulled out his calculator from a pocket Fran had sewn onto his T-shirt, and he started pushing buttons. He stopped suddenly to smile out at the trees, then he fingered his beard, and pushed more buttons.

Fran smiled at Walter, and waited for him to smile back, but he seemed to be busy.

"I'm relieved you're finally getting some furniture instead of sitting on that rusted outdoor set," Mrs. Krull said. "Is it outside?" Mrs. Krull stuck her neck around the corner in the direction of the back porch.

"In the spare bedroom," Walter said, without looking up. He was still involved in a calculation.

"Did Walter tell you how we put an egg in the microwave, and it exploded?" Fran said quickly, hoping to divert Mrs. Krull. Walter had been frequenting junk yards again, and he'd been storing his objects d'art in the spare bedroom.

"And he's supposed to be a scientist!" Mrs. Krull laughed and clapped her hands once, powerfully, and her entire body jiggled. "I need to bring over the microwave's instruction booklet so you don't kill yourselves."

"We won't do that," Fran said quickly.

Fran really didn't feel well.

Fran needed to rest.

Then Fran watched Walter slowly turn his head and look at his mother. The two pairs of eyes were the exact pale gray color, and at that moment, Fran thought them indistinguishable. Walter returned his calculator to his pocket.

"We planted five hundred baby cherrywood trees," Walter said, his voice high and excited. He started pointing outside. "See? See?"

Everyone looked out the bay window to the forest of pines and cherrywood and the rainbow-shaped pond that Walter bathed in when it wasn't ice-covered. There was a thunderclap in the distance, then it began drizzling.

"Our cabin will be surrounded by trees," Walter said. "You know what they say about simple pleasures?"

"Simple pleasures are the best," Fran said. When they sang together (they used to sing a song called "Partners" to the melody of "Sisters"), Fran knew she loved Walter more than she ever loved anyone or would ever love anyone. At the same time, Fran had been a persnickety librarian with thick glasses, large jutting bones and a perpetual frown, the latter because she was always on the lookout for potential book thieves.

Whenever Walter appeared at the Mentonville Library, the senior librarian, an older and distinguished man, would take Fran aside and shaking his head, he'd whisper: "That Walter Krull, he's very strange. An interesting person, but very strange."

Fran's parents, both high school teachers who read voraciously, and still lived in Iowa, told Fran: "He's a visionary, yes. A genius. But geniuses—they often have these quirks. They tend toward extremes. Sometimes they have these God complexes. You have to know when to stop them." But Walter had brought to fruition the playful side of Fran's personality (she hadn't even realized she'd had one), and for that, Fran was more than grateful:

she felt forever indebted to Walter.

In twenty years we'll harvest the trees," Walter said. "And Joe McGurdy and I already poured the cabin's foundation."

"You didn't hire a professional?" Mr. Krull said.

"Dad, you always told me: 'If you want something done right, do it yourself.'" He tugged at his father's arm.

Fran saw Mr. Krull glance at his wife and shake his head.

"You have enough money to hire a professional," Mr. Krull said. "The Survey pays a damn good salary—especially after fifteen years. What are you going to do with all your money?"

"Save it for a rainy day," Walter said.

"It's raining now!" Mrs. Krull cried exuberantly.

"Drizzling, Mom," Walter said.

"Don't you think you're being a little extreme?" Mr. Krull said.

Fran looked up.

"Extreme? Come on!" Walter laughed. It was one of those laughs that went to the core of Fran's being, a laugh that implored: 'Trust me. Believe me. I know what I'm doing.' Walter looked at Fran, and Fran laughed, then Mrs. Krull laughed. Well, Fran thought, if everything seemed okay to them, then everything must be okay.

"Dad, Mom, listen: we're getting out of the rat race. You know? Rampant consumerism? Three-hour commutes? Isn't that crazy?"

"There are lots of people," Mr. Krull spoke carefully," who do crazy things, and who don't understand the consequences."

"George," Mrs. Krull said.

"It's like Thoreau's *Walden* here, except that we call it Walt's and Fran's." Then Walter went to the couch and put his arm around Fran's thin shoulders. She'd been feeling cold; the closeness of Walter made her warm again.

"Walt's and Fran's," Mrs. Krull said.

"Walter's Fran," Mr. Krull said absentmindedly. He was sitting on an unpadded rocking chair reading the dog-eared paperback that he usually carried with him.

"Not quite as poetic as Thoreau's Walden," Fran said. She had a theory that what people read gave clues to who they wanted to be. Mr. Krull read his paperback: *Jokes and Their Relation to the Subconscious* and Mrs. Krull read the stock market pages and religious propaganda. Fran read romances, and Walter, since starting his woodworking projects, he hadn't been reading much of anything.

"It's functional," Walter said. "The name, I mean."

"We're not dense," Mrs. Krull said. She was in the kitchen, putting the roast in the microwave.

"Money will give us freedom," Walter said. "The more money we have, and the less money we spend, the more freedom we'll have."

Fran saw Mr. Krull raise his gray eyebrow with skepticism. Mrs. Krull came out from the kitchen and frowned.

"I'm not sure about that," Fran said. "I'm not completely sure."

"Fran! Fran!" Walter jumped up from the couch. "No one's

ever completely sure about anything! Come on, Dad." Walter playfully waved his hand between Mr. Krull's paperback and his eyes so he couldn't red. "You can read anytime. Let me show you my new saws."

The two men left the farmhouse, and the door closed behind them. The barn, where Walter did his woodworking, was only a few feet from the house. Fran listened closely as Walter began his demonstration: circular saw, table saw, radial arm saw. Next would be the band saw, then the saw with the extra-strength tungsten steel blade.

Mrs. Krull whistled and puttered around the kitchen, putting things away and taking things out. She rattled a can of bent nails and laughed. The nails, Fran remembered, they'd salvaged from an abandoned house that had been struck by lightning and partially burnt down; the wood had been too rotten, and they'd left it. The linoleum squeaked as Mrs. Krull puttered about.

Fran looked outside to their only ornamental tree, a mountain ash, which Fran had identified from a guidebook she'd gotten at a garage sale. She'd been a regular garage saler before she fell ill. Last spring, the mountain ash was covered in white flowers that resembled cauliflower. Fran decorated the house with them and Walter made them for dinner once, but Fran couldn't eat them. The tree also bore red berries, and luckily, Fran thought, the berries were poisonous to humans. Mushrooms, which Fran had persuaded Walter not to eat, outlined its root pattern. The tree wasn't old, but it was dying.

"You could use a modern sink," Mrs. Krull said, trying to turn on the faucet. She knocked over the can of nails and bent down to pick them up and her voice became nasal, her breathing labored. "I know you two ...want to do things ...the natural way ...but a little convenience...never hurt anyone."

Fran felt as if every clatter was something physical hammering on her head. She was getting a horrible headache.

"Is Walter taking you out at all?" Mrs. Krull had recovered, and was getting out the dishes.

"He takes good care of me."

"Do you get out?" Mrs. Krull turned toward Fran, a chipped plate in her hand.

Fran was silent.

"It's not good to be alone so much, Fran. If you don't get out, you forget what the outside world is like, and how other people live."

"Walter bought me a cordless phone so I can call people, and a beeper so I can get a hold of him."

Leaning down, Fran put her hand beneath the couch and produced the phone. It was black, and dented around the edges. She bent down again, stretching her fingers, but she couldn't find the beeper.

"He bought you something?" Mrs. Krull said.

Fran understood that tone of voice. She believed that children, to compensate for their parents' obsessions, developed equal but opposite obsessions. Walter's parsimony was perfectly explainable in light of Mrs. Krull's wastefulness. The Krull house had numerous useless knickknacks that stood on numerous useless table tops. Every cupboard was named and every wall was filled. Moreover, they had a condo in Florida that was so inundated with things that one could barely move.

"Men," Mrs. Krull said, and Fran understood the implication. "Sometimes they are so insensitive."

"Walter takes good care of me," Fran managed to say. Lying back down, she pulled the pink comforter up to her neck. She looked at the ceiling and saw a water mark directly above her.

Fran couldn't remember which had been there first—the couch or the water marks—and it annoyed her because accurate observation had always been one of her virtues. Her memory had been infallible.

Fran couldn't wait till they were gone so she could watch TV and Walter could rock and meditate: every night that he was home they did that. And they never fought, not like Walter said his parents did. Describing to Fran the screaming, name-calling episodes obviously caused Walter pain, yet in spite of it all, Walter admitted the fights seemed to settle something. Still, Fran believed she and Walter had a wonderfully amiable relationship, except that Walter got preoccupied with his woodworking or his extension classes. Walter had explained the necessity for a strict routine to Fran.

"Fran," he'd said, "what's stable?"
"The trees you just planted."
"More stable. More psychologically stable."

"The house?"

"Say we were to flee, Fran," Walter said. "Say because the country was collapsing." Walter was fond of theories of government collapse: Fran knew that Armageddon attracted him. The government's collapse would allow him to rise to his full potential as a scientist and free thinker.

"I don't know, Walter. Tell me."

"Bullion. Gold bullion," Walter said, his eyes animated.

"Is that where all of our money's been going, Walter?"

Walter raised his blonde eyebrows and stroked his pointed beard.

"Is that what the hole near the compost is for? Do you have a pot of gold in the compost?" she asked, her eyes now glittering, like his.

Walter grinned. "Money doesn't lie. It tells you who you are."

"I already know who you are, Waltie," Fran said coyly.

"I'm not finished, Fran. Now if the country goes to hell, what do we need that we can't produce?"

Fran thought a while about that. "Zippers?"

Walter laughed with abandon. "Who's going to care about fashion when the country is going to hell!"

"Okay. Tell me, Waltie."

"Medicine."

Walter believed he was on the brink of an important discovery. He explained to Fran how he had cooked the mountain ash's white flowers, distilled the liquids and was now culturing them. In addition to his biochemistry degrees, Walter kept current on medicinal herbs. Walter's discovery—a miracle medicine—would not only save Fran, but would make them unbelievably rich.

Fran didn't want to sound negative but hinted around that medicines sometimes took decades to develop, and required the efforts of hundreds of researchers.

"But we have need on our side," Walter said. "Need."

"They just don't realize," Mrs. Krull said. "Sometimes you have to spell it out. Men don't like to talk. They don't realize talking helps them solve problems."

Mrs. Krull kept talking as she set the table.

Fran closed her eyes and imagined warm blood circulating through her muscles, soothing the cramps and aches. She was drifting off, fantasizing about Walter and herself holding hands, laughing, singing. She was almost asleep when she heard: "Fran! Fran! Are you all right?"

The found face was six inches away from her. At first Fran thought the gray eyes examining her were Walter's, but this close she saw that Mrs. Krull's eyes weren't as steely as his. The eyes looked concerned. Fran felt ashamed of herself: Mrs. Krull had some intelligence, although it was an odd intelligence.

"I was just thinking," Fran said sleepily.

"You think too much. It's not good for you. That puts you in a rut."

"A rut? Do you ..." Fran began, putting her elbow on the couch, almost leaning against Mrs. Krull, only the pink comforter between them, and she smelled the roast and fresh peas on her and that scent of laundry detergent that her clean clothes exuded. "I mean, here, out here, in this farmhouse, do you...I mean. . ."

The comforter fell and Mrs. Krull groaned elaborately as she bent down to pick it up, and Fran thought Mrs. Krull looked like herself again: the stiff brown hair in little knots that circled her pinkish pudgy face. Fran decided not to pursue the matter.

"Fran, I should tell you." Mrs. Krull neatly folded the comforter and placed it at the end of the couch.

Here it comes, Fran thought. She lay back down, but forced herself to look at Mrs. Krull.

"Everyone in my group has been praying for you."

"That's very generous or you, Mrs. Krull." If she agreed with her, Fran thought, Mrs. Krull wouldn't be as persistent.

"Praise the Lord, Fran. But I have a feeling something's going to happen."

Fran really believed Mrs. Krull was some kind of loony.

"Something big," Mrs. Krull added expansively.

"We're going to have an earthquake," Fran said. She'd been reading about Japanese earthquakes. Reading and sleeping was how she spent her days.

"As long as I've lived in New York State," Mrs. Krull said,

"which is all of my life, we've never had an earthquake. My feeling is about you, Fran."

"Praise the Lord." Fran didn't want to hear anymore; sometimes Mrs. Krull's proclamations spooked her, like the one about the almost-dead woman who suddenly regurgitated black liquids after being prayed over by Mrs. Krull's delegation.

Fran looked at the ceiling, her eyelids fluttered, and they began drifting close when Walter and Mr. Krull returned. Walter went immediately to the couch and grabbing Fran's hand, said, "How are we doing?"

"We're doing fine."

"Look at all that food," Walter said, pulling Fran up into a sitting position. "Just smell it. Wonderful, huh?" Fran saw Walter's gray eyes open with pleasure and thought that the night could still go well.

"Roast beef, peas, carrots," Walter said. "Salad. Rolls. Real mashed potatoes. Gee, Mom: this is great!" Walter gently squeezed Fran's hand.

"Wonderful," Fran said.

Walter lifted Fran's elbows and she tried not to lean on him too much as the walked to the table. She tried to smile. When they all sat down, the table wobbled.

"An early project," Fran said. She had to talk, to let everyone know she was okay. They passed around the food and the table continued to wobble. Everyone started eating when suddenly Mr. Krull said: "Look at your son eat!"

"George," Mrs. Krull said sharply. "Use some tact."

Mr. Krull shook his head and grumbled.

"Working outside all day gives Walter an appetite," Fran said.

"Great food, Mom," Walter said, when he got the chance.

"Do you have an extra fork?" Mr. Krull held up a salad fork that was missing its two inner prongs.

"Let's see." Walter grabbed a roll and got up to search through the silverware drawer. Silver rattled. "Guess that's what happens when you shop at Goodwill. You get these surprise bags. Surprise! Surprise!" Walter giggled.

The silver rattled again, the Walter shook the drawer with more vigor and gave Fran his sly, elfish smile. "How about a soup spoon?"

Walter held up a bent spoon.

"That's okay," Mrs. Krull said, shaking her head silently at an exasperated Mr. Krull. "We'll share."

"Okay." Walter returned to the table to eat.

After one tablespoon of mashed potatoes, Fran gently pushed aside her plate. Her teeth didn't feel well. Her hair had been falling out, but she'd heard cortisone, which she'd been on for two years, could do that.

"Finished," Fran said crisply.

Mrs. Krull paused mid-air with the gravy ladle, and Mr. Krull's mouth opened slightly.

"Stress," Fran said. She knew stress could be invoked to explain almost anything. She didn't want an involved discussion on her state of health.

"Stress," Walter echoed. He was working on another helping of potatoes, lading on the gravy.

"I didn't say anything. Not a word," Mrs. Krull said, and she seemed to close her eyes.

After dinner, Mr. and Mrs. Krull cleaned up, then Mr. Krull announced it was time to go: he hugged Fran and Walter, then went outside to warm the car.

Mrs. Krull kissed Fran good-bye and told her: "Take care of yourself."

Fran nodded weakly and attempted a smile. She watched Walter walk his mother to the door and step outside on the porch. Holding onto the furniture, Fran quietly lurched and hobbled over to the doorway.

"She's very depressed," Fran heard Mrs. Krull say.

"It's her medicine, Mom."

Then you have to take her back to the doctor. I don't care how much it costs. Didn't the doctor say that the new medicine could have dangerous side effects?"

"She's read every book that's ever been published on the medicines and the disease. She's intelligent. We both know what's going on."

"Thirty-six years old and she's an invalid!" Mrs. Krull said sharply. "She should be in a hospital. She's starving herself to death. You can't leave her alone. Ever."

That last word shook Fran's entire body. She breathed so deeply she hurt.

"Mom," Walter said, almost whining. "We know what we're doing. Fran's just having a relapse. She'll be better in a few days."

"She needs help. She needs therapy, Walter. She can't do it alone. You don't understand how far it's gone and she won't tell you herself. She has too much pride." Then Fran heard Mrs. Krull kiss her son on the cheek. "I don't mean to interfere. We'll see you next Sunday."

Fran made it back to the couch. She heard the Krulls' car drive off, and Walter's measured step on the porch's old floorboards. The front door opened slowly, and remained open, letting in a gush of damp night air, and Fran knew Walter was turning around, giving them one last wave. The door closed, and Walter walked over to the couch.

"That wasn't so bad, was it, Hon? We had a great dinner and Mom even cleaned up the house. But my mother's worried about you." Walter patted Fran's head, then went to his chair and started rocking.

"She's always worried." Fran's words trembled; the fast retreat back to couch made her breathe harder. "It's just my new medicine."

"How much was it?" Fran told him and Walter stopped rocking. "If you'd let me call around, we could have found it cheaper." Then Walter started fingering his beard, and Fran thought he was going to prove something to her with his calculator, but he didn't. He glanced outside at the trees and said: "You know what they say, Fran: A penny saved is a penny earned."

"I did some calling, Waltie. But that phone you got me—sometimes it works and sometimes it doesn't. It's so temperamental. Like the beeper."

"You have to remember to recharge it, or replace the battery."

"I'm sorry. My brain hasn't been working properly."

"Use the other phone."

Fran nodded, unable to admit that she couldn't always make it to the other phone.

Walter rocked. He was upset, Fran knew; it was, after all, his money. And he'd nursed her like a guardian angel. Fran didn't have any friends in New York; for the last two years, she'd been too ill to leave the farmhouse. Most of her knowledge about married couples she gleaned from the romance novels or the women's magazines Mrs. Krull gave her. If a couple had to disagree about something, she believed it might as well be money; she never wanted to whine, or God forbid, turn into a shrew.

"I'm going to sand the door," Walter said, rising. "I also need to check on my cultures."

"This is your only night off, I thought that since..."

'Fran, I love you, but the sooner I finish the cabin ...you know what they say, Fran."

"Time is money. Money moves the world. But sometimes, Walter, you can worry about money so much that it becomes a disease. A real disease. A physiological part of you."

"Where'd you get that idea from? One of your romance novels?" Walter laughed.

95

Fran tried to laugh with him, but her entire day had been off, starting when she work up that morning from another nightmare about falling into something black. The nightmare had been so strong and vivid that it moved like an aura around her. It was something she could feel and touch, and it left a lingering smell, like the way Mrs. Krull's roast did, but the smell wasn't as palatable. Fran knew something wasn't quite right.

"Walter," she said, swallowing hard. "Walter, I have this feeling."

Bending down, Walter brushed his lips against Fran's sunken cheek. "Beep me if you need anything." He patted her shoulder and walked towards the door.

"Walter," she said, her voice shrill and wavering. He stopped briefly, and she saw the lines beside his mouth harden.

"I have work, Fran," Walter said sharply. "I'll be right here." Then he added softly, "Only a few feet away."

Fran heard his determined footsteps, the door closing behind him. Very soon she heard the sanding machine. With the pink comforter up to her neck, Fran lay on her back, staring at the ceiling's water marks.

Her premonition of disaster was more powerful than ever, so she started singing "Partners": "Part-ners ...part-ners ...there were never such devoted part-ners. . ." As she sang, she looked outside to the mountain ash, but the ash had faded into the gray twilight, and it was as if the tree never existed.

A chill ran up her spine.

It was raining now, but Fran could still hear Walter's

sanding. The sanding wasn't nearly as soothing as his rocking. The sander would slow down, and sometimes stop. She worried about Walter, what he would do if she ever…maybe that was what started her heart beating, beating wildly, as if it wanted to jump right out of her rib cage, as if it'd had enough of this confinement.

It wasn't just her hair falling out, or her teeth wobbling; the illness was in her muscles, as deep as her heart muscle. It surprised her that it had gone that deep. She reached beneath the couch for the beeper to summon Walter; he would joke with her or sing "Marion The Librarian" from *The Music Man*.

She stretched her arm, then her fingers as far as she could. At last she felt the cold plastic. Breathless, and overcome with joyous emotion, she brought the beeper up to her chest and pressed the tiny square button. She pressed it again.

It was dead.

Her heart pounded more furiously and there was a reciprocal pounding in her head and she felt faint and thought maybe she could crawl to the door; just like a baby, crawl, crawl to the door. It wasn't that far. Then scream. But she was very dizzy, so dizzy that if she lifted her head, she'd probably faint. The room got darker and darker, almost black, and at first Fran thought it was merely a thunderhead moving over the farmhouse. She did hear thunder. Then she felt as if she were falling, and she wished that someone, anyone, even Mrs. Krull would burst in and cry: "Hell-lo-oo! Anyone home?" Or maybe Walter's generous side would assume control, and he'd appear before her. She thought if she willed it hard enough it would happen; yes, she knew how strong the Will was, and Mrs. Krull, certainly a woman of strong Will, had saved her before.

The fall was getting slower. It was turning out to be quite pleasant. The sanding became fainter and fainter, even fainter than the rain. The smell of pine and musty dampness was getting stronger. Would anyone come? Fran wondered. Was there still time?

Genomes, Quarks and Brahms

They had just left the airport and were driving south toward the lake in a mud-colored Dodge. There were certainly newer and more beautiful cars on the road, Fran had to admit, but the old Dodge was reliable. She knew what to expect. And it being one of a kind—well, no one would ever dare steal it. Amy, Fran's freckle-face niece, was sitting in the passenger seat, admiring the fields of weeds, the sparkle of the blue Finger Lake, the occasional squirrel who dared to descend from a pine tree and play chicken with four tons of steel moving at 50 miles-per-hour. Her niece had to sit up front because Walter had removed the back seat. He could never leave things as they were, it was as if he had to personally mark them so that he would not be forgotten, not even for a minute.

The warm summer wind was blowing through her thin hair, and Fran was having a grand time thinking of all the fun and extraordinary adventures she would take Amy on, when Amy suddenly cried out:

"Stop! You have to stop!"

Fran pulled over so abruptly that a frayed bungee cord holding the car trunk closed somersaulted in the air. Gone forever.

"What's wrong?" Fran's eyes followed Amy's and she stared with dread at the child's wrist (where Amy was staring), expecting to see an escapee from one of Walter's insect experiments eating into her tender flesh.

"It's exactly, three, two, one: four o'clock! Oh no!" The girl's expression became suddenly despondent. "It *was* four o'clock."

"Something special about four o'clock?" Fran said. "Tea time?"

The little girl became silent.

Fran parked the old Dodge in college town, beside a three-story stucco house painted a bright shade of orange. Even though it was August, there were no flowers, and the spotty grass could have used a good trim.

On the porch roof, which leaned at a precarious angle, was fully functional lawn chair and giant prone stuffed cat, grinning, welcoming all visitors to the humble abode.

"Leaning porches are not so unusual in the Finger Lakes," Fran said, ducking as she ascended the porch's steps. Having wacked her head numerous times, she knew when to duck. "Hills make everything lean. Lean — a joke there! And the house — a little briefing here, Amy — it's grand in design, but not what you'd call in suburban shape."

They entered through the front door, Fran cautioning Amy about the porch's floorboards, not because the holes were large enough to cause one to lose footing, but because of the moles, the mice and occasional skunk that periodically inhabited the netherworld below.

"They are, however, tame," Fran assured Amy. "Previous renters had been Animal Rights Activists," Fran continued. "They had — shall we say — pets? Then the students moved out, and left their pets behind. Students!" Fran rolled her eyes. At least she had Amy's attention. "Wonder why, eh? There were other unanticipated guests—too many—and Uncle Walter could have had them exterminated or trapped and removed—it was getting to that point—but it's against his principles to pay good money for something he can do himself, and more importantly, something he can do *better* than someone else." In response to Amy's look of confusion, Fran added: "There's always a price to pay for living in the center of action. If you ever live in the middle of nowhere, you will understand."

"That's okay, Aunt Fran," Amy said shrugging. "My Mom said that intellectuals like you and Uncle Walter are always willing to try anything."

"Anything?" Fran's hands trembled, and the hurt deep inside her threatened to seep out. She needed courage, the kind of courage that romance novel heroines were famous for. Reading romance novels was Fran's greatest passion. Her present novel, set in India (the publishers like exotic venues), involved a heroine seeking not only the perfect mate, but seeking leaders of pseudo-scientific organizations who believed they could cure infertility. Belief and suspended belief were the innate elements of such novels. Heroines with political savvy, personal problems and courage—the courage to be hurt—were in demand by publishers and readers alike. Fran admired these heroines for being everything that she was not, and she loved them all unreservedly.

It was dark inside the house, yet through the hazy light (the windows were tiny, high, not clean) Fran made out the image of

Walter: his rigid shoulders, the slumped belly. On his wooden rocker he went, back and forth, back and forth. He was thinking.

"Hello Walter," Fran said.

"Hello Uncle Water," Amy said.

Continuing to rock at pace, Walter raised his right hand a few inches in a gesture of recognition. His lips were pursed, the eyes closed in concentration. Perhaps he was thinking through a complicated problem that involved making fast food as healthy as fresh vegetables. It was obvious to Fran that she should not disturb Walter. *Do Not Disturb* was one of his unspoken rules, and Fran knew enough not to break any of his rules. She led Amy into the kitchen to offer her a glass of cold cider and wheat crackers, which were accepted.

The kitchen was not in the best shape: the linoleum was upbowed and the wallpaper was impossibly greasy. It should be removed (the landlord encouraged beautification efforts), but Fran did not have the energy. Previous renters had cooked up all sorts of concoctions for their little friends, and the kitchen, despite a strong bleaching, still expelled an odor of grease, sugar and unusual herbs.

Walter had a penchant for decrepit houses, and the more decrepit the better: rotted wood, water in the walls, tiny interior spaces that functioned as hideouts for insects. Fran believed that living where they did fulfilled an essential psychological need of Walter's to be confronted with dilemmas. Had it been up to Fran, she would not be living at the base of a steep hill in a moldy, dark basement apartment where flooding was a concern.

Fran had not appreciated the full extent of 'water running downhill' until the torrential rainstorms of June. One night the rain had come so fast and furiously that they had to set the furniture up on concrete blocks. Dirty water littered with flotsam of indeterminate origin swirled beneath their bed.

Walter, with extraordinary calmness, had said: *This is truly a unique experience, Fran. Unique experiences often inspire one in unexpected ways, and allow one to see the world differently. Mysteries of the world, Fran.*

Unbelievable, Fran had thought, that it could rain so much, but Walter had explained the horrendous precipitation in terms of temperature, pressure, the good old *PV equals NRT, great bodies of water and rotation of earth. The exquisite geometry of water transport.* It was a good enough explanation for Fran, and she did not pursue the issue of finding more amenable accommodations.

Fran watched Amy study a group of ants as they hiked down the greasy wallpaper to the sink, risking death for microscopic food tidbits. The constant dampness and pervasive smell of grease and sugar encouraged the Ant Heaven. Because Fran cooked mostly beans, lentils and rice, it occurred to her that perhaps *these ants,* who resided in an intellectual town where anything was possible, possessed long term memories. Fran made a mental note to discuss this with Walter. He was always receptive to new ideas, especially ideas associated with the mind.

"Have you lived here long?" Amy asked.

"We're renting. We'll be here only a few years while Walter teaches his native medicinal plant classes and does research with the great scientists from all over the world, so we figured...we figured. . ."

The little girl smiled, and for a moment, the ancient kitchen with its single leaning cupboard and asthmatic refrigerator seemed to vanish. Amy did not appear to be a ten-year-old having difficulties with her parents' divorce. Amy's mother had mentioned fragility, fears about the night, and fears about swimming, although Amy had passed every swimming class at the Y. Fran had promised to take her niece to all the beaches and pools within a hundred mile radius of the city. *Maybe she will talk to you,* Fran's sister had said. *She's always talked to you. She won't talk to either of us.*

Fran led Amy through the front room where Walter contentedly rocked, eyes closed, his face transfixed in the Zen state. From the position of his hands on the chair's arms, Fran knew he was emptying his mind, an activity akin to shoveling snow or deleting unused computer files.

Into the spare room they went, entrance accomplished via a narrow path through leaning towers of books and papers. Hundreds of books from the Entomology Research Library filled the room which certainly meant overdue fines, but knowing Walter, he would never pay the fines. He would get away scot free.

"Is there a bed?" Amy smiled cheerfully, as if in anticipation of an adventure.

"Living with greatness, one must expect eccentricities." Fran smiled with pride. Then she noticed a new ant infestation in a corner where someone (Walter?) had left an egg-encrusted frying pan. Surely this greasy pan was here for a reason? Although a jar lid with Walther's new human-benign-but- insect–deadly white powder sat nearby, the ants still went on their merry way, lugging itsy-bitsy bits of white egg up the wall. But Walter was a genius and a firm believer in trial and error, and whatever Walter believed in, so too, did Fran. She let the fry pan stay.

"You know what they say about cleanliness and God, well, Walter and I decided long ago to search for – "

"Aunt Fran." Amy's index finger pointed to her red-banded watch. "It's four-forty-four. Look! Four-forty-four forty, forty-one, forty-two, forty-three, forty-four!"

After a dinner of rice, lentils and beans, Walter, Fran and Amy sat outside on stuffed chairs recently jettisoned by the frat boys. But the chairs were comfortable, and they had been free. The sky was clear and blue. Sparrows chirped in maples. Fran's adorable niece was beside her looking with awe around the tiny backyard, hemmed in or formed – depending upon one's perspective – by the backs of other dilapidated houses. Could life get any better? For the time being, Fran was content.

"What exactly do you do at the university, Uncle Water?" Amy said. She tucked her feet beneath her, making herself comfortable in the stuffed chair.

"I'm refining my medicines."

"He's creating medicines destined to change the world."

Fran was overjoyed that Walter had emerged from his trance to join them.

Often his trance lasted through dinner and into the night, and then in the morning he would walk zombie-like onto the campus bus and that would be the end of him until the next dinner. Fran was not sure how Walter would react to Amy, his perspective being that children consumed money and time, and without time and money, how could a person control his life?

"I'm helping people who are sick," Walter said.

Amy nodded and sipped her cider. Walter was given all the free cider he wanted because he was helping the university's apple orchard develop a fungicide to combat the venturia inaequalis – which everyone in Fran and Walter's circle knew was responsible for apple scab.

"What kind of sicknesses?"

"Diabetes, asthma, rheumatism, AIDS, cancer. At some level," Walter narrowed his green eyes, and his voice became sonorous, "they're all connected."

"If anyone can do it Walter can."

Walter smiled. Then he went over to a wooden keg from which a balloon protruded and drew himself a drink. He held out a cup to Fran, but she could no longer drink cider, hard or soft.

"So all those books in the spare room are for your medicine research?"

Walter laughed as he returned to his overstuffed chair. The chair was patterned with raised red roses that matched the pattern of the ripped wallpaper in the front room. One renter had attempted to strip the wallpaper, but had given up. Whatever chemical the renter used had started eating through the wall, and it was responsible for the holes in the floor.

"Walter's research is also in preparation for a book," Fran said proudly. "Walter *never* stops." She thought to qualify the statement with 'where intellectual pursuits are concerned,' but she liked hearing Walter laugh, and she wished he would laugh more.

"My Mom said you were multi-talented, Uncle Walter. She said you could do *anything*."

At the suggestion of anything, Fran became suddenly alert.

"The tentative title of my book is <u>Rules of the World</u>." Walter loved to talk about his book. "It's going to be bigger than the Bible. You've read the Bible?" He looked at Amy intensely, as if it were the first time he had set eyes on her.

"Parts of it. My parents aren't very religious. They don't seem to be much of anything at the moment, except divorced."

There was that word, again, Fran thought. *Anything*.

"<u>Rules of the World</u> will be bigger than the Bible, and more profound than Shakespeare. Shakespeare was a lightweight." Walter grinned so that his long incisors showed from beneath his red beard. He had a theory about the increased use of nose rings vs. the decreased length of incisors within certain populations. It had to do with compensation, bone density and material selection. Walter had never had a nose ring.

Seeing the look of confusion on Amy's face, Fran said, "Do you ever wonder, Amy, how the world works?"

"Sometimes," Amy said disconsolately. She looked down at

her watch, her dark lashes covering her eyes.

"Ru-uules," Walter bellowed, edging out onto his rose-patterned chair. He spilled some cider on his cutoffs. Crows congregating at the garbage bins nearby cawed. "So people can exercise control over their lives."

"What did you say, Uncle Walter?"

"People need control over their lives, so they can control *themselves*."

Amy glanced at her watch, but only briefly.

"Let's see, how many books do you think one needs to read to develop a sense of how the world works? I remember being ten, wishing I'd had such a book." Walter eased back into the stuffed chair, tilted his head back and gazed skyward. His tone became avuncular. "Today kids grow up much quicker — you can't help it: adolescence comes faster with hormone-infested meats and milk. You drink milk, don't you, Amy?"

"My mother makes me." Amy was now studying her watch. "But she's forgotten lately. She's forgotten a lot of things."

"Growing bodies require calcium. You might consider a supplement rather than the real product, which I believe to be tainted. Poisoned."

Amy looked up suddenly.

"But no one can prove it."

This was a familiar argument to Fran: the data were not in, the data likely never would be in because of the impossibility of isolating all contributing factors. If you could put a human in a sterile environment, like David The Bubble Boy from Houston (he finally succumbed to an infection after living in absolute sterility for twelve years), and monitor everything ingested, inhaled, absorbed, then perhaps one could deduce the effects of hormone-tainted meat and milk on an individual's physical and mental growth. The nefarious and subtle influences at work on an individual's physiology were of paramount concern to Walter.

"Let's return to our original argument. How many books would one need to read in order to simply *acquire an appreciation* for the rules of the world?"

"Two hundred?" Amy said.

"A thousand?" Fran said.

"To develop a sense of how the world works." Walter raised his green eyes to heaven. Fran and Amy, too, looked heavenward. "That depends," Walter went on, his gaze becoming more direct. "Which world? White world? Black? European? Asian? Present world? Future? How do we project to the future?"

"That's a little too much for Amy, Walter. She's only ten."

"I'm pushing her," Walter said, grinning.

"I can give you some rules." Amy looked down at the weedy grass. "Never fall in love. Never get married unless you plan on being married forever. Nothing good lasts."

Fran and Walter exchanged glances. Fran had mentioned the divorce, but had Walter been listening? Fran's sister, a therapist, had asked Fran to encourage Amy to talk, even if it was painful because talking helped one recognize problems. Then her sister interjected some unflattering observations about Walter, but Fran dismissed her concerns: if you did not live with greatness, then you did not know.

"One subject at a time," Walter told Amy, wagging his finger at her. "Back to my question: how many history books would you have to read to get an appreciation for how the world works? How many science books? *Rules of the World* will summarize all the great concepts. In addition, there will be an option to continually incorporate new data."

"Look!" Amy cried. "Uncle Walter! Aunt Fran!"

"What?" Walter said, astonished at the girl's sudden turn of mood.

"It's exactly, three-two-one: eight o'clock!"

"Bedtime?" Walter offered raising his red eyebrows.

"It *was* eight o'clock," the girl said morosely.

"It will be eight o'clock again, tomorrow," Walter said crisply. "And the next, and the next."

Amy shrugged.

Glancing suspiciously at Fran, Walter finished his cider, then went inside to his rocking chair, leaving the two of them outside, and alone.

The next day Fran and Amy set out in the mud-colored Dodge to explore the city.

"Do you think it will start again?" Amy said, taking a precautionary bounce on the passenger's seat.

Fran laughed gaily. There were holes in the dash where the knobs should have been. There was no radio, no heater. Fran pulled at her flowered polyester blouse in an effort to circulate the humid air. "You're very observant, Amy. See in New York State, the cars, well most cars share certain characteristics. It's the harsh environmental conditions. The salt eats away at the metal. Now if cars were not made of metal . . ." Fran raised her thin eyebrows and sighed.

Amy nodded and her pigtails bounced. Her eyes were bright.

"Screws fall out, seams break open," Fran offered. "It's a wonder a car lasts as long as it does. Just watch where you sit. There's a loose spring and you don't want to get lock-jaw on vacation." Fran laughed again: it had been years since she had been in such great spirits. She laughed so hard her stomach ached.

Fran pulled out onto the narrow street. The little freckle-faced girl sitting beside her made her feel maternal, and queenly, as if Amy were *her daughter*, a miniature manifestation of her flesh and blood, genes destined to survive into perpetuity. There was nothing more in the world that Fran wanted than a child. Women could have babies into their forties, and drugs existed to produce fertility in septuagenarians, but Fran did not want to wait *that* long. Fran was thirty-eight, and not in the best of health. A year ago she nearly succumbed to her disease — a rare intestinal, immune disorder — and was saved at the last moment when Walter discovered her passed out and barely breathing, and he injected her with one of his experimental drugs. The miracle drug revived Fran, and very slowly, her health began to improve. Then rather than buying expensive prescription drugs, he put Fran on a regimen of his drugs. *By eliminating the FDA, EPA and OSHA from our lives,* Walter told Fran, *I have been freed. Consequently I now feel capable of making significant advances in the cure of human disease.* With a bit of levity, Walter would inquire, *Teeth coming in red yet, Fran? Notice any quills sprouting on your knuckles?*

Fran drove past the university's experimental corn and soybean fields, vast green fields whose superior plant sizes signified ingenuity, and the ability to solve any problem. Then they entered a part of town where roads narrowed and red brick replaced the asphalt. The gray stucco houses with their chocolate-colored trim and tiled roofs seemed to have been plucked right out of a Grimm's Fairy Tale. Other houses had ornamental windows, eyebrow windows or bay windows, cupolas, steep pointed roofs, buttresses, but the most extraordinary to Fran were widow's walks atop the century-old houses. Whenever she saw one, she searched for the long-haired damsel in black, walking to and fro, pining for her long-lost love.

Then they came onto campus and its maze-like foot-paths with their suggestions of endless, perhaps unfocused, energy.

"We are entering a Medieval City," Fran declared in a solemn voice. "These miniature castles, believe it or not, are where the college students live, and listen to lectures from Nobel Prize winners. Now recall that in Medieval times women were drudges, destined to a life of servitude. They were allowed no opinions and had no control—none—over their lives. In our enlightened age, however, we have men and women sitting side-by-side—the future scientists and artists—learning together about genomes, quarks, and Brahms." No response from Amy, so Fran continued. "Genomes are about cytogenic maps, mutations, polymorphs, DNA and clones. Building blocks of the cell. Life. Quarks are high energy physics particles related to skyrmions and pions, particles that experience deep, inelastic scatter. And Brahms—he wrote the lullaby tune?" Fran hummed a few bars. "Today, Amy, a female Brahms would be possible."

"The bell towers are okay," Amy said quietly.

Fran did not give up so easily. She focused on the buildings they passed, reciting to Amy the mottoes chiseled in stone above entrances that promoted ideas of justice, honor and truth. Such ideas Walter had attributed to a time when humanity had little control over nature. *People had to adapt, and accept. Today we control nature. And each other,* Walter had said ominously, *in ways that are often nefarious.*

Merely to drive through the campus made Fran feel part of the progressive and diverse intellectual elite that inhabited the Finger Lake city. The twisting road along the valley plateau offered spectacular views of the lake below, whose waters were deep green and blue in summer, colors that surprised Fran with their intensity. As she drove along this road, Fran felt as if she were truly on top of the world, and her heart overflowed with love for her niece.

During Amy's visit, Fran took a few days off from her job at the reproductive center, where she transcribed doctors' notes.

She was intrigued by the stories of women who desired

sperm. Many were wives of high-powered college professors, men whose goal in life was not to produce progeny but to acquire tenure. The women were prepared to undergo whatever necessary humiliation to obtain this white, liquid gold. *There are strategies,* one nurse would tell the weeping women. *Inviting over friends who have adorable babies or well-behaved children helps, as well as certain movies. Aphrodisiacs. Wine, certain foods. Then you can use syringes — like turkey basters. Whipped cream. You'd be surprised,* the nurse said gaily, *about what turns a person on. It can be anything. Understand that we live in a town where people think too much, and it behooves you to learn your mate's vocabulary. If he's a geologist, communicate in terms of eruptions, subduction, hot spots. For a mathematician, it's vectors and angles. Guaranteed, the idea will seep into his dreams.* Fran thought the nurse's theories preposterous, but she could not help herself from listening to every single word she said.

 Fran mulled over this white, liquid gold as she ferried Amy to museums, farmers' markets, playgrounds, pools and lakeside swimming spots. Her niece put not one toe in the water. And when it rained, Amy would refuse to venture out until her watch reached an exact time—determined by Amy. Fran skillfully hid her anguish. At day's end, they would return to the decrepit rental and eat a dinner of rice, lentils, beans. Amy never complained about the monotonous fare. Afterward they would all sit outside on the cushioned chairs, or inside if it rained, and Amy and Fran would give Walter suggestions for his magnum opus.

 The last day of Amy's visit, Fran treated Amy to a roast beef sandwich at a deli near campus. Painted on one wall was an elaborate mural of chunky people of Italian descent who seemed overjoyed at the prospect of baking bread and planting tomatoes and peppers in straight rows. As Fran contemplated the contented, rustic, earth-is-good life, Amy cried out, "It's exactly one o'clock!"

Afterward they went for a walk alongside a creek. The path steadily descended, and soon they were in gorge sided by black shale. The summer day was warm and calm. As they walked, the creek became more robust as many smaller streams fed into it. Turning a bend, they suddenly came upon a magnificent waterfall. Several feet beyond the falls, at the stream's center stood a large, smooth, flat-topped slab of shale.

"Looks unreal, doesn't it?" Fran said. "The perfect place to daydream." If truth be told, Fran was disappointed: she had failed to help Amy in any substantial way and she had anticipated a victory somehow related to her quiescent genes of motherhood.

Amy slipped off her sneakers and rolled up her jeans, and to Fran's surprise, she entered the water.

"Be careful," Fran said.

Thin arms outstretched, Amy walked toward the waterfall, the water slowly climbing up her pale legs. She teetered on some of the sharper rocks. A fine mist from the waterfall settled around her head, and water droplets in her auburn pigtails glistened in the sun.

Turning around suddenly, Amy said, "Aunt Fran, I had the greatest time with you. I've never been to so many playgrounds or museums."

"Me either." Fran closed her eyes, trying not to feel sad. She would be alone again, and now more than ever, she found herself wanting a child.

"In Minnesota we swam at a lake almost every day during the summer. In winter we swam in an indoor pool that had a giant mushroom-like fountain. It was so much fun, Aunt Fran. You just wouldn't believe. But...I don't remember the last time we swam together. My parents spend all their time fighting."

"Adults aren't always the smartest people," Fran said.

"Right. My parents could use a book like Uncle Walter's Rules of the World."

"Nothing intrigues Walter more than solving a problem." Fran felt it unfair to add that Walter was equally intrigued by money. A fascination with money ensued, Fran knew, when one grew up poor.

"You and Uncle Walter don't seem to have any problems."

"Well-lll ...." Fran's voice wobbled, but she refrained from saying more.

"But you know what, Aunt Fran? There's nothing in Uncle Walter's book about divorce. It's as if it doesn't exist."

"There isn't?" Fran couldn't recall anything about procreation either, and she looked away from the child, at the swiftly moving water. Apparently Amy had overcome her fear of water, and that was good. And Fran should have felt an intimation of victory, but she didn't.

The water's gurgling reminded her of Walter in the bathroom, and she wondered if he ever thought of her during the day's odd moments. She couldn't force him to think of her. Her nature was to be passive, yet was she destined forever to achieve love through romance novels?

Love is psychological. Completely made up! Walter had said with glee, squeezing this most essential emotion into a tiny abstraction. That she could not recall the last time they had made love made her feel ashamed.

Walter always claimed to be busy. Such were the disadvantages of a passive nature, yet aggression required energy, and the hope of achieving something. *Anything.*

"I read his entire book."

"You did?"

"I think I could give Uncle Walter some insights."

"Certainly you could." Fran remembered being ten, a painfully shy, sickly ten, a social pariah. She would never have had such a conversation with an adult and she admired Amy for her forthrightness. Looking down into the stream, Fran saw treacherous, slippery moss-covered rocks. A frightened face stared back at her. Was *she* afraid? Of what? Or whom?

"Walter," Amy said. She took another two steps. "He knows everything."

"No one knows everything." The comment startled Fran: hadn't she always believed Walter knew everything? Hadn't she deferred to him on most matters because of his superior intelligence?

"I can still tell you about divorce, Aunt Fran. It hurts." The girl looked into the water again and blinked rapidly.

"I'm sorry, Amy. Healing takes time, a different kind of time from what your watch measures. It's gradual, and not very exact at all. But you will heal." Time, Fran thought: how it ran so many lives, and in its own secret and insidious ways without regard for anyone. It marched on, heedless of birth and death, of fortunes created and fortunes destroyed. Amy stopped midstream. As they assessed each other across the expanse of green water, Fran had an idea. "You know Amy, there are things and events a child can't control. And there are things and events that *an adult* can't control."

Amy had climbed up the slab of black slate, and was walking its perimeter, testing the rock's solidity. "Like what?"

"Weather. Can't control."

Amy stopped pacing and said quietly, "What else?"

"The sun burning out. Can *not* control." Fran flicked a pebble into the stream and heard its clear kerplunk. She liked the sound, so she flicked in another one. "Your turn."

"The length of the school day."

"Can't control," Fran said.

"I know!" Amy exclaimed. "The ants in your house."

"Can't control!" Fran laughed with abandon. And perhaps Walter would *never* perfect his insecticide? He was involved in too many projects.

"Rules. Can't control," Amy said.

"But some are meant to be broken."

"They are?"

"Rules of the person, personal rules. See, Amy, everyone has

119

her own private rules that only she knows about. Even Uncle Walter. And me." Fran looked sideways at the child.

"Huh."

"People always have problems, Amy. If not one thing, then another. All your life. As soon as you solve one problem another takes its place. That's the human condition." A fertility doctor at work was fond of this phrase. Fran put her hand over her eyes, shielding them from the sun's glare. Amy was sitting cross-legged on the rock, her eyes fixed onto her watch. Although Fran could not see her expression, she knew well the look of expectation. It was nearly three. Even Fran was keeping track of time now. Goose-bumps had formed on her arms. Ignoring the ritual, or even distracting Amy with M&M-topped ice-cream cones had not worked. She looked toward the black slate, this thought of defeat freshly in her mind when she noticed that Amy had removed her watch and set it beside her. Reaching for a flower petal flowing downstream, she knocked the watch into the water. Amy stared briefly at the watch, then said, "Oh well."

The two waited in silence, Fran expecting the watch to jump out of its watery grave and reattach itself to Amy's wrist. Closing her eyes, she heard water bubbling and tinkling everywhere. A sudden wind rose up, shifting the waterfall's spray so that a mist cooled her arms. Fran removed her sandals and rolled her polyester pants up just above her knobby knees. She stepped in and shuddered at the water's sudden coldness. Holding out her arms, she balanced herself on the moss-covered rocks. The water had become transparent and colorless. Looking up she saw Amy holding out her hand. Touched by the gesture, she took Amy's hand and it was then that Fran imagined herself running off with Amy, staying in a cheap motel along the Florida coast, sitting in the sun and eating fried shrimp and French fries, no more beans and lentils! But the idea was only a dream, a plot twist that she might find in a romance novel. In a romance novel, the episode would have worked.

"So you know what my mother said before I left?"

They watched more flower petals floating downstream, the clear water sparkling in the sunlight. Fran had climbed onto the black slate.

"She said that if you hold onto your pain too long, it can become a part of you. I didn't know what she meant, but I think I know now." Amy stared into the water where the watch lay. Fran saw it too, the hands still moving. "Uncle Walter wrote a note to himself inside the front cover of his book. It said, 'Anything is possible if you think it is. Try, try, and try again. Never give up.'"

"Walter said that?" Walter doubting himself would imply that he was fallible, or even wrong. Walter wrong about something? Never. Walter fallible? Interesting. And was it true that one required an entire book of rules to know how to live? Maybe, just maybe, there were a few simple rules. *Don't give up so easily. Don't hold onto your pain too long.*

The two sat down together on the rock. The rock was smooth and warm. It was pleasant in the sun, not too hot. Fran laid back. Her muscles instantly relaxed.

She sensed changing shadows and knew that Amy had laid

down too. Simply to be close to Amy gave her a feeling of peace. Strange how that worked. Perhaps it was possible to learn something from a ten-year-old. Fran listened to the steady movement of water. Turning her head she saw pockets of turbulence where the water frothed white, and it made her think instantly of the white, liquid gold. Water continued to arch from the waterfalls, and she imagined herself engaging Walter in a conversation about *PV equals NRT. Great bodies and rotation. The exquisite geometry of liquid transport.* Certainly Fran could insert such non-threatening phrases into their nightly discussion on Rules of the World?

There would be a half dozen gently-scented candles in the bedroom, clean sheets, and Fran, with the greatest of stealth, would present this idea of white, liquid gold to Walter, how it mysteriously came up at the waterfalls when she was with Amy, and hadn't the past week been just wonderful living with that adorable, pig-tailed cherub, who not only took it upon herself to read your book, but to hold onto your hand, and hold onto and savor your every word?

You Be You

Fran stood silently in line at one of the many, many entrances, the hot December sun slowly baking her bare shoulders. Back home in central New York, a winter snowstorm had closed roads and shut down malls for the third consecutive day. No skiing, no snowboarding. It was December 25, 1999. No doubt her neighbors were sitting inside in thick sweaters, the air and conversation becoming increasingly stale. How many times could you watch "Miracle on 42nd Street"? Answer: it depends: are there kids, or no?

"Magic Kingdom," Morris whispered, his little hand in Fran's hand. He was wearing his moose antlers and as long as he had those antlers, Fran knew Morris was happy. Morris was at last at The Magic Kingdom: land of castles and kings, cartoon characters, unlimited ice-cream, and candy. Adults attired in ornate costumes sang and danced as if that was all they ever did, and all they ever wanted to do.

"Forty-five dollars," Walter, Morris' father, hissed, repeating the price quoted by the cashier. "Let's see . . ." Fran watched as Walter removed his calculator from his shirt pocket and began pressing buttons in rapid succession. "At a million people a day. . .365 days a year..." The shirt pocket also held a tape measure, mechanical pencil, black marker, miniature high-powered flashlight, Swiss Army knife, the latter which held Walter at bay whenever he went through metal detectors at airports. Setting off detectors, however, Fran knew, gave him the opportunity to proclaim his views on individualism and the consequences of relinquishing personal freedoms. The security guards were not amused. Once Walter was sequestered in a back room and he almost missed his flight, but he emerged with a triumphant smile, and an upgrade to First Class.

When the final number appeared on his calculator's display, Walter blinked rapidly. "Per person? That's an *obscene* profit."

"Magic Kingdom," Morris whispered. Morris' profound enchantment at being allowed through the hallowed gates had made little impression on Walter. Walter always seemed preoccupied with his own ideas, and sometimes Fran thought he was just a wee bit selfish. Expressions like 'wee bit' and 'naughty' had become standard vocabulary for Fran. Vocabulary was known to change after hours spent watching children's videos and reading children's books. Yet it *was* a kingdom: just look at the many people standing in line to pay homage! So Fran had to wonder: where was the king? There must be a king, and worshippers, just as in every conventional romance novel, there must be a man and a woman. Fran, as usual, had brought a romance novel, wedging it between the water bottles and PB & Js in her lunch bag. Neighbors had warned her there would be lines, that Disney was not like the grocery store. In Florida, there were many grocery stores, but only one Disney.

Obscene profit or not, Walter peeled back his wad of bills, and with trembling hands, he held out the money to the cashier.

Never once did he glance at Morris. Then they boarded the train and traveled over a body of blue water, its shore lined with expensive white condos. Pleasure boats floated lazily in the calm waters. The view was flat, white and blue. A dark cloud flitted by and Fran remembered Walter's earlier missive: *There will be a tremendous electrical storm over Disney in the afternoon.* This he predicted based on meteorological information he had had obtained from NASA. They had been to NASA the day before, and had Walter ever been so joyous? So vast was his knowledge concerning the Vehicle Assembly Building and the International Space Station that Walter was offered a job and awarded an honorary lifetime pass to the IMAX movies. Walter unreservedly loved NASA.

"Isn't this a nice and friendly place, Walter?" Fran said. "First they showed us where to park, then where to pay, and finally where to get on the train."

Walter was staring at the ribbed rubber floor of the train and muttering. Walter, Fran understood, craved high-powered intellectual dialogue. He missed his colleagues and fermenting petri dishes. Adjustment for Walter was never easy — not so for Fran: she was having the time of her life sitting on the hard plastic and eavesdropping on everyday conversations.

"It's the way to go, Fred," a woman behind Fran said. "You can make a lot of money if you have the skills."

"Betty," he drawled, "I'm just a plain, everyday ordinary hair cutter."

Walter rolled his eyes.

"Beautician," Betty said. "Never underestimate your abilities. Every beautician is going to be doing it. Cutting into the scalp will be as routine as winding hair around curlers."

"What bothers me is inserting the roots."

When the train stopped, the families leaped out with maps in hand, routes marked in red. Never had Fran seen such energy and enthusiasm and she was about to call attention to this when Walter, screwing up his green eyes, said: "Hair transplants."

Then he grinned in pain at the swell of people and the brightly painted huts.

"Try to remember what it was like being a kid, Walter," Fran said.

"Magic Kingdom," Morris whispered. His dark eyes were wide. His eyes were so dark that his irises appeared to be black. The black eyes and black hair complimented his somber demeanor, and his eyes always seemed to be open, perhaps because he had forgotten how to blink, or maybe his eyeballs did not require the liquid refreshment eyelids gave. Morris was an extraordinary child, and Fran knew this. He kept his hand securely in hers as they trotted upon Disney's hallowed ways and stood at their first line before *It's a Small World*.

Walter fidgeted and wiped the sweat from his neck. He pulled on his red van Dyke beard and rocked wearily on his heels.

"We are walking on land that has been shown all around the world on TV," Fran said.

As a child, Fran had dreamt of visiting Disney, but her parents always took the family to authentic and cold places, like the Coast of Maine or middle Canada. They camped in tents or slept in a rundown Nimrod popup and Fran often came home with pneumonia. The closest she got to Disney was Sunday night at 7.

"Who cares?" Walter said.

"Try to enjoy yourself, Walter. Relax. Don't forget Morris," Fran whispered, indicating the awe-struck boy.

Walter grunted.

The line moved and soon the water canal appeared, then the small boats, and lastly, the many well-organized feet, numbered and painted in red on concrete. Tending the feet was a man in a red vest festooned with Disney characters. Every few seconds, he would say: "How many in your party? Take feet one ...two ...three. Next. How many—"

Fran, Morris and Walter (reluctantly) took their assigned feet, and when the signal was given, they jumped down into their boat, with Morris squished in the middle.

"It's a Small World," Fran said, smiling. They bobbed along the water canal, becoming gradually acclimated to the idea of a simultaneously dark and brightly colored, but small world. Puppets sang in shrill voices, yet in unison, united despite custom, language and attire differences. The singing puppets, lined up on both shores, appeared to be feverishly enjoying themselves. They trotted, walked, bowed, skated, skied and balanced on tightropes.

"Cute," Fran said.

"Magic Kingdom," Morris said, his wide eyes slowly taking everything in.

Walter slumped down into his seat. Behind them sat Fred, Betty and their two kids and they were all singing to "It's a Small World." Fran started singing also because she believed that the physical act of singing made the heart sing too, but Walter gave her such a look that she had to reassess this belief.

"Why don't you do something useful, Walter? Like figuring out how much water evaporates from the canal every hour?"

Walter removed his calculator from his pocket. Ever since Morris' second Halloween, Walter had seriously considered some of Fran's ideas, such as varying the diet: eating beans, rice and lentils only three times a week. The impetus had been Morris' moose costume with the reusable antlers.

Morris looked from one parent to the other, and whispered, "Small World."

That Morris had added a new phrase to his vocabulary made Fran think the trip worthwhile, despite cohabiting with Walter's parents. Every room in the Krulls' three-bedroom condo had a TV. Mrs. Krull, who fancied herself as an advocate for the everyday person, watched CNN nearly continuously.

She did not approve of the government taking control of a person's life. *Corrupt liars! Look at the pensions they get! The health care! They don't have to beg to see a doctor! All those pork belly deals. They don't even read the legislation anymore – they have corporations write all the legislation. Somebody has to know what's going on!* Mrs. Krull would say.

She mixed up the opinions of key Cabinet players and the platforms of the Democrats and Republicans. She even thought there was a Socialist party. In addition, Mrs. Krull had the habit of relaying events reported by publications of dubious repute as if they were true. *Well – lll,"* Mrs. Krull would backpedal, her ample body trembling, *I'm not saying every, single word is true, Fran. There are not many publications in which every, single word is true.* Then she would tell Walter, as if he were seven-years-old, that the most appropriate literature to read a child , e.g., Morris, was The Bible. *The greatest book ever written*, she pronounced, nodding her tightly-knotted brown head of hair. God is the one in control.

Before leaving for Florida, Mrs. Krull called Walter and Fran numerous times reminding them that planes fell out of the sky every day, without warning. Mechanical failure, drunken pilots and now terrorists! Thus, Morris needed to be baptized. *You don't want him to go straight to Hell, do you? He won't even get a chance at Purgatory. Everybody deserves a chance, Walter. Fran.*

But Fran knew Morris was bright, perhaps brilliant, even though he was predominantly non-verbal. For instance, he never once said the word *Daddy*. This worried Fran but she realized there was not enough time in her lifetime to worry about everything and thus, she was obligated to pick her worries. People often equated silence with stupidity, but Fran knew silence was often times the opposite of stupidity.

Those who had had firsthand experience with Morris' talents suggested that Morris be tested for his IQ, but Walter, who was busy with his own scientific projects, vetoed the idea.

Verbal acuity, ability to think abstractly, memory: that's not all intelligence is, Fran. The idea of IQ and what it does is like a warped and shattered crystal ball that you bounce light rays off of, trying to predict angles of reflection and refraction. If doctors give Morris a high IQ then he'll go off and start his own cult. A low IQ and he'll take up residence in a cardboard box in the bad part of town inhabited by college dropouts strung-out on Ecstasy.

Fran said, *That sounds a mite extreme*, and Walter calmly countered with: *Extreme? Hah! I'm defining boundaries.* Never had Fran thought of IQ in quite that fashion. *Right here on your Internet, Walter, it says that IQ predicts success or failure in school. Is that equivalent to success or failure in life?*

Nevertheless, Morris was unusual, in part, Fran believed that because from the day he was born, she had read to him. Reading was one child-rearing strategy that both she and Walter agreed on. Walter, however, eschewed the traditional fairy tales and instead read him Spinoza, Kant, Hieldegard and Buber. Or it could be said Fran was assigned this task as Walter's fabulous mind was in demand at the university.

Yet Morris did talk. *Be who you are,* was one of his key phrases. Fran was not absolutely certain that Morris understood the philosophy behind the phrase (this transpired when Walter was reading Buber aloud), but he seemed to intuit the sense of what was read to him.

And then Morris had a way with animals. Neighbors and college students brought their ill-behaved dogs and depressed cats to Morris. Concerned about putting their pets on Ritalin or antidepressants prompted their actions. Morris' approach was behavioral, and entirely intuitive. The sessions consisted of Morris and the patient down on the floor, staring at each other, raising eyebrow or paw, slowly, in an attempt to understand each other's unspoken language and worldly perspective. After a few sessions, the pet was cured of biting, chewing, peeing on couches and other behaviors associated with separation anxiety. Both Walter and Fran encouraged this interest of Morris', but for different reasons.

"Doesn't make sense," Walter said, his mouth downturning. "The ride takes 10 minutes, you wait in line for 50. Now if we extrapolate to an eight-hour day, most of the day is spent ..."

"Magic Kingdom," Morris said, contemplatively, savoring each syllable. "Small World."

They went on more rides, and the procedure of lines, ropes and fences soon became second-nature. When the boats came into view pulses began to race, but the numbered red feet were so nicely laid out that everyone knew his place. Sometimes while waiting, a fake bird would warble, or a fake squirrel would run across a brick wall, and Morris's green eyes would brighten with enthusiasm.

"It behooves man to delineate the minds and hearts of animals. Eventually," Walter said in his deep voice, "the world will be taken over by other living beings. Microorganisms, Fran. It's inevitable." Walter looked down at the broken pavement where ants were congregating on an abandoned cookie.

"Already, they outnumber us. To conquer or better yet, cohabitate, we must understand. Microorganisms are found in our deepest oceans and in the outer reaches of the atmosphere. Ebola," he sniffed, "is nothing in comparison to what could happen. Best now to consider microorganisms as sensate and measurably intelligent — even though their intelligence defies our means of measurement. Think of them as sufficiently intelligent so as to in some way *organize*, Fran. Let us now learn how to get them on our — humanity's — side." Walter worked with microorganisms. He had written a very persuasive paper, **The Unseen Micro-Society**, which both *Nature* and *Scientific American* rejected, suggesting that Walter submit it to the *National Enquirer*. "The common folk are always blind to great ideas," Walter commented. The rejections compelled him to redouble his efforts to find intelligence where conventional thought predicted little intelligence existed. "The power of thought is not an insignificant power," he often said. "The power of thought of The Self."

"You be you," Morris said. A fake robin appeared on the bench behind him and started warbling.

Fran smiled and said, "But it's not as though you have to leave *The Self* behind." Fran and Walter had had many fruitful discussions about The Self. The conversations had become more frequent since Morris' birth and complimented the various philosophical texts that Fran read to him. Sometimes when Walter was at his lab, however, Fran read Morris excerpts from her romance novels. She wanted Morris to know about *love:* the different types of loves, its intensity, its power to motivate a person to do great things and things that no one would ever have thought possible.

Walter was sitting on an aqua-colored bench outside Mickey's Gingerbread Hut waiting for Fran to pass him a PB & J. It was lunch time at the Magic Kingdom.

Walter thought about everything, and issues that in a lifetime would not have occurred to Fran.

Consideration of esoteric issues required time, and Fran's responsibilities, which included management of a bug-infested, rundown house, a patchy lawn, and Morris, kept her busy.

She continued to work part-time for the Reproductive Center, in part because without a nurse's advice, she would have never gotten pregnant and Morris would never have existed. Quite frankly though, Morris wore Fran out. If she did not read to him day and night, he coughed. At first Fran thought Morris had croup or asthma but every time she brought Morris to the pediatrician, the cough mysteriously vanished. Many nights she read to him until midnight, his alert eyes encouraging her belief that he understood the texts. Then every morning he woke at six, refreshed, in wonderment of what divertissements his mother had planned for the day. Based on Walter's lectures on the insidious and dangerous influences of substitute Moms, Fran decided she could not hire a sitter. Thus, Fran's sole reprieve during the day was when distraught pets arrived for a session with Morris, and Fran could lie down for twenty minutes. Inevitably the pet was helped because of Morris' undivided devotion; he gave the animal his total attention, an intensity of attention. He gave them love.

Fran's and Walter's discussions followed a simple pattern, beginning with Walter sitting imperiously, sighing, then intoning, "What is The Self?"

"The self is manifold," Walter said. "There are no easy answers."

"I'll agree with you there, Walter."

"The Big questions, Fran. Fate and destiny. Beliefs such as life after death."

"Sounds oxymoronic to me, Walter."

"God." There was a faraway gaze in his gray eyes. Walter smoothed his red Van Dyke beard, a gesture that indicated submersion into in deep thought. "Go—ooodddd," he crooned. Then he completely closed his eyes, his head bowed, and his large incisors became hidden inside his mouth.

"Are you…having a spiritual experience…at Disney?"

Walter grunted. Clearly, Walter was developing his spiritual side. As one approached the half-century mark, serious contemplation of mortality ensued.

Presently Walter's closest colleague at the university was a mystic from Pakistan. Walter had invited the Pakistani man for dinner and the man, whose accent was exotic, spoke an English superior to most of Fran's friends. Fran baked meatless lasagna. There was a lettuce salad with red and green peppers. The red peppers were not in season and they had been three dollars a pound, but Walter, demonstrating that everyone has the capacity to change, allowed Fran to buy one red pepper.

Fatherhood had truly transformed Walter. Along with inquiries of spirituality, and loosening of the purse strings, came the necessity to become attentive to Morris' mother, Fran.

Fran finished her PB & J, declaring it the best sandwich she had ever eaten, then Morris jumped on her lap. He preferred to have a lap to sit on, or a shoulder to put a hand on. He spoke only when necessary, fine, Fran thought, because Walter always had enough to say for the three of them.

Fran had left most of the thinking to Walter—until Morris came. In fact, after the baby's birth—two weeks early—she had not yet chosen a name for the baby. Luckily Fran received a book from her sister, *Morris the Moose Goes to School*. Whenever not reading philosophy or romance novels, Fran read Morris the story, adding commentary, such as how nice it would have been to have had a moose visit her school. *Such a moose would have made the classes more entertaining.* Fran often thought that perhaps it was she who planted the seed of animal attraction in Morris' nascent brain. Ever since Morris's second Halloween (when Fran created the moose antlers), he insisted on trick-or-treating as a moose. That he had this presence of mind at such a young age to know *what* he wanted to be indicated intelligence. *He has a presence of self*, Walter had declared with a grin, even though he declined to take the toddler trick-or-treating. That he was a moose every year pleased Walter immensely. The antlers, which Fran fashioned from cardboard, Velcro, elastic and felt, were reusable.

"What do you believe in most?" Fran asked Walter. She wiped a dollop of jelly from her hand onto a napkin.

"I believe in The Self," Walter said solemnly. Having finished his PB and J, he plucked another squished sandwich out of Fran's bag.

"Oh. The Self. Is there a circularity to our conversation, Walter?"

Walter laughed. "I like a conversation with geometrical qualities. Geometry gives an added dimension to any issue. That's what the world needs, more dimensions. The dimensions of self."

"The self's all good and well, Walter, but people still need other people. Even Frankenstein had friends." Once while at a used bookstore, Fran heard the clerk pronounce Mary Shelly's Frankenstein a romance. Fran went immediately to the library and took out the book. Not your typical romance, yet Fran found the story immensely absorbing.

They finished eating their sandwiches and went on more rides. The day became hotter, more humid, and the crowds were so thick that Fran once lost Walter (who had all the money, but not her romance novel) for several minutes. As the crowds grew, and the heat solidified, Walter's good demeanor deteriorated. He announced what Fran dreaded most: "One more ride. Then we go."

On Morris' face was a subtle, pained look.

For the briefest moment, Fran wondered if she and Walter should have had Morris. Walter's work—which seemed to be always on his mind—required a huge commitment of time, and submersion into a world that neither she nor Morris could understand. Fran did understand that a person could not be everything: great scientist, adoring father, lover—yet at times, sometimes Fran wished Walter would set aside his desires, and consider the needs of someone else.

It started raining so they ran inside *Pirates Caribbean* because there was no line. The water boats gave them the complete, relaxing, passive experience of a thematic adventure. Seated behind them once again were Betty, Fred and their two kids.

"Ain't you lucky," a red-vested youth with a thin black mustache said to Walter. "Lead boat."

In *Pirates Caribbean,* life-sized men in striped shirts and shredded pants sang bawdy songs. They shook their whiskey bottles in the air and guffawed. The family behind them tried to sing along, but the lyrics were nearly incomprehensible.

On one bluff, damsels in slinky dresses stood nervously on auction blocks as ribald men sold them to the highest bidders. Other women screeched with glee as men pursued them. To Fran, the puppets seemed more real than the people in the boats. Fran closed her eyes and imagined herself being pursed by a dark, muscular man, a man who would take her by her bare shoulders, and kiss her on her lips, deeply, a kiss that would make the nerve cells from her toes to her hair roots shoot off sparks.

No sooner had she imagined the fantasy than she heard a tremendous noise. Sparks of light shot off everywhere and for a second, Fran believed it was the power of thought that had created the magic. The raised arms of puppets froze midair, and except for the random sparks, and glowing red exit signs, there was no light. Their world had stopped completely, without warning, and for a moment, Fran did not know where she was. After hours of waiting and walking in the heat, of being jostled and stepped on, of hearing countless people sing, the ensuing silence surrounded her softly, like a blessing. Fran had a sudden and urgent desire to close her eyes and sleep. Then something overhead fell into the canal. A wire broke loose and danced on the water's surface throwing out more sparks, people cried out. Behind Fran, a boy whined, "I wanna' go home! Now!" The boy, who was about the same age as Morris, started to rise in the boat.

"Elroy!" the mother said.

"Just stay where you are," Walter said suddenly, turning around and facing the boy. Fran would never know what made Walter speak up: maybe it was the sudden release of free electrons, or the deep darkness which favorably affected Walter's mood. "Were you ever in a haunted house where suddenly ...everything seemed real?" Walter addressed the family (all of whom wore mouse ears) immediately now, before him, but others listened too. Walter did have a commanding voice. He flicked on his pocket flashlight and positioned it beneath his chin so that his red Van Dyke beard glittered. Little did Walter know that that morning Morris had risen early and found Mrs. Krull's glitter makeup. Morris asked a snoozing Walter for permission to "make him up." Taking his father's snort as affirmation, Morris busily applied himself to the task of transforming his Dad. Rarely did Walter look at himself in the mirror in the morning as his time was better spent on other endeavors. Now Walter grinned and some of those in the boats chuckled. In addition to the glitter, Walter's incisors glowed blue and purple, colors that manifested his teeth's intricate biochemistry. Walter and his dentist, Dr. Lobrogini, were developing a new toothpaste. (Many people whom Walter associated with mysteriously became valued colleagues.) Walter had met Dr. Lobrogini during a cavity filling, an experience that Walter elected to undergo without the benefit of Novocain. Walter laughed, then cried out through the blood and the cotton: *Doctors have never understood the power of the imagination! The power of thought!* The doctor had been so impressed with Walter's self-control that he offered to drill and fill future cavities for half price. This progressed into a discussion of effective toothpaste application — one of the least-desirous properties of common toothpaste. Thus, their experimental toothpaste, which Walter was developing (and would eventually obtain a free life-time supply of), was applied using techniques that mimicked those of a sloppy tooth-brusher's.

"Welcome to the second portion of our show." Walter gazed down at Elroy. The boy looked up, beguiled by Walter's blue and purple incisors.

"But you must keep your hands on your lap. Everybody. Even adults. This is the part of the show that you take back with you as a memory." Walter moved his flashlight around in laser-like fashion. "Everyone here is lucky. This is not the typical Disney ride, and not the typical Disney theme. The theme here is ...ah . . ." Walter was losing his ability to think clearly — which was exactly what Walter had told Fran would transpire if he were obligated to spend time in a mind-numbing theme park. It was like the carbon dioxide slowly diffusing from an opened can of soda:

eventually the soda went flat and was no longer tasty. "The theme of . .ah. . " Walter blinked on and off his pocket flashlight.

"Gravity," Morris said.

"Gravity...yes. What?" Walter peered down at little Morris' dark eyes.

"The Universal Force," Morris said in his fragile, five-year-old voice. "Attractions of bodies. Mass over distance squared."

Fran smiled and squeezed Morris's hand. His inner genius was surfacing, and at Disney of all places where one did not normally contemplate the universe of genius except in a suburban sense. Walter managed to keep everyone in their boats by explaining how gravity kept the water in the canal, and kept the boats in the canal, and kept them in the boats. Interactions of electricity and gravity was a more subtle subject.

"Without gravity, we wouldn't be here." Then Walter played a game that Fran often played with Morris, but Walter –had he even heard her play? – never played. The game was *Imagine*. Anything was game: you could experience what it was to be like a hamster on a wheel, or world class chess champ who ate fluffernutters before each match.

"Imagine," Walter said. "Close your eyes and imagine that that earth's gravity becomes diminished by some fraction, determined by the imaginer, and related in some fashion to the unpredictable motions of magnetic currents near the earth's iron core. Keep those peepers closed! These motions are exacerbated by stellar interactions millions of light years away. Now, imagine the earth as having reduced gravity. Greatly reduced."

Everyone's eyes were closed.

"Imagine leaves not falling down in autumn, but falling up. We wouldn't have Fall anymore, we would have ....Rise."

"Rise?" Elroy said.

"Rise," Walter said, cocking an elbow, then elaborating on the theme of rise and fall, as related to the famous PV equals NRT, then spicing it up with socio-political implications.

Suddenly a generator rumbled and the chains along the canal's bottom tugged the boats to the ride's conclusion. There a Disney manager awarded Walter a ceremonial pair of Mouse Ears, and coupons good for a year.

The ears were scarlet red and gold and big so they fit perfectly on Walter's massive head — it gave him an Attila The Hun look. As Walter walked away, Fred stuck out his hand and told Walter how much he appreciated his efforts.

"Got some advice for you," Walter said, smoothing down his red beard.

The man grinned, and the grin in combination with mouse ears made the man look slightly absurd.

Walter described to Fred a new biotech startup working on hair growth – on any place on the human body.

"You're kidding."

"Sir, Walter Krull never kids." Walter's incisors still glowed blue and purple, and this was what Fran loved about Walter: the odd ways in which his true character radiated. "I'll call it a technique – for the sake of simplicity. See, the technique was initially tested on mice after we convinced the Animal Rights

Activists that each mouse would be given kingly or queenly accommodations and infinite supply of brick cheese and organic peanut butter." Walter gave Fred his card.

"Thank you." Fred shook Walter's hand again, and then he departed with his family, their four sets of Mickey Mouse ears bobbing off in unison, until they became lost in the crowd of other bobbing ears.

"Hair growth," Walter said mysteriously, patting his red goatee. He removed his calculator and began crunching numbers.

Fran stared at Walter, knowing that when they returned to New York, he would be engaged in a new project.

"Hmm..." Walter said, staring at the calculator's display. He had not noticed that Morris had led them to a scary roller coaster ride, *Earth's Odyssey: 2001*. The patrons' screams became more profound as they approached the ten-story metal edifice. Screams could be heard well above the hum and drum of the crowd, and they were not happy screams: they were screams of pure, unadulterated terror.

Walter was not good on roller coasters rides: the violent rushing of blood nonplused him and the high-frequency oscillation of cells impacted on every nerve in his body, so he had confided to Fran.

Potential for brain cell damage was tremendous. To subject oneself to excessive physical stress was not only illogical but detrimental to the life of contemplation. Some individuals were simply not made for roller coaster rides. But there Walter stood, in line, Fran beside him, Morris between them.

Then Morris took hold of Walter's hand and he gazed at the askew Mickey Mouse ears said, "Daddy, you know what? I love you."

The Neighbor Who Gave Me Flowers
Published in "Oasis" 1995

A year after Doug and I bought our house, I was walking down Fifth Street. The night was brisk and still: no wind, no cars, no people. It was as silent as the inside of an eight ball. You often get nights like this on the northern prairie, but you aren't always aware of them. There was just enough moon out to show there was land, and the land looked as if it could extend forever. I know flatness bothers some people — it makes them feel lost, that there is no end and they're never to going finish or get anywhere soon. There's no place to hide. To me flatness is openness. It means opportunity. Most visitors will dismiss the northern prairies as wheat and weeds, missing the bigger picture. I feel sorry for them, that they can't see the subtler things, things that might be little, but things that are important all the same. You have to be careful here.

So I was out walking, without a hat, the mid-February cold penetrating right down to my skull. I was worried about getting frostbite on my ears, but I snuck up to my neighbors' front picture window anyway, and I peeked in. They had the same Bob Dylan poster tacked on their wall that we have on ours, except that ours is in the kitchen. Big Ears was slumped on a spongy couch, drinking beer, staring comatose at the TV. I thought about what I was going to say, something like: "Thanks for the cheese curls and beer." Or, "Thank you sincerely for your kindness," but it sounded so corny and silly that I rapped against the window instead, pretending to be a squirrel. Then I hid.

For that first year that we had the house, nearly every morning at five, Big Ears would be outside, gunning his Oldsmobile. Without the cottonwood there, the glare from the Oldsmobile's headlights comes right in through our bedroom window. Their lemon-yellow heap, which they park beneath our pine tree, the best tree on our lot now, never starts first try, so Big Ears is out there for fifteen minutes.

Doug, my husband, has to be at Emerson's Meat Market by seven. He works twelve hour days so he can buy a new car, and he needs his sleep. He stands in front of the bedroom window (if I stand up with him, on my tiptoes, I can see right into their kitchen) and shakes his fist out at the glaring lights, but I'm sure they never see us. Even though he has a thin chest—Doug is asthmatic—his arms are thick and strong, from cutting through flesh all day.

"Dammit," Doug says. "What the hell is wrong with those guys? That's what happens when you get transients in the neighborhood."

Out of their pickup they get the jumper cables, and Big Ears generally connects them wrong. You'd think that coming from Michigan they'd know more about cars. Then Toothpick Legs, he comes out in an army supply trench coat and blanket like some chief. The dawn is lit up with sparks and punctuated with Toothpick Legs' screams: "Are you trying to kill me? I said wait. Wait!"

Doug lies down, molds the pillow around his head and mutters: "Go ahead, kill him. Maybe I'd be able to sleep past five." Then the Oldsmobile dies, and it starts all over.

We moved out of the trailer court because we wanted space and privacy. Who can sleep at night with some guy yelling at his girlfriend? With some jaded mother slapping her kids around? I was so excited about owning a house, and owning land, that last spring (our first spring in our house)

I planted a huge vegetable garden: tomatoes, peppers, squash, beans. I'm not a flower planter; Doug and I think flowers are too frivolous, too fragile for the northern prairie's climate. We'd always had vegetable gardens in Darvy, big ones that my father used his tractor and cultivator on, so I knew what I was doing. I planted the seeds at the proper depth, and I watered and hoed.

Everything died.

That wasn't all: that spring I also found out we had bought a house next door to Big Ears and Toothpick Legs. Who would ever have thought of checking out the neighbors after all the problems we'd had? We initially bought the house because of its huge cottonwood. Its limbs had stretched from one end of our house to the other, like a mother, opening her arms wide for her children.

Big Ear's real name is Sebastian.

"Sebastian—another beer! Hey! Did you hear me?" That's the neighbors' buddies: dark sunglasses, helmetesque stringy hair, cutoffs, basketball stomachs and white skinny legs covered with mosquito bites and scabs. Leg acne, Doug calls it.

"They're disgusting slobs," Doug says. Doug changes his shirt at least twice a day. Every morning, and it doesn't matter if we're visiting relatives in Darvy, he washes his feet in the tub.

"They're also transients," he says, looking suspiciously at their big cars and those Michigan license plates. "They'll work a year or two, then they'll be gone. And they drink all the time."

Doug had spent his life getting away from lazy people who played black jack and drank so much that Mondays they rarely made it to work. That's why we left Darvy. "Inbred and without ambition," Doug says. "You and I, Rachel: we're different. We're going to do more with our lives." Doug didn't want anything to do with that other kind of person. And now look who lived next door.

That summer I got pregnant and I quit work at the grocery store. It had taken me five years to get pregnant, and now, we wanted to do everything right. We didn't want any harm to come to the baby. We knew this baby was going to change our lives, and we were both ready for this change.

When I got bored of shopping and watching TV, I started driving around. I found out that Sebastian worked at the convenience store off of Highway 94. Sebastian's store gets a lot of cosmopolitan-type customers: small families from the big cities out East driving to Yellowstone or Glacier. Toothpick Legs works at the convenience store near the Missouri River. That store has a camper dump, and sells expensive bait to the tourists. Their friend with the North Dakota plates, I later gleaned, was the regional manager, and he could be found at stores all over the city. The convenience stores have infested our small city like the prairie dogs have infested the wheat fields.

When not working or sleeping off a hangover, Sebastian and Toothpick Legs would be in their kitchen, hunkered over, guzzling beer and slapping down cards so hard their kitchen table would wobble.

After cleaning the house (Doug has a thing about cleanliness), I would be in the bedroom resting, and their voices would come in through my window, and it was as if we are all in the same room.

"Anything happen at work today?" Toothpicks Legs would say.

"What?"

Toothpick Legs would raise his voice: "I said: anything happen at work today?"

"One real nice looker."

"Yeah?"

"What?"

"You, Sebastian, have a hearing problem."

"What?"

Toothpick Legs would be just about screaming. "Who was at the store?"

"Red mini-skirt. This red eye shadow, black hair. It was becoming though. Black midriff. Breasts like. . ." They would start whispering, as if they knew I was listening.

"My God," Toothpick Legs would say. "Then what did you do?"

"What could I do? Her husband was there. But she had class. And she was right there in front of me. This far away. She smelled wonderful. Like soap."

"You, Sebastian, watch too much TV."

Two or three swigs and they'd crunch their Old Milwaukee cans. They'd shake their heads, slap down more cards, change the radio station and get another beer. Most mornings I would find their beer cans in our backyard, near the swing set. The swing set has two metal seats that are slanted so steeply they're almost impossible to use. The metal is a speckled green and red rust, but it was a freebie along with the half-filled sandbox from the previous owners. Doug keeps meaning to take the swing set away. I tell him it doesn't bother me.

Once Sebastian put up a sign on their crabgrass and dust front lawn. It said: "Camper For Sale—$200." An eggshell camper, white and baby blue exterior. I walked past it several times. From the end of their dirt driveway, I made out a stove, a bench, and a bed and a fridge as big as a full grocery bag. A camper for two, maybe three. It must have been thirty years old, as old as me, but for two-hundred dollars! Everybody here has campers. I had been wanting to go to the Badlands for the weekend, and with a camper we could go in style. Doug believes tents are dirty. "How can you possibly stay clean in a tent?" he says. The tourist hotels are too expensive.

I was walking toward the camper, prepared to bargain, when I suddenly felt shy and scurried home.

The next week I popped in Sebastian's convenience store. Although I was pregnant, it wasn't yet visible. I was wearing my best jeans. Doug says they fit me like a glove; if they fit, wear them, is our motto. We have other mottoes too: Try, try, try again; Laugh and the world laughs with you; and Cry and you cry alone. Remember the Alamo! Sebastian's pin-prick eyes examined me through his amber aviator glasses, maybe thinking he knew me. But we kept to our house, and he and Toothpick legs kept to theirs. Then he sees so many people in a day. How could he possibly remember them all?

During that time that I was pregnant, I thought a lot about our cottonwood. In winter, although it had no leaves, it protected us from the Canadian Northwesterlies. In spring and summer, robins used to stand on the branches, near the tree's insides, and peep. They had decided our cottonwood was the last majestic tree on the prairie; it was their stronghold, and they meant to keep it.

In September the leaves would clap against one another making music when a breeze came by: stop and go, a rustle, a full tree patter, then a crescendo of rustles. It was a pure, soothing music you could listen to day and night. There was something concentrated and powerful in those leaves, but you had to pay attention, to know it was there. Life is subtle, sometimes tenuous on the northern prairies.

That tree was so loaded with life. It would make me laugh: I too, had felt full of life, brimming over, like a soda poured on ice cream. But these feelings came too early, like my contractions.

When the leaves just started turning golden, I knew our tree would look like something from a fairy tale. But then I noticed, and this I did not want to admit, that about half of the cottonwood had no leaves, or the leaves were shriveled. I examined the cottonwood every day, looking for signs of green. But the branches were dry. When you snapped them, they weren't moist inside.

Shortly after my discovery, Doug and I were outside barbecuing ribs, and he looked at the tree and said: "It's dead. No two ways about it. It's dead."

"Look at the leaves over here, Doug," I said, grabbing his arm in a persistent way. "You can't find healthier leaves this side of the Missouri. Maybe this part of the tree is dormant. It's recovering from something." That even sounded good to me.

"I can tell when something's dead." He went back to the grill and turned the ribs. He cooked all our meat thoroughly. He didn't like the sight of blood; it reminded him too much of his job. His job makes him an authority on what's dead, so I respected his opinion. "It's dead," he said. "Believe me. It's dead."

I called the city wildlife services and they sent out a forester.

"Could be that blight from Minnesota or Wisconsin," the forester said. "Even as far away as Michigan."

Michigan, I thought.

The city forester looked like he knew a lot about trees. He

was lean, and his face was sunburnt and his hair was whiter than the cotton that the tree shed.

"You could prune it back, and it would take a couple of years to know if it would make it, but in the meantime," and he paused and looked at the stubby pines Doug had planted, "it would look funny. In fact, it would probably always look funny." Then he took a sample of a dead branch and a sample of a live one which he sent off to a university.

Whereas I sit around daydreaming, in states of indecision, Doug gets things done. In this way we complement each other. In retrospect, I probably should have fought Doug harder, but I was still so happy about the house, and being pregnant, that I didn't want anything—not even the smallest thing—to come between us.

The next week four men came out. My best jeans, the tight ones, were drying on line near the tree. I let them hang there. Using one arm each, the men moved the swing set. They brought out their power saws. In two hours they had the tree down. I stood at the back door the whole time watching them with their ropes and saws, hearing the drop of heavy branches: thump, thump, thump. Like bodies falling. I watched hundreds of leaves, some still green, flutter to the ground. It was the leaves that hurt, the fact that they were still green. I wanted to go out and tell them to stop, that it was a mistake, that the cottonwood, at least some part of it, was still alive. As they pushed and pulled I imagined the tree aching. It took another three hours to cut it up and haul it off.

Where were they taking it? What happens to diseased trees? When only a few inches of trunk remained, they brought in a trunk-eating machine.

After they left I went outside to investigate. There were two small piles of fresh shavings, and moist dirt raked into it. I knelt down and felt the dirt. Then I felt sick, as if something inside of me had died.

Leaves and twigs made a trail from where the cottonwood had been to where the men had parked their trucks. That too, would be gone: blown into nothing by the wind. Dust to dust. I shuddered, thinking that maybe they had taken out the roots too, although I knew this was impossible: the roots were too expansive; you'd have to dig up the whole house to get to them. Still, no one would ever guess that a great cottonwood had stood here. No one but me would remember it.

In early February, not quite a year after we bought the house, a terrible cold front blew in. Thirty below for days and the wind blowing cars off roads. The air was so icy and dry it couldn't snow. It hurt your lungs to breath. The naked sun made your eyes ache. The snow on the ground was dirty, and old.

I have always had uneasy feeling about February. February three years ago Doug had broke his arm playing ice hockey. February was when my uncle, who farmed up north, drowned himself.

I should not have been getting contractions for another month, but suddenly I was in the hospital with Doug beside me, squeezing my hand as if he believed that would expedite my labor. Things happened too slowly, then too quickly because when the doctor asked me if I wanted to hold my baby, I told him no.

"Look," the doctor said gently, holding up the baby. He was used to holding up babies, but not this kind.

Doug couldn't look; he could barely talk, and he left.

The baby, a girl, was just like a doll, except her eyes were closed. She didn't cry. There was nothing wrong with her, except that she was stillborn.

"The cord's twisted." The doctor couldn't come right out and say: you killed your baby, but this was what I thought back then, that I killed my baby.

He held the baby out once more, then he took her away.

Only after the baby was gone, did it become clear that I'd made a big mistake, one of the big ones of my life. I wanted to ask for her back, but what if they said no? What if they had already done to her what they do with such babies? Right then I decided I wasn't going to make any more mistakes.

When they stopped giving me tranquilizers, I told our relatives: "Go home. Go back to Darvy. Leave me alone. I need to think." I didn't have the energy to explain or defend myself. For Doug, especially, this had been torture. This event was out of his realm. I didn't want anybody telling me what I should do or how I should feel; I certainly did not want the hocus-pocus stuff about God and faith and destiny. "Save it for somebody else. Share it with them," I told my relatives. Because it wasn't worth it to talk anymore; there just wasn't anything else to say.

At first no one wanted to leave, but I made it clear if they didn't leave, then I would. "Doug," I said quietly, "Go back to Darvy. Take them with you." I only asked him once, and he left.

In retrospect, it was partly my hormones going crazy. My breasts were impacted with milk, so some part of my body still thought there was a baby. My thoughts were not consistent. I brooded over the occasional Diet Coke I'd had, and how I had salted my corn at lunch. When night fell and I was alone, I worried about the baby appearing before me, so I slept with a light on.

For a week I got up and drank so much coffee I don't know how I slept, but I slept, and I slept a lot. After the coffee I walked to my convenience store, and it didn't matter if the wind chill was 60 below; I went to make sure I could still go out. Death was hovering around me, waiting.

Once, in an act of great courage, I gathered up the sheets—I was sweating a lot—and went to the laundromat. As I listened to the mothers scream at their children, I came close to tears.

Back home, I slept. Every day I slept and I slept all afternoon, until evening. Then I sat on our new rocker and I stared at the Oldsmobile, which sat immobile beneath a street light.

I was staring into the twilight as it became night, staring inside and outside, trying to find what I had missed, what had eluded me. For sure there was something for me to learn, and I had to learn it before this time of my life passed. After several days of my routine—and who knew when it was going to end?—I woke up from a nap and found a note from a delivery service saying they had left flowers for me next door.

Sebastian answered the door. There was a fine orange dust on his upper lip, just below his mustache. Right away he gave me flowers, red roses. The flowers were alive, and I considered leaving them with Sebastian because I had so little skill with living things, but I did not think he would understand, and I could not explain. The flowers made me feel discombobulated—like being in a new apartment and being unsure of where to put things. Today should be my birthday, I thought, or I should be going out to dinner.

"Something bad?" Sebastian looked down at the floor. He was flustered, unused to talking to women.

I nodded because I had a hard time talking. Having not talked in days, I wasn't sure I even had a voice. A small card, impaled on a clear plastic pitchfork said, in black cursive writing, Doug's writing: "Can I come home?"

"I'm sorry. Here." He pulled out a chair for me. Something from the floor stuck to my shoes. When I sat down the table wobbled, even more than ours. The kitchen smelled like cheese curls and beer. I was right about that: Sebastian offered me a beer and indicated a bowl of cheese curls. It didn't look like they had much other food. The cheese curls were stale, but I hadn't eaten in days and they tasted surprisingly good with the cold beer.

His kitchen was an exact duplicate of ours: the white hastily painted cupboards, the hummocky linoleum floor, the plastic on the windows. It struck me then that all the houses in our neighborhood were built from exactly the same plan. A track house. I felt cheated, but more than that, humiliated.

Sniffing back my tears, I drank the beer. Sebastian drank his too, looking away whenever I started to raise my head. This was the first time I had seen Sebastian up close and he didn't look like the disgusting slob Doug had made him out to be. He looked younger too. When he took off his aviator glasses to rub his eyes I saw how soft his eyes were. I hoped he had a girlfriend, a person who would not take unnecessary advantage of his good nature.

Then to my surprise, I said: "You need a block heater in your car. You plug it in at night and it keeps the oil hot. Then your car starts in up the morning. Even when it's thirty below."

"Huh?" He looked around, startled, as if he didn't believe the voice came from me.

"You probably don't have them in Michigan. They're about fifty dollars."

"Block heaters?" he said, so I could tell he could hear me.

"Any mechanic can install one. Doug—he's my husband—might even put one in for you."

He nodded.

"You don't have big ears," I said.

"Big ears?"

I smiled, just a little.

When I finished the beer he offered me another, but I shook my head no. I had already said enough, and I was feeling low again. As I was getting up to leave, he said, "Wait."

He went into the closet, and in our house this is where we keep our mop and vacuum cleaner, and brought out an industrial-sized bag of cheese curls. No labels on the bag. It stood from the floor to my waist.

"Here." Sebastian held out the bag. Then he put two cold Old Milwaukees in my coat pockets, gave me my flowers, and opened the door.

That night, I sat on my rocker eating the cheese curls and drinking the beer. I put the roses on the windowsill where I could see them. There, I fell asleep, a deep sleep, and I woke up with the sun, and proceeded out to the grave. I took a flower with me.

At first I got nervous, thinking that it was the cemetery near the strip mall. It was all concrete, no trees. But it wasn't that one. The one we put the baby in was remote. There was a barn in the distance. And there were some trees.

The grave was in the baby section and I found it easily as it had no snow on it. It was as big as two sheets of notebook paper. The ground was frozen, and I could tell they'd had a hard time digging. I don't know how they did it. It was very cold that morning, and my breath moved away from me like whispers. I knelt down in the snow and laid down the rose. The grave was filled with clods of dirt, hard as rocks. It came to me that I could easily remove the clods; they probably didn't need to put babies six feet down. And there was no one around: no one but me and the wind and the snow, but I let it go.

The Ride

The kids were sleeping upstairs, the blinds down, when she opened the garage door and wheeled out the old bike. The boy, the youngest of the three, still slept with a fan on because he found the white noise soothing. The bike was her older daughter's and it was a little small for Elaine, but she was an adjustor, believing that a measure of intelligence was one's ability to adapt. It was July, the sky blue, the air cool, but once she started down the hill, there'd be a cold wind that would cut right through her. The roads were that steep. It was downhill all the way into town and in winter, with the snow and ice, she'd take a roundabout way, avoiding the 30-degree grades and hair-pin curves. Once on those curves you couldn't see a thing until it was right on you, and by that time it would be too late.

Six a.m., Sunday, and Elaine was the only one out, except for the insomniac in the rusted blue pickup vibrating with *Credence Clearwater Revival* and driving on the wrong side of the road. A tattooed arm and the *Sunday New York Times* periodically emerged from the pickup's window. There had been a time before kids, many years ago when she had lived in Texas and biked everywhere: to the university, the grocery store, the park, even to her first white collar job in the city's center. She had driven alongside the cars and trucks then, daredevil that she had been. Now *that* was dangerous.

As she adjusted the helmet, she imagined the world full of bikes rather than cars, a slowed-down, gentler world where people had the leisure to think about anything that came to mind; or maybe in this slowed-down world, people watched birds not as an obligation but for pure pleasure. Imagine.

In this leisurely life, individuals had time to think beyond how the next bill would be paid, maybe even think of how not to generate the next bill. Maybe have time to ponder what was good and what was bad about the world. Then, say you had an overabundance of time, so that rather than reacting to the next newscast, you might read in-depth articles on an issue, the Mideast war for instance, and consider the damning consequences; and maybe, if there were enough involved people, they could persuade the country's leaders that war lead to misery and bankruptcy for us, and profound misery and bankruptcy for them.

Bikes rather than cars. But then what would families do on weekends? Saturday mornings at the bagel shop Elaine stood behind the freckle-faced children in shin guards, tight socks right up to the bony knees, numbered jerseys. Dressed to intimidate. Even Elaine, who had played soccer in school, felt meek, diminished in their presence. They were cramming down oat-and-walnut muffins with orange juice, fortifying themselves for the three-hour drive to Buffalo, to the next tournament.

Wheeling the bike to the road's double yellow line, she looked over at her front yard to the euphonium, the forsythia— none of that had existed nine years ago when she bought the house. The grass was a little long and she needed to pull weeds, otherwise it was a fine house, although small by some standards. The side yard did not have as many day lilies as she'd like, but that was okay. Day lilies sprung up everywhere along the central New York roadsides. Now they were in full bloom, the neon orange color especially striking against the deep green grass. There had been rain this July, and so the grass had not turned brown. Some years it died. And there she was standing in the middle of the road, a premonition lurking that would not quite cohere into a thought.

She pushed off, passing the tattooed arm (taking a longer route than the blue pickup), passing a farmhouse, an old barn, a trailer nicely kept and mostly hidden by a grove of maples.

Any other day Mary Woods, who grew organic potatoes and garlic, would have been out walking her four-mile route and Elaine would have ridden beside her, asking if the garlic was ready because she was running out. There was nothing like fresh garlic with onions, olive oil on whole wheat pizza crust topped with melted cheddar cheese. Or Ralph Evans, a music professor, would be walking his black lab, Lightning, and they'd talk about their kids and baseball.

Her lower leg muscles clenched up, her shoulder muscles too, as her hands depressed the brakes. A cold wind knifed through her T-shirt. The T-shirt, which the school district had given teachers last September, had a slogan on the back: "All students achieving their dreams—and I helped." Elaine wanted to believe it.

Biking down hills at neck-breaking speeds required attentiveness, you could not check out the way you could while you were running. On a bike you could be going 30 miles-an-hour.

She knew this after having followed a biker, maintaining a two-car distance behind the red-shirted man, his hands strategically on the brakes, as they descended the long winding hills together. Yes, well, she had a job interview Monday with a high-tech firm and her prospect for employment looked good.

She passed the Bennetts, their rooftop solar panels generating electricity today and Susan King who was writing a screenplay on grave robbing. There were the Ruebens whose 15-year-old son had cystic fibrosis and rarely ventured outdoors. Her parents, both math teachers, were saints. There was no other word for it.

Elaine had made for herself a comfortable life, she thought, as she sped around a bend, leaning (10 miles-an-hour, she estimated), but it had not been easy. Her divorce ten years ago had been long, and expensive, and not without suffering.

Each of her children had gone through a depression that exacted more from her than she thought she had, yet each child had emerged triumphant, and with a resiliency earned from overcoming unforeseen ordeals. She owned her house, the mortgage paid. Most of her friends were not as fortunate. There was some college savings for each child only because of an inheritance bequeathed to her when her father died two years ago of pancreatic cancer, many of his dreams still unfulfilled.

She had reached a relatively flat and disappointing section

of the road and she stopped for a few minutes to adjust her pannier, and in her mind's eye the image of Scott appeared: tall, green-eyed, salt-and-pepper hair, but it was his original mind and open heart that had attracted her; his marriage he dismissed with "We'll work it out."

She met him after her divorce imagining that when her kids went to college, they would be together. For nearly seven years they talked on the phone or by e-mail about her kids, her job, social and political issues, but nothing about him.

Except for the occasional walk, they went out twice: once for coffee, and once for French fries. After the fries outing, Scott remarked: "That was fun." Too much fun apparently, because they never repeated the French fries outing. Yet he continued to ask her questions that made her believe that he still loved her; and he did, for many years. "We'll take it slowly," he said, after his divorce. Yet a week later, he expressed an interest in seeing other women, and Elaine was unable to believe that his feelings for her had changed. A typical story, and because of that, all the more wounding. Recently she had heard that his firm was having financial difficulties. A case of his was stalled and he could not, it was alleged, make a decision on a key issue.

At the first crossroad she stopped. Three deer were lazily grazing on Lynn Wilbur's day lilies and orchids, moving steadily from one flower to another, an assembly line of destroyers, and Elaine shouted at the brown monsters.

Not even one bothered to raise its dumb, lozenge-like head. They chewed constantly and contentedly. *Leave us alone, human.*

Sometimes they went right down to the root. Bastards. When she saw them near her plum trees or tomato plants, she shot at them with her son's air gun. They always returned. The next step was a BB gun, then ...venison barbeque. She'd heard venison barbeque was quite tasty. Once she opened the backdoor of her house and caught a huge brown thing from the woods chomping on her Cortland apples — apples she'd picked only an hour ago from the apple orchard. Frightened, she retreated behind the kitchen door, then after a moment, annoyed and indignant, she opened the door and cried: "Go away, beast!" The deer twitched its snooty nose at her and stared, as if to say: *I'm going to fight you for these. Stay outa' my way, woman!*

Elaine was entering — no, had created — a new phase of her life. Imagine, starting over at 51! At 51, her own mother had relocated to Florida to start over as a pool bobber and patron of the early bird specials.

Elaine had not been back to Florida since her father died, and she wondered if she would ever go back. Her new life began with her dismissal from the high school: from the outset, she fought against the Principal's standardization and lockstep policies instituted to increase test scores; the policies handicapped teaching and murdered a teacher's incentive. The Principal was a sloganeer. Posters of "You Make Your Day" and "Your Attitude is All it Takes" festooned the school hallways. He advised Elaine to begin her classes with a slogan. So she stapled her students' polymer ball advertisements to the bulletin board outside her classroom that said: "Our balls bounce higher!" and "No one has balls like ours! Try them!"

"Pretend to be one of them," Scott had warned her. "They'll keep you as long as you are useful." So she chatted with the other teachers and smiled when an administrator passed by.

She did everything they assigned to her, but also some things not assigned to her. Once the administrators decided she wasn't playing the game, they required her to attend twice the number of regular meetings and when they observed her, they never had a kind word to say about her teaching. Their Observations became her Performance Record, and thus, Elaine lived in constant fear of losing her job.

The Principal came to observe her once while teaching during the T.W.I.N.K.I.E.S. Lab: Testing With Indestructible Noxious Cake In Extreme Situations. This was with her high-risk kids: D- and F-students, the potential dropouts. Her students measured the Twinkie's dimensions, dissected the Twinkie, taste-tested the Twinkie, hypothesized what elements composed the Twinkie (cream versus the shortcake), measured its non-air volume (two milliliters!), combusted it, bounced it, pressed it against a ceiling tile (demonstrating its adhesive characteristics), and ran an electrical current through it. Yes, a Twinkie could light up a diode. Twinkies were electrical conductors! Even she was amazed. Who would have imagined?

"What does this have to do with the state standards?" the Principal asked. His head bobbed, the folds of skin around his mouth wobbled. She told him, and he replied: "I'm sure you could get the same material across in a 20-minute worksheet rather than a double lab period. The other teachers do it that way. So can you."

Taking a left at the next crossroad, she started on the second hill, a much steeper one. Every summer there was a rollover involving a teenage driver unfamiliar with road, showing off then getting in trouble. As far as she knew no one had ever died, and as long as she kept her hands on the brakes, the steep hill was no problem.

Elaine was watching a curtain of fog move up a hillside of evergreens and was not alarmed when from the corner of her eye, she saw Fuzzy trotting across the road, right where she was headed. Fuzzy's fat, tiger-shaped body. Things would have been different had she been going slower.

Fuzzy's family lived in the purple-painted Greek Revival, across the street from a low-income housing project where police were often summoned to manage domestic disputes or soured drug deals. Fuzzy's family loved him dearly. There was Mom and Grandma, who were housebound with sun allergies, and a very shy boy, Tyler, who had been Elaine's student, an A student.

Elaine had just enough time to change her trajectory to avoid hitting Fuzzy.

Then there was sudden loud music — *Credence Clearwater Revival* — the music of her youth. In the next millisecond she saw the blue pickup, backing out of a driveway right at the road's curve. Her front tire impacted against the pickup's rear, which the driver, groggy from having been up all night, never even heard.

As the bike was propelled into the air, Elaine did not think of Scott, the Principal, her parents, her ex, or even what the bike was doing. The thoughts came rapidly, one right after another, uncontrolled.

Then there was the thought that had been flitting at the edges of her consciousness.

It was last summer, an unbelievably hot and muggy day. The kids were irritable and bickering — a visit to their Dad had gone wrong, and they had been disappointed — so Elaine took them out into the country to pick blueberries. It was hot, no shade, and they must have picked 12 pounds of berries and eaten another two. The bushes, and there were acres of bushes, were heavy with the fat, sweet berries. Afterward, they talked to the man who planted and pruned the bushes.

At home they made a pie using the berries right from the plastic containers. Her daughters made the crust, and her son helped with the filling. Then it was so hot inside the house that they went out in back and sat, staring at the woods. Crickets chirped away. As the sky turned that violet blue that it does in July, they watched the phosphorescent lights of fireflies.

"They're all over," her son said, awestruck.

"I like this, Mom," the younger daughter said.

Then the oldest child went inside and emerged with the pie, plates, forks, ice cream. It was the best food she ever ate. So she had done something right. Then they were all watching the fireflies darting here and there, lighting up the backwoods, listening to the soft hum of crickets.

This Good Life

Even though the students are inside, the classroom windows face Cayuga Street so that they can still look outside and see the blue sky and clouds, and know that some things in life never really change. The sky will always be there and most of the time it will be blue.

Yes there could be snow and quite a bit of snow: snow on roads, snow on the sidewalks making them impassable, snow softly blanketing the cars in the parking lot, so much snow that schools would close early. It has happened. And there would almost always be cars speeding along on Cayuga Street attesting to the fact that people are involved in life a significant way, in getting things done and in going somewhere.

People, every day ordinary people, are doing everyday, ordinary things: shopping, depositing checks, getting their hair cut or meeting a friend for coffee. There is a purpose to life and these everyday, ordinary people know that. Not only a purpose, but solid goals and a sense of moving forward.

Yes, although the students are crammed in this small room, they can feel that they are a part of a larger world, that their ideas will be heard, their actions acknowledged, and that if they keep their eyes on their books and can memorize The Seven Wonders of the Ancient World, then the good life will almost certainly be theirs. But what is this good life?

It's December. Snow falls rapidly, thickly, dusting the small city, a city with sledding hills in such abundance that everyone who lives in this glacial enclave feels lucky and safe. Safe from earthquakes, floods, hurricanes, tsunamis, torrential mudslides, rattlesnake infestations, terrorists. What more could a person ask for? It's a safe, safe, safe place. What need one fear?

"You're not screaming at me," Joh says gaily to Edith. Was that a wink? Joh, a small-boned 13-year-old dressed in T-shirts and jeans, is a good-natured kid. There are several T-shirts but they all have holes in them, and these aren't the fashion holes. The material has thinned so much that the stress of stretching the shirt along the wrong trajectory could bring about its demise.

He rips another page out of his notebook, wads it up, tosses it into the garbage can. He misses. Joh doesn't rise to pick up the wadded paper, but at the period's end he will. A nice kid Joh is, respectful, despite for him what has been an inconsistent and peripatetic life. He lives in a rundown house adjacent to the Salvation Army meeting hall. Rumor has it that he plays the trumpet during Sunday services.

The other students glance up from the history and math books and blink. The content area support lab, or CAL, consists of students with learning disabilities and/or behavioral problems: the high-risk students known by the other students as stupid, disrespectful brats who do everything possible to disrupt class. To Edith, they are the presently unreachable students and are considered by many to remain unreachable.

During this period, one or two will put his head down on the desk and sleep. "I'm tired," a kid will say dismally. Who knows how late this 13-year-old was up last night and what he was doing?

What is true about all of them, unequivocally, is an inability to concentrate, yet to be successful in the American society one must be able to concentrate. All else follows from that. You need to be capable of holding a thought in your mind for longer than a few minutes. You need to remember the mechanics of long division, and remember that *their* is not the same as *there*. Or where. Or here. Hear?

You need to remember what words mean.

"That's right, I'm not screaming at you," Edith says cavalierly, although she keeps one eye on the hallway. A substitute teacher who fails to maintain adequate control is a substitute teacher soon to be unemployed. Yet if a student chooses to rip pages out of his notebook, what right does she have to stop him? It's his notebook. *Other teachers would stop it,* is not only a flawed rationalization, but an excuse. All day, every day, and every minute and every second of the day she must be aware of making excuses.

"Why aren't you screaming at me?" Joh says, wadding up another sheet of paper.

"I don't know you well enough." She gives them the opportunity to speak and act. Opportunity, in Chinese, has a connotation of danger.

To order him to work (Can ordering him achieve what she wants? And what is that exactly — what she wants? Is that morally defensible: *what she wants*?) will undermine the genuine connection she seeks to establish with him; teaching often fails to achieve anything worthwhile unless there is a connection, a true interest in understanding who the other person really is.

Edith doesn't scream at Joh, but she screams at her own children, although she wishes she wouldn't. She wishes she had more time with them. She wishes that she knew what to say to them during a crisis. The right words have to be right there, at the tip of her tongue, in fully-formed sentences, good words like responsibility, respect, accountability, learning, limitations.

For the past few weeks, Edith's 15-year-old, Denise, has been coming home every day slamming doors and shrieking. Her petite, intelligent, creative, ambitious, opinionated, straightforward — perhaps too straightforward — daughter has lost her tolerance for frustration.

Her normal melancholia — and there's nothing wrong with some melancholia — has mutated into despair. If the English teacher fails to appreciate the nuances of her essay on Emily Dickenson, then Denise suffers, as does everyone else in the house. Yesterday she came home crying because the Math teacher told the class, *If you failed the test, then you should drop down to a lower level. Don't ask me for help: I don't have the time. You simply shouldn't be in the class.* And Denise followed this by: *I don't know what's wrong with me! Maybe I'm just like Uncle Felix. No*, Edith has told her daughter. *You are not like Uncle Felix.*

Trish, a beautiful girl with wavy brown hair and blue eyes, sits with a sleepy, vacant look on her face. A week ago in a science class Edith attempted to help her graph a time versus distance plot, spending 15 minutes of a 38-minute period with the girl. It was clear to Edith that the girl would never master the meaning of a graph: how X and Y change together and create a pattern that means something. If the gray matter wasn't there, it just wasn't there. What was one to do? Tell her to read the posters on the wall? *Attitude is 90 percent.* The reality is that gray matter is 90 percent, but there are no posters on the walls indicating this. Holding a moderately abstract thought in her mind more than a few seconds was impossible for Trish, so why has the school demanded this impossible feat? The blue eyes stare back at Edith not with hostility or need, but with bland acceptance, and a little less enthusiasm than what a pet exhibits for a TV show. To believe all students can succeed is naive, stupid and dangerous.

In another part of the room, Nathan pulls crumpled papers and multicolored folders out of his backpack. He'll do this for most of the period then he'll produce his Gameboy which Edith will tell him to put away. He'll argue, then attempt to try engage Edith in conversation on any subject except his school work. Why? He's known in the schools as a 'consumer.' He has learned how to work the system. So he does think and learn, but not what the school intended.

In another corner of the room A.J. sits warily, a blue doo-rag snug around his head. Edith's seen him riding his dented bike along the busy streets of downtown, playing chicken with the college students in their shiny Accords and BMWs. Last week Edith was A.J.'s social studies teacher. He strolled up to the front of the classroom and plopped his fulsome body down in the teacher's swivel chair, and initiated a series of back-and-forth movements. Edith asked him to return to his seat.

"Say what?" he said, not quite belligerently.

The students became suddenly silent, perceiving impending drama. All of them stared at Edith.

"Why can't I sit here?"

Edith sincerely believed in equality of people and mutual respect. She knew he wasn't going to throw the chair at anyone or spin it into outer space.

"What's wrong with me sitting here?" he said, raising his chin, then spinning around a complete 360 degrees. Just let the Principal walk by and see that, Edith thought.

A.J. gave the class a marvelous, triumphant grin, his teeth very white against his brown skin. Edith chose to ignore the tone of insolence, if that's what it was, because it could have been a breath, a small inhalation and exhalation of freedom.

She didn't know A.J. at all, except that she occasionally sees him on his bike, challenging cars and trucks. Surely there must be a parent somewhere? Edith asked him again to sit down, and suggested that they could talk after class. He sat down and for the remainder of the period he sulked, and Edith could think of no way to bring him out of his sulk.

She had to be patient. The motives and emotional needs of the students are almost always buried, rarely revealed to a sub.

And she isn't nearly as perceptive as she needs to be. Edith's list of flaws is two miles long. A sub was compelled to make broad and often erroneous assumptions as to who her students were, who their parents were, if they had a quiet, well-lit place to read at book after dinner. Edith has learned never to take insults personally.

Even so such situations make Edith uncomfortable; she isn't as strict most other teachers and perhaps in part, this is why she has not been hired as a regular teacher.

Every morning just before six (the sub coordinator begins calling at six), Edith talks herself into the job, and the talk goes like this: *Not much is expected of me. What I am expected to do is keep the students safe and maintain a modicum of order. If they allow me to teach, wonderful; if not, then not. I am not going to change 24 students I've never met before in 38 minutes.*

Another part of the talk is about jobs in general. *Is there anyone who loves her job? Yes ...but such individuals are far and few between. Such people, such jobs are the exception. This is the situation I am in now, and I must accept it. Do the best I can.*

Edith spent all of last week at Ryden Elementary, sitting in a cold, dark, 4th grade classroom with faded posters on the walls that said things like *Think Positively* and *Always Do Your Best. Together we'll succeed.*

The posters, some hanging by one taped corner, peppered the hallways and inadequately covered the walls of bold green paint. The school is a half-hour drive out into the country along icy roads that threaten with every hairpin curve to turn the driver into a paraplegic.

Many students here live on ramshackle dairy farms. Their families are poor. For them school is something to get through, not an opportunity (with its connotation of danger, and risk) for a better life.

A mile from Ryden, near a creek that overflows every April, sits a trailer court where a young man was beaten over a period of hours, then subjected to the terrors of the murderer's pit bull. The beating was in retribution for an unpaid debt. Identification by DNA was required because the man's face was gone. Drugs were involved. The dead man was unemployed, but engaged to be married, and said by a neighbor in an unwashed coat and thick glasses to have *Been a nice guy who trusted people too much. Way too much!* The man died inhaling his own blood.

During Edith's week at Ryden, the 4th grade boys were required to use the bathroom in pairs: some students, rather than aiming at the urinals, preferred the floors and sinks. Why? Edith, who grew up with brothers, knows boys sometimes play games with their pee.

This was something she never understood, although she concedes that girls play games too. Starting in 4th grade they loiter in the hallways, then at the last moment, dance into the classroom in their two-inch heeled black shoes, their tight blouses threatening to pop off buttons.

They dance to a beat belted out by the rap music coming incessantly from their key chains. Edith disliked taking away personal possessions, but she asked the girls several times to turn the damn things off.

When Edith started an English lesson, these girls, not quite young women, declared: "I can't do it."

"It's too hard."

"I can't understand it."

"I don't need to."

Edith told them to read it slowly. Read the passage aloud. They countered with: "It's *too* hard." Period. "We're not going to do it." (Arms crossed beneath the emerging breasts.)

This disinclination to concentrate, or to try isn't supposed to happen at nine-years-old. These girls had the gray matter, but they chose not to use it. They had what is known as a learning block, and the blocks varied: bad parents, peer pressure, social dysfunction, poverty.

Edith, having grown up in the country and played Barbie dolls with a neighbor who lived in a perennially cold house, knows this type of child. A kid left on her own. A house with chickens milling about the yard—a place of dirt and scabby trees that never produced fruit. In winter, the chickens would come indoors.

Edith cajoled the girls: "Try just one sentence. Just one. I'll help." She attempted patience, logic, and was close to a threat, when she capitulated: there were 25 students in the class, not three. And in that moment, she violated one of her guiding principles: to teach the students at least one useful piece of information during the period that she has them.

Edith read from the book, the pages assigned by the teacher. Their atonal, unmusical key chains will become obsolete in a year or two (only a year or two: you must be tough, because only the tough survive), replaced by the charms of cigarettes and bars. Doublewides and babies. Rusted pickups and sodas at the neighborly GassFill. Drugs, pit bulls and sex, because sex is cheap and free entertainment.

These are not the kind of girls whose parents will take them to the free programs at Cornell's Art Museum, or who have season's tickets to the kids' plays at the Hangar Theater. If these students are lucky, they'll get a job as an aide ($12,000 year) rather than attendant at GassFill ($7.50-an-hour, tops).

"My father passed out this weekend," Jackie, who met Edith just moments earlier, said. "Me and my stepmother tried to dress him up like a girl. But he's too fat—we couldn't get a bra around him."

Look at your kids, Edith wants to say to these parents. *Look what you're doing to them. Do you want them to be like you? So hungover Saturday morning you don't know your kid is trying to put a bra on you?* She wants to say: *Help them now to get out of the rut and tell them that succeeding in school is important. Help them aspire to something more than a retail job at the mall. Get them off the poverty track and impress upon them the importance of homework and learning. Understand the weight of inertia and habit, that it's easy for a student to descend, hard to ascend. Help them defeat fate.*

Of course Edith says none of this. She doesn't know their parents; it is unlikely she ever will.

A little self-righteous, aren't we? a voice inside of her says. As if you have no problems with your own kids. Edith's Denise went a week without speaking to her. And the week before was horrendous.

At ten p.m. Denise was banging a pot around — against the stove, the table, the sink. Why? She was cooking broccoli for tomorrow's lunch.

Denise was very meticulous about what went into her body. She turned on the radio — loud rap music — but she wasn't singing along. The idea was to disrupt. It was an announcement: *You're never going to get rid of me. Hah!*

Edith's bedroom, a former porch, shares a wall with the kitchen, and thus Edith asked Denise — nicely — to finish up. Denise commented with words that Edith never would have used with her own parents.

Times have changed and children are different, and Edith, with sadness and longing, accepted this. The young women these days put rings in their belly buttons and spike their hair neon blue. Edith doesn't mind that, in fact, she respects such manifestations of individuality, but it's the *"bitch, fuck-off* that she can't adjust to. How have things gotten so cruel, so out-of-hand? At the same time, their high school math is the same math that Edith sweated over in college. Edith can only imagine the stresses they endure. *I do not plan to have kids*, Denise has said in a tone that does not invite discussion.

The night of the pan banging, Edith comfortably reclined in bed while reading a short story by Robert Stone. She was at a part where two pot-smoking, heavily drugged couples were on a boat in the Caribbean, waiting for a signal to deliver the drugs on an island. The stoned adults jumped off the boat—for an impromptu swim—unaware that nefarious individuals had severed the anchor's line.

In their drug-induced state, the stoned adults neglected to lower the boat's ladder, making escape from the water impossible. *The boat was drifting away and one of the swimmers felt something—*

"Mom," Denise said, suddenly appearing at the door, a pan of steaming broccoli in her hand, "I want to talk with you."

"Okay." Edith glanced back down at her book.... *drifting away and one of the swimmers felt something rubbery. It was —*

"Okay, Mom!" Denise slammed her mother's door so hard that a water color (a Madonna-like Mom walking with two children) on the adjoining wall shuddered. Her lovely daughter shrieked, pounded up the stairs, and once in her room, turned on the radio full volume.

In seconds, Rob began screaming: "Foureyes-dingledorf-thongwoman-nosepicker! Turn off the radio! Foureyes-dingledorf-thongwoman-nosepicker!"

An hour earlier Edith had talked with Denise about the consequences of screaming, slamming and radio blasting. Denise screamed back at Rob using the most imaginative and inventive strings of four-letter words. (She'll be a writer, Edith thinks.) Edith dropped her book and began climbing the stairs.

"Get out of my room!" Denise screamed. "You bitch!"

This was not the first time; amazingly, each time this happens Edith's heart is seized with terror. Grabbing her daughter's shoulders, Edith wrestled her to the bed, that wonderful young woman who gave Edith so many of her meaningful moments of the day; that kind teenager who loved the neighbors' young children and whom all neighbors wished were theirs; that intelligent, dangerously independent woman, unafraid to speak her mind. Edith slapped her face.

"You have to stop!" Now Edith was screaming. "This can't go on! The rest of us need to sleep at night!" Breaking free, Denise ran helter-skelter out of the house, weeping, slamming doors.

Edith turned toward the door, then decided against it. In the hallway Rob was standing, his arms hugging his Penguin, last year's holiday present from Felix. His face was flushed red from the excitement.

"I'm glad that's over," he said.

Edith looked at her son, the bags under his eyes, thinking: yes, I'm glad it's over too, but it's over only for *now*. Giving him a kiss, she tucked him and Penguin in bed. Then Edith went to bed. She couldn't sleep: too much adrenaline still pumping through her veins. There was too much that she had not done right. She should have put the book down immediately. She should have walked Denise to the bus stop when she was in first grade. Second grade. Third. She should have volunteered at the schools more often.

A half hour later, Denise returned, and quietly ascended the stairs. Edith still could not sleep. Sometime during the night it occurred to her that Denise had no defenses.

Something terrible, Edith was sure, has happened to her fragile daughter. Something in that high school of 1,600 kids. Last week while subbing there, a fight broke out in a hallway in G building. Edith, standing on the fight's periphery, shielding other students, keeping them back, saw from the corner of her eye, a white jersey jump up in the air, arms outstretched, big boots landing on someone on the floor.

At 6:30 the next morning, the shower went on. Later that day, Denise would begin to talking to her mother. "I don't know what's wrong," she would say, "I'm having such a hard time, but I don't know why." Every day, Denise revealed a little more: "Sam isn't the same person he used to be. He has no convictions."

Sam, so that's it, or part of it: Denise's boyfriend who lives a few houses down the road in a well-kept house with new wood floors, gleaming white tile in the kitchen. Two Subarus, waxed outside, vacuumed inside, wait in the paved driveway for the next excursion to Maine.

He's a polite kid with two parents, both of whom have good, steady jobs. They don't worry where the money will come from or how they'll buy gas or groceries. Without fail his parents attend all of Sam's baseball games and volunteer at school. He hasn't lived through what Denise has. Why should he have convictions?

A.J and Joh have gone to other classes, and Edith goes to lunch, to the teacher's lounge which shares a wall with the gym, finds a spot on a couch set against a wall packed with 20-year-old textbooks, and nibbles on some pecans that she brought with her. She never buys the lunches. One-by-one the teachers enter and take their place at two tables, one long, one short, set together to make an L. They laugh and waste no time starting in on the tacos that smell faintly meaty. Edith eats her pecans and listens to the conversation. She likes the teachers. Good, hard-working, caring people these teachers are. Their nights are spent correcting papers, and planning for the next day.

"You just have to work a little harder with Joh," the English teacher says.

"Joh's a nice kid," the Math teacher says, "but he'll eat up 95 percent of your time if you let him. Then that's only 5 percent for the other 22 students. No matter what I do, and I've been teaching math for 20 years, I'll never be able to get him to add. Adding is something you have to learn at a very young age, and if you never get the opportunity when you're young, you miss that window of opportunity, you can't make it up. It's gone. Give him a calculator, and he can do it. But he can't do it in his mind, and I don't think he'll ever be able to."

"The poor kid has had such a rough life," a counselor says. "He practically lives at the Salvation Army. He's over there most of the time."

"I know he's had a tough life. And I know he's a nice kid," the Math teacher says, "but you still can't devote 95 percent of your resources to one kid. Kids need parents. Ideally, they should have two parents. Two responsible parents, otherwise the kids are at a disadvantage, sometimes an extreme disadvantage, and you can't expect the schools to makeup the gap. We're not parents. Most of us have 100 students."

"You can't just abandon the kid," the English teacher says.

"I didn't say abandon," the Math teacher says. "He's a kid who's going to fall through the cracks unless there's some special adult out there — and I don't see any right now — willing to adopt a 13 year-old biracial boy. Not many people are. He's too old. It's too risky."

"We can keep trying," the counselor says.

"You get people who become foster parents not for the love of a kid, but for the love of money," the English teacher says.

"Right now he's with foster parents, and they're good people, but they have their limitations. They can't give Joh as much as he needs," the counselor says.

"He's going to fall through the cracks, and we need to accept it," the Math teacher counters. "There are just too many needy kids walking through that door. We need to distribute resources over the range of students. Look: we're teachers here. We're not parents, and we're not God. We can't save everybody. I wish we could, but we can't. Remember that: we're not God."

The next morning Edith is up early, rocking blissfully in a

chair in the backroom, which used to be a porch, but new windows and insulation have made the room habitable year round. The windows on three sides make it the best room in the house, especially when there's a full moon at 6 a.m.. In the woods out back, a half-dozen deer trot past the wire mesh fence, a 6-foot tall fence that will protect the tomatoes and zucchini that she'll plant in late May. She's reading an autobiographical novel, <u>This Blinding Absence of Light.</u> A group of Moroccan prisoners have been sentenced to life in tomb-like cells beneath the earth's surface, and are let out only briefly for funerals of fellow prisoners, almost all who've died horrible deaths. Many of them seem to die of craziness.

It's six-thirty. Edith goes to the small kitchen, puts a mug of water in the microwave. Water surges through the pipes and Edith registers that Denise is up and taking her shower upstairs. The microwave beeps and Edith removes the cup and drops in a tea bag in and a spicy aroma of cinnamon fills the small, cold kitchen.

The thermostat is set to 60 degrees for economical and environmental reasons. Beyond the warm walls of the house, snow blows furiously. Through a window, the glow of a streetlight on the desolate road quivers in the gusts of wind. It could be the Arctic out there, or Antarctica, continents she has vicariously visited on videos she's shown to classes. She wouldn't mind not subbing on this cold, cold December morning. Then she sees something on the road: a shadow of December frigidity. The shadow moves uncertainly, falling in the deep snow, rising, staggering, falling again, retrieving something and that is when Edith makes out the outline of a man. An entombed man, she thinks, a man grasping for something that will always be beyond him. A skimpy jacket flaps open in the wind and blowing snow. No gloves, no hat, and he must be cold, but he doesn't seem to feel it. Blowing his hair straight up, the wind seems to lead him on.

In the sudden illumination of the porch light, Edith recognizes Felix. As he climbs the slate steps, he squints back the light, and falling on one knee, looks up uncertainly.

"Cold," Felix says, as he rises, opens the door and casually walks inside, into the kitchen, as if there is nothing unusual about this dark, deadly, pre-dawn visit during a snowstorm. He doesn't bother to brush the snow off of his pant legs or remove his snow-covered sneakers. Edith hasn't seen Felix for months. Felix comes when he wants, when he is lonely. His sole acquaintances seem to be doctors.

Gaunt and unshaven, his hands shake as he stands in the middle of the kitchen, and to quell the shaking, he reaches for the refrigerator door. The light above illuminates the kitchen and every blue-black hair on his head, casting his face in steely shadows. He opens the door, peers inside, moves a jar of mayonnaise around, and apparently finding nothing appetizing, closes the door. He thunks down a worn paper bag filled with bottles on the blue card table that serves as the kitchen table.

"It's early, Felix." Edith's tone is non-judgmental, non-confrontational.

"Kids." It seems hard for him to talk. He opens the refrigerator again. Maybe it is the sound of the motor revving up, or the blast of cold air that soothes him.

"Do you want something to drink?"

He closes the door, sighs. "Of Gods and Devils," he says, staggering onward into the house, suddenly oblivious of her presence. There's a couch, but the couch presents a problem: to sit or not to sit. This seems to be his dilemma. He sits. Looking out the picture window across the snow-blown road where an evergreen glows with strings of bright, multicolored lights, Felix appears entranced. The lights give the snowy dark landscape a wonderful warmth and mystery. This is the place to be on a snowy December morning. There's hope. New beginnings. Warmth and peace in the midst of cold. She hears his breathing, labored, the catch, and thinks: he's been abusing his medication again.

"Is everything okay?"

Felix, sitting on the couch's edge, stares blankly at Edith as if trying to remember who she is, or why he is here. Then, staring into the middle distance, he says,

"One must have a mind of winter
To regard the frost and boughs
Of the pine trees crushed with snow."

Exhausted by the effort, he sits back and stares out the window again, his hands on his knees. "I have to tell the kids — about 'the pine trees crushed with snow.'"

"They're getting ready for school."

"I have to tell them. Now, in person. It's very important. They need to know this. There isn't much that is important, but this is. Wouldn't you agree with me, Edith?"

She looks at his bloodshot eyes, wondering where he has been. "That's right, there isn't much that is important."

"I don't want to forget this."

"They may misunderstand you."

"This is where you're wrong, Edith, and where you've always been wrong. I can make them understand." Felix: as if by the sheer force of words—his words—could move continents. At times he certainly believes this.

The wind howls and rattles the windows downstairs. Drafts move through the house and send a shiver up the spine. The windows, which are at least half a century old, should be replaced. There are other things the house needs too.

Rising, Edith stands at the base of the stairs, and calls Denise and Rob, announcing Uncle Felix's arrival. Overhead, a bed creaks and a child's feet thud on the wood floor. Stairs creak as Rob walks haltingly down, arriving for inspection in Scooby-Doo shorts and a bright pink "Save the World" T-shirt. He's still rubbing the sleep out of his eyes. Denise follows, her hair wet, the scent of shampoo and perfume filling the tiny front room. Felix tries to smile as he gives them each a hug, his thin arms shaking. The kids don't notice—they're still half asleep—or they're simply used to Felix's eccentricities.

"I took the path less traveled," Felix announces. Then he sits back down, nearly missing the couch. "How many times," Felix says, his eyes widening, "do you think a person can get lost between here and Syracuse?"

The sharp tops of his teeth align themselves into a smile yet again, although Edith knows this is not meant to be a joke.

"None," Denise says, giving her uncle a condescending look. "It's all route 81 then route 13. It's impossible to get lost."

"Denise, Denise," Felix says. He rises, pulls the chord on the overhead fan, and he watches the blade spin, making sure the spin is right (his head nodding with each blade revolution) before returning to the comforts of the couch.

"Ten times," Rob says, trying to be helpful.

"Four, I got lost four times. Or I think it was four times. It could have been three. But I know I slid off the road twice. That I'm sure of. First time, I got all four wheels stuck in the snow, in the middle of nowhere. How did it happen? The roads are treacherous. Icy. There's the black invisible ice that kills and permanently maims."

He stops suddenly, his eyes stare at the fan overhead as his lips silently move, while Edith considers the treacherous icy roads.

If they are as bad as he describes, then it seems to her miraculous that Felix survived the roads. But from Syracuse? What was he doing in Syracuse?

"Too much ice and too much snow," Felix continues. "I decided to stay in my car. You don't want to go out unless it's absolutely necessary. It was three in the morning. I was in the middle of nowhere, not even sure how I got there. There was nothing around but blackness. I was completely surrounded by snow: blowing, packed snow, howling snow. It was right out of a movie. At times, the snow looked black. The snow was high and the sky black. I could have been on another planet for all I knew."

Felix looks out the front window to the bright holiday lights on the evergreen, shaking in the wind. All eyes follow.

"Which is the sound of the land
Full of the same wind
That is blowing in the same bare place."

He pauses, then says, "You remember the poem?"

"The Snowman," Denise says. "Wallace Stevens."

"Yes! Yes, you don't forget, do you? Good girl, Denise. See, I decided to stay in my car where it was warm, but then I thought: hey, wait a minute: if the snow's up to my door, then it must be way past the exhaust pipe and I don't want any of that exhaust coming into the car. Car exhaust is mostly carbon monoxide and too much carbon monoxide will kill you. Puts you to sleep. Drift off into Z-land and you never know what happened."

Edith had a cousin who did it that way, but his act was intentional.

"Uncle Fe-lix," Rob pleads.

"I'm okay!" Felix says, his voice hitting an odd cadence, so that Edith worries more. The cadence is on the verge of cracking. "A joke. Nothing serious! I calmly evaluated the situation. See, I couldn't move the doors. Too much snow. I thought, a-hah: sunroof. So I climbed out the sunroof, and that's how I ripped my shirt." He raises his right arm, showing everyone the ripped blue-and-green flannel shirt, some dried blood on the sleeve. "I must have walked a couple of miles in the snow until I found a farmhouse and called a tow truck."

"Why were you in Syracuse, Uncle Felix?" Denise says. Her annoyance has modulated into curiosity, which often happens in situations involving Felix.

"Your Mom didn't tell you?"

Edith shrugs. She is never quite sure what to tell the children. Too much, she hurts them; too little, she hurts them. And Felix's reliability as an unbiased reporter is often questionable.

"I was getting my brain shocked."

Edith watches their reactions. Nothing. They have no idea what he's talking about. But Edith is starting to understand. He's been self-medicating again.

"Doctors do that sometimes—give shocks to their patients. It helps crazy people. Almost forgot." Rising from the couch, shaking again, his arms making small angular movements, he hobbles out to the kitchen and returns with a brown paper bag. From the bag, he pulls out a Coke and hands each kid one which they immediately open and drink half-way down before Edith can object.

Edith doesn't give her kids Coke. Felix smiles at Edith, a smile that says: *See, I don't think solely of myself. You're wrong about me, Edith, and you've always been wrong.*

"Gee, Uncle Felix, thanks a bunch," Rob says, slinking back into the easy chair, positioning himself to better enjoy this rare caffeinated state. "You know what, Uncle Felix? I would invite you to my basketball game, but our coach had to stop the games because we don't have a person to who knows how to use a defibrillator."

"When I was offshore last summer—remember that? Analyzing critters in ocean sediments? I learned how to use one." Felix smiles, a rubbery smile, but a smile all the same. "Anybody can do it. You simply need to know what voltage to use. You don't want to fry the person." Felix laughs. Edith can tell Rob wants to laugh along with him, but isn't sure if frying people is something to joke about.

Denise's eyes narrow and Edith understands her daughter is annoyed, and at the very least, wants to go to school. School follows a routine. It's predictable and often rewarding. The teachers are fairly stable adults with organized plans of what they will accomplish each day.

The wind has died down, and if the front picture window were open, they would hear the snow falling softly, accumulating and producing that idyllic pattern on trees and roads, making the world appear untouched by anything untoward, as if this part of the world were newly created just hours ago. A pure, significant and beautiful world.

Felix suddenly jumps up from the couch and makes for the kitchen. Cupboards open and close, cups clatter, a glass coffee pot bangs—without breaking—against a counter. "Ow!" Felix cries. Then, "I'm okay! No worry! Just spilled a little coffee. Nothing to get upset about." The with a bellowing voice, he recites

"For the listener who listens in the snow
And nothing himself
beholds nothing that is nothing

and nothing....and nothing. That might not be right."

He walks back in the room with a mug of coffee, cold coffee that Edith made yesterday, and says: "I almost didn't make it here."

Edith is again reading. It is at that time of year when the sun shines for a few hours then sits on the horizon for the rest of the day, waiting. The phone has not rung and she reads, intently, because she believes that the answers to life's problems will be found in books; not all answers, but surely some.
    And what would she do otherwise? Paint a room? Scrape mildew off the bathroom tile? Could she learn from housecleaning what she has learned from Greene, Cotezee, Gordimer, Proust, Stone, Jin and Joellen?: faith, dignity, courage, desire, humility, forgiveness? Learned such things from scraping off mildew from the tub?
    In some sense, perhaps, but she reads for pleasure too, for the pure pleasure of discovering an author who can weave words together in such a way that the words sing out from the page and invite her in. *Welcome to this world that you've never before experienced, and likely never will again.* Men kept below ground in

horribly tiny, dark, dank cells. Those who died, the author declares, died of hatred, not hunger. For herself, for her children, she needs to remember that. If even one small nugget of wisdom can be incorporated in their brain each day, then the day is a success. She needs to do everything possible for her and her children's souls.

Edith's parents never read. Reading was an odd thing to do—only very odd people read—and certainly reading was not important to success in life. Her parents had their own ideas of whom and what they were, and never sought anyone else's perspective.

Out of laziness, ignorance or fear, they became who they were, her mother more so than her father. Was she curious about how other people lived? People on T.V, maybe only those people. Reading, for Edith is not just a way to idle away the time; indeed, reading for her is often equivalent to eating: she needs the sustenance of ideas flowing through her veins.

Then the phone rings.

"I don't have my medicine!" Felix screams. "They took them all away when I was in the hospital. Now I have nothing." He starts to cry. Listening to him makes her eyes water and she's on the verge of tears herself.

"Felix, listen to me," Edith says firmly. "Call the hospital. Or better yet, go back to the hospital. Go back now. Today. Right now. I'll call a taxi for you."

"I don't know what's wrong with me. I'm so lonely and so sad. What's the matter with me? I can't go back there. Don't tell me to go back there. If I do, I'll go crazy! I *need* my medications. If Frank were here, I'd have my medications. He'd get them for me. He'd figure out a way."

Felix sobs as he gives her details, scattered details but enough for Edith to piece together his story. Felix checked himself into a hospital in Syracuse for electroshock treatments. Apparently he was given two of the required ten treatments before fleeing in the middle of the night. He simply walked out. Typical Felix. The doctors took away all of his meds, meds that he had been on for years, type and quantity varying over those years before Frank died, but Felix's problems accelerated after Frank's death. Frank was Felix's brother, Edith's husband. When Frank died, Felix filled in as surrogate father: ferrying the kids to music lessons, reading them Wallace Stevens and watching over them the year Edith attended night school. Without Felix's help, Edith never would have gotten her teaching degree.

Suddenly, Felix is no longer crying, rather, he's asking Edith's opinion of his girlfriend, Marilyn.

"I think I fucked everything up with all that legal action," he says. "I probably shouldn't have charged her with larceny."

"I wouldn't know." Edith doesn't know the details, but she suspects Felix acted rashly and emotionally; Felix rarely acts with logic or care. She has learned to be very careful with Felix: he is not the same person he was three years ago.

"Edith, you should let me take the kids out to dinner, or to the Y to swim."

"Hmm." Again, Edith is careful not to mention the Ford

driven into a creek and totaled, the black BMW driven into a tree and totaled. Apparently he was on new medications. Edith never knows when he's switching medication. Neither does she mention the prolonged hospital stays, the suicide attempts. Did those too result from a medication adjustment, or something else? How would she ever know? He tells her only what he wants to.

"What am I doing wrong, Edith? I need a girlfriend. That's all I really need. Just a girlfriend." The essential Felix: *I need.*

"She doesn't have to be a good cook. I can teach her how to cook. Do you know anyone, mid-thirties, medium to slender build, intelligent, kind, good sense of humor. Yeah, that's important. And clean—a little cleaner than you, Edith. You let things go longer than they should, Edith. And that coffee. You never knew how to make coffee."

"The only single women I know are teenagers."

Felix seems to consider this. For Edith, it's hard to reconcile the new Felix with the old Felix, Dr. Felix Rambrand, who published scientific papers in respected journals and gave talks at conferences. He's a smart man, this Felix Rambrand, yet he never understood what makes a person happy.

Happiness: this intangible quality of being, a way of existing. It's there or it's not. Happiness *is* an issue because it forms an umbrella over your life, letting in just the right amounts of rain or sunlight, and keeping whatever is needed in, in. At some level, Edith realizes, all novels are about happiness, and Felix, being the voracious reader that he is (another reason she and Felix get along well), shouldn't he have understood some of these ideas? Doesn't everyone learn from books and poems? Frank would have said she was being naive, too eager to generalize.

"I don't know about teenagers. Teenagers are too fucked up. I remember myself as a teenager. Goofing off. Drinking too much and taking too many drugs. Having a good, old time. It was a life dominated by hormones."

Edith remembers what Frank said, that they had all gone to the best schools, right up to the Ivies. Summers they spent in Switzerland, skiing on top of glaciers. Winter break was snorkeling in the Caribbean and identifying fish in the neritic zone.

Every few years they moved, following the career of a college history professor, never staying long enough anywhere to make friends. They led a privileged life, yet somehow, Felix got lost along the way, or maybe he was always lost and no one noticed, like Joh who never had the opportunity to learn to count, and never will. Or maybe it was little things that built up over the years, unacknowledged, not reflected upon, and then suddenly, these little things cohered, and gaining momentum, they became overwhelming. The umbrella collapsed. Some individuals are just more sensitive than others, and they end up broken, their lives disrupted and diminished, emptied of resources.

The image of A.J. swirling around in the teacher's chair takes possession once again of Edith's mind. She should have let him sit on the chair. He wasn't harming anyone. What damage could he have done? What damage did she do?

"I can't go back," Felix says suddenly. "You don't know what it's like there. It's everything you can imagine and more:

people walking around like zombies, walking around in pajamas that open up the back. I can't do that. People with bibs tied around their necks, like a noose. They treat you like babies. I had a roommate, Edith, and he kept calling up his wife, screaming at her, telling her she bought the wrong kind of jeans for him. He wanted Levis. Nothing else. He reminded me of me and Marilyn! Was I that cruel to Marilyn?"

He starts crying again. "It's supposed to be a brain eraser. But nothing fundamentally changes. That black cloud is always there, always hovering over me. That's my black cloud, and it's never going to go away. My problems are still the same. They will always be the same. They're never going to change. Edith. Never."

No one has called her to sub, and so Edith has been home reading the entire day, stopping twice more to listen to Felix. He called in tears again, asking her what was wrong.

When Frank was dying — pancreatic cancer — he asked her to watch out for his younger brother. It seemed at the time, a small thing to do.

It's nearly three, time for the buses to climb the hill and return students to their rightful homes. Edith sits in a rocker enjoying her last few minutes of solitude.

The room with its many windows gives her a view of snow and woods and she remembers what fun Frank had making sled runs in back for the kids. He was always doing something with them: taking them to movies, buying them ice-cream, swimming at the park below the waterfalls.

Frank died within months of his diagnosis. Pancreatic cancer does that. Always, Edith will ask herself: did she tell the kids too much? Too little? She'd like to think they're more resilient and forgiving than adults, but it seems that they're not: most of the time they're angry with life, and angry with her. Cheated feelings and disappointment rule their lives: they feel cheated that her father died and disappointed because Felix is an inadequate substitute. What worries Edith is how easily long-standing anger can turn into indifference and bitterness. The only reason Rob didn't argue with her about getting up for school this morning was because Felix appeared. Rob won't argue in front of Felix. Felix and Frank have (had) the same blue-black hair and intense eyes, and maybe that's what stops Rob from acting up when Felix visits. To convince Rob to do anything: brush his teeth, take a bath, change his clothes, requires huge amounts of emotional energy, and Edith often starts the day drained.

And weren't there things Edith could have done to have made Frank's last few months more comfortable? Couldn't she have waited before returning to school?

At the time, she felt overwhelmed with death and responsibility, and she needed a release. It was Felix who sat with Frank and the kids when she went to class. And if Felix has a black cloud hanging over him, then Edith has one too, but this cloud is one of guilt. She will never be forgiven for those last few weeks of Frank's life.

Edith hears the bus' groan, then an idling engine as high schoolers saunter off the bus. Large snowflakes speed past the windows. The front door opens. Edith listens to the thunk of the backpack on the kitchen table. She listens for the howl of teenage rage; instead, there's sweet talk to the dog. Edith's tensed back relaxes. The refrigerator door is opened, a half-gallon container of milk removed and milk drunk without the benefit of a glass. The backpack is unzipped, a paper pulled out.

"Mom," Denise says, coming into the back room, wiping her mouth with the side of her hand. Her winter jacket is still on, the boots off. "I got an A plus on my essay. Do you believe that?" She places the essay, *Light of the Middle Ages* on her mother's lap.

"Thanks for your help. Read it, and look what the teacher said about the last quote. Go on, read it."

Edith picks up the paper. *"The best thing for being sad," replied Merlyn, beginning to puff and blow, "is to learn something. That is the only thing that never fails. You may grow old and trembling in your anatomies, and you may lie awake at night listening to the disorder of your veins, you may miss your only love, you may see the world about you devastated by evil lunatics or know your honor trampled in the sewers of baser minds. There is only one thing for it then: to learn life is not so bad."*

"See? My teacher wrote, right here: *You saved the best quote for last*. That was the quote you gave me." She gives her mother a kiss, grabs the phone and heads upstairs to call a friend.

Edith rocks and re-reads the quote. It's not a bad quote. She copies it down and plans to bring it in with her the next time she subs, and if the moment is right she may just read it to her students and ask them what they think of it, and then maybe, if the day has gone well, they will feel that some of this bounteous, good life was meant for them.

14,000 Reasons

First published in Emrys Journal, Volume 14, Spring 1997

This time, I'm prepared. Rather than being supersensitive, I'll be generous, yet firm in my resolve. My skin's tough because I've made it that way. So we have our differences! — that doesn't mean that anything has to go wrong. But when I see my parents trundle off the plane in a bowlegged roll, my mother wearing wraparound sun glasses with yellow feathers on the edges, book in hand, and my father in pink floods (undoubtedly my mother's doing), with both of them glowing that brutal Florida bronze, maybe, I think, only a little will go wrong.

"Hello! Hello!" Arms outstretched, they come at Gail and Jean, besieging them with juicy kisses and hugs. Gail, almost three, lunges behind me, digging her fingers into my leg. John, the baby they have traveled 1,500 miles to see, cries.

A neon green plastic arm with a hand on the end reaches out from my father's sleeve and scratches Jean's back. When the arm is tilted, it makes a noise that sounds like indigestion.

After putting the final touches on her groans of exaltation, her energy spinning off in all directions, my mother says: "I'm starved. Let's go out to lunch."

"We just had lunch," my father says. He straightens up, and gives the neon green arm to Jean. Jean moves it up and down, trying to make it burp.

"You call that lunch?" With feathered sunglasses propped on her head and new black eyeliner, my mother looks like a traveler from a distant solar system. I feel a white, fluidized, super-critical heat, a heat that surrounds and engulfs; a heat you never get away from—not even in Minnesota. People look at us, and they look more intently when my mother bends down, grabs Gail's hands, and gives her a cackling witch laugh.

Gail pauses, then laughs.

"Remember the last time," my mother cries, as if this is a great pronouncement, "we went to Cafe Late!" Rising, she looks at me. "The Late Cafe?"

"Cafe Latte," I say slowly, evenly, giving her a gentle nudge with my hip, and her ample hip bumps me back—a prelude to a dance—and she cackles again.

"That place with the two-dollar coffee," my father says, grumbling. He adjusts his black-rimmed glasses. The glasses are new.

"Don't be so negative, George." My mother, a wellspring of infinite optimism, holds up her book to me—<u>14,000 Reasons to be Happy.</u> Eager to convert the unenlightened.

"Don't you want to check in at the hotel? Take a nap while the kids take theirs?" I casually glance at my watch. "See, the kids sleep until four. At six we eat dinner. At seven—"

"The Late Cafe for a late dinner!" my mother cries, like someone shouting "Bingo!" To five-year-old Jean, she says: "You like shrimp, don't you?"

"What's shrimp, Mom?"

My parents are dutifully picking up the slack while Ray, erstwhile husband, father of three, and ambitious scientist putters away in a research lab in California: Bad timing, but it couldn't be helped: The day the lab was ready, the baby was born. Anyway, Ray doesn't get along with my parents. "They're tasteless, ignorant and dangerous—TIDs," he claims. "TIDs!" When he says that, his thin lips tighten, his dark eyes narrow working up into a full-face sneer. The vein going up his forehead starts pulsing. "Brainless TIDs: you look through one ear and see out the other."

After snatching up the airport's free weeklies and posing (with devil horns and smirks) for photographs with the kids, I drive my parents to their hotel so they can rest.

When I get home, I put everyone down for naps. I run downstairs to my office, a mole's hole: narrow, dirt-colored walls, one low-watt light bulb. In my chair I lean back, stretching out my legs. I close my eyes.

There's not a sound in the house except for my computer's efficient hum. I count backward from ten, and feel my body turning into liquid. Lulled by my computer's hum (I call it my "Song of Myself"), I finally relax, every cell limp.

After thirty seconds of nirvana, I hook into the net and find an e-mail from Ray. It says: "How're the kids? How're the visitors from the distant solar system? Has anyone blown up yet?"

"The hotel's toilets flush and the TV has cable," I e-mail back. "They couldn't be happier. And Ray: intelligent adults do not 'blow up.'"

That night, to prove I am the dutiful, self-effacing daughter of their dreams (I am their daughter, but I am <u>not</u> them), I take my parents to an outdoor concert.

We sit on a terraced, velvet green hillside facing the outdoor theater and watch the Ding Dongers—a group of septuagenarians costumed in red and white. Behind the theater, ducks waddle in a pond.

My parents are enthralled: Outdoor concerts are definitely their turf. Geese fly overhead, some even honk, making them feel like they're back in the country of upstate New York, cultivating the garden with their tractor, or shoveling six-foot snow drifts off the front porch.

The Ding Dongers serenade the polite crowd (mostly elderly women perched on lawn chairs) with "Let's All Sing Like the Birdies Sing." My mother, sitting Buddha-style, sings and sways as if she's in some religious trance. Then the Ding Dongers put their hands to their mouths, where they've cleverly concealed whistles. They warble together. My father whistles with them.

"How do they do that?" Jean asks.

"How do they do that?" Gail repeats, savoring each word. Gail's at that stage where she doesn't know enough about words to use her own.

"I don't know," I tell them.

"What do you know, Mommy?" Jean says.

Emerging from her trance, my mother says: "That's one of the mysteries of growing old."

"Like the mystery of the universe," I say, without looking up.

I brought my work: a computer printout of the parts-per-billion of benzene in soil near a landfill. "You know, Mom? Gasses accreting in the Big Bang?"

"What are you doing?" asks my mother.

"Looking for glitches in patterns." Ruler and pencil in hand, I go down columns of data, then more columns of data.

"You're missing everything," she says.

I look up. On stage a Ding Donger steps out of her red skirt, revealing silk pantaloons edged with flowered lace. She holds her arms out chest high, like she's getting ready to hypnotize us, and starts tap dancing. Another one languidly plucks at an electric keyboard. One in a motor-powered wheelchair shakes a tambourine.

"We did that tap dance in seventh grade," my mother says.

"You did? You remember that?" I say, wondering if she's going to demonstrate. Already her arms are rising.

"Everybody took dance then." My mother's still swaying. Jean and Gail start swaying. "It was in the curriculum. We didn't waste our time on sex education. Sensitivity training." My mother snorts. "That's what choice should be about, not this other choice. Life used to mean something. No wonder your sister is home schooling."

When my sister, mother of five, lectures to me about the school system dumbing down and the government making us into automatons, I nod, and make the perfunctory "hmms." If I didn't know her, I'd think she were a fanatic, or had a persecution complex. But obsession is a trademark of my family.

"What's that on your shirt, Mr. Gerk?" Gail asks, pointing to my father's dark blue, short-sleeved shirt. The shirt shows off his arms, which like his legs, are slim and tan. They've nicknamed my parents The Gerks, a throwback from last year when Ray called them The Jerks. When my mother asked how they chose The Gerks, I told her it's after Gerkian motion: the motion of small particles in fluid, the impact of liquid striking the particles moves the particles.

"That's his moon shirt," my mother says. "It shows the moon."

"How come the moon isn't round?" Jean says, frowning. She touches a white sliver on his dark blue shirt.

"The moon has phases," my mother says.

"Phases. Right, Mom," I say. To Jean, I say: "The moon circles around the earth, and the earth circles around the sun."

"And the knee bone's connected to the thigh bone, and the thigh bone—"

"Mo-om," I say. "The moon is always whole, Jean—always—but it gets its light from the sun. Not the earth. The earth can block off light, making the moon *appear* to be not whole."

"That's what I said," my mother says. "It's a matter of phases. Appearances."

Waving pastel hankies, and wiping sweat from their wrinkled foreheads, the Ding Dongers bid the crowd adieu. My mother waves, too—big waves—and Gail and Jean do likewise. The girls are watching my mother closely, wondering what she's going to do next.

Next up is Uncle Jim Slim and his three-piece band. A kiddie band, so all children including Jean and Gail, swarm to the stage and help Uncle Jim sing the ABCs. I'm left with the sleeping baby, and with my parents, one on each side, which could be good or bad.

"How did you like those tomatoes we had for dinner?" I ask my father.

"OK," he says, as if he's doing me a big favor. He starts whistling the ABCs.

"There's nothing like a tasty tomato," my mother says.

"They used to have good tomatoes," my father says reflectively. Growing up on a dairy and vegetable farm, he should know, but ever since the steel plant gave him the golden handshake, he's had moments of melancholia.

"Remember the tomatoes we used to grow?" my mother asks. "They were so good." A former self-reliant country type, she used to pick cucumbers and haul slate from the back woods to put around the house. Now, down on her knees, she plants flowers. She organizes the condo people to protest bulldozing the nearby jungle.

Not to let a good opportunity pass me by, I tell them: "I grew tomato plants recently."

My parents look up, impressed. Maybe their daughter is not the vain, polo-shirted yuppie from the suburbs: gravel surrounding the shrubbery, the kitchen host to an army of dangerous-sounding vegetable machines.

"I bought biodegradable cups—made of peat moss." I nod, raising my eyebrows, and they raise theirs. My parents are great fans of peat moss. "I watered them. I sunned them. I babied them. Then Jean pulled all the plants out." I nod again, waiting for them to raise their eyebrows.

My parents look at me: So?

Then my mother starts laughing because Uncle Jim is doing an accelerated rock-and-roll version of Itsy Bitsy Spider: the rain coming down, the arm rolls, the sun coming up. He's losing half the kids, but he's not losing my mother. Jean and Gail are back up with us, watching my mother, their small hands moving in wobbly circles, trying to imitate her.

As she does Itsy Bitsy Spider, she tells my father: "You have to teach her, George. You don't have anything better to do. Go buy some plants for Kate."

"Mom," I say sharply, "I don't have any place to plant them."

"We'll find a place."

"What else do you need done?" my father asks. Swallowing, he looks up to the sky as if he's calculating the amount of radiation the grass is absorbing. "I could paint the front door. Or give your windows a grease job."

"You don't have—"

"It will give him something to do, Kate."

When the concert is over, my mother says: "Come on over to our hotel room."

"That's OK, Mom," I say gracefully, as if the visit is an invaluable privilege, which is exactly what the girls think. They can't get enough of The Gerks.

Their hotel room is like a giant hamster's nest: several editions of *USA Today* (shredded and unshredded), candy wrappers, apple cores, half-filled cups of orange soda. There, my parents prop themselves up on beds for the night and gradually become soporific, the TV blasting away, potato chips in one hand, Coke in the other. It's their at-rest mode, the essential complement to the going-out mode.

"Sure you don't want to come? I think *Homeward Bound* is on. It's so funny." My mother starts convulsing with laughter. "They have this dog—" Her eyes become tiny stars. Spit flies in projectiles from her mouth. "This dog who talks."

"Gee, Mom," I say, coolly, lowering my eyes, "I have to put this baby to bed. See how cranky he's getting? He kept me up last night." I jiggle him, and he smiles at my mother.

During the next few days, we eat dinner out. We eat lunch out and sometimes breakfast, as if being "in" manifests a failure of the spirit of adventure.

"Why work?" my mother asks.

"Work?" I say. It's more work trying to keep the kids entertained at a restaurant than making dinner, but I take the invaluable opportunity to tell her: "Mom, you work to get ahead." I've already shown them my state-of-the-art computer station, and explained to my dad (he has an analytical mind, unlike my mother, whose mind is likely engaged in some out-of-body, extraterrestrial traveling) how I can access thousands, maybe hundreds of thousands of databases on just about any subject under the sun: knowledge at my fingertips.

"But we're on vacation!" my mother says, punctuating this with her witch laugh. "Who cares about databases? We need to go to Cafe Late. The Late Cafe! Isn't there a parade somewhere?"

She nudges my father and he says: "Yeah."

"The mall," she says to me. "The biggest mall in America."

"Yeah!" the girls scream and start dancing around.

"Mom, the traffic will drive you crazy. That mall is a black hole of traffic—the cars go in, but they never come out."

Most times, I weasel out of the parades and the two-for-one breakfasts, claiming that if the baby spends his life in a car seat, then he'll grow up with a hunched back. Or I tell my mother: "I have to make some phone calls."

"Relax, Kate, you just had a baby! Take it easy!"

"I have a job, Mom."

"The job can wait."

"What job?" my father says. "I thought you stayed home with the kids."

"I work at home, Dad."

I don't pretend to be the mother my mother is. For the next four days, however, I will ease up on the job; I need my energy and intelligence to outsmart them. But my parents are persistent.

"Chicken," my mother says, when I decline still another dinner invitation—as if I am a defector. As if I am abandoning the kids. Or them?

They've gone back to the hotel, the kids are napping, and I'm in the basement, cushioned by darkness and silence, a hot cup of coffee beside me. My computer screen glows blue.

I hunch my back, click on my e-mail and see four new messages. The moment is perfect. The last message, from Ray, says: "Are the TIDs driving you nuts yet?"

"A lot you know about people!" I bang on the keyboard, and send it off.

That night I find myself at Fun Time; it's the least I can do after all my father's painting and greasing. No sooner do Fun Time's glass doors swing open than cheerleader music blares out at us. High-pitched sirens scream and lights of all colors flash at us, as if in warning: Enter at your own risk; leave your mind behind.

"We never had things like this when you were a kid," my mother says, unsure for once what to think. The kids stare, goggle-eyed.

"These places are everywhere, Mom," I tell her casually. "I predict they will replace the swing set."

"Remember the swing set we had for you kids?" my mother says, wistfully. "Our swing set was the center of everything."

She twists on her legs and I feel her absorbing the place's karma. She likes the place; in fact, there doesn't seem to be any place she doesn't like.

"I remember putting it up," my father says, groaning.

"The people that bought our house—he owned a bank in town—they took the swing set down," my mother says.

My parents, pausing mid-thought, tilt their heads, together, like the cardinals in our backyard. I get the feeling they're intercepting a secret message. Suddenly a giant polar bear with glowing pink paws grabs Jean's hands and bobs his enlarged head. Gail crouches behind me, and the baby howls. If it were just me with the kids, I'd make some lame but logical excuse and escape; but it's one thing fooling the kids, another fooling the parents.

"They should put this in <u>14,000 Reasons to be Happy</u>," my mother says. She gives the polar bear a cackle, and he cackles back.

"What?" I can barely hear her.

She repeats it.

"Yeah, yeah right, Mom." Every day after dinner, when the kids are screaming, or during dinner, when they're screaming (the screaming is a recent development), my mother opens <u>14,000 Reasons to be Happy.</u> She reads a passage then laughs uncontrollably.

We've gradually moved ourselves away from the noise center, toward the restaurant section when my mother suddenly cries: "George! Talk to your daughter. You never see her."

"I have a routine in Florida," my father says, his voice deadpan. He's watching Jean and Gail as he talks, maybe trying to find the resemblances between them and me. Or maybe he just wants them to come over and pinch his nose, or pull his hair—something he actually encourages. "I get up at five and bike to the bagel shop in Cocoa. Then I play golf. Then I swim. Then I make lunch. Then I eat lunch. Then I take a nap."

"Huh," I say, nodding, hopefully reflectively, not wanting to hurt his feelings.

"Then you eat dinner and go to sleep at five," my mother says, putting her hands on her ample hips and jutting out her chest, as if after forty years, she's ready to break in another husband.

"I don't go to bed that early," he says, slowly raising his gray eyebrows at my mother. He looks sad.

"You can get a jumbo pizza, a pitcher of pop and twenty tokens for $19.95," my mother says, sticking out her stomach.

My father snorts.

"We don't need a jumbo," my father says. "Anyway, I thought you were on a diet."

My mother gives him her evil look, which closes that matter.

Behind the counter, the at-attention teenagers are sweating, watching my parents for signs of decisiveness. A line has formed behind us, a line of busy, time-crunched people — like myself.

"What are you doing?" my mother asks my father.

"I'm reading the menu."

"He's in one of his moods," she says to me. "A phase."

"What do you mean by that?" he says.

"It means you can't make up your mind." My mother jabs my father in the side. "Get the goddamn pizza, George. Just get the goddamn pizza," she says louder, and the mothers in line behind us try to stare her down.

"What kind of soda?" he asks.

"No Coke," I say. "They've eaten so much sugar recently," I pause slightly, "that it's a wonder they still have teeth. We never got Coke. Remember, Mom? You used to give us lectures about how the pop molecules got beneath the gums and rotted the teeth—in no time at all."

"One night of Coke isn't going to kill them," she says. She orders the food and my father pays the relieved teenagers. Then I watch my parents and the girls play games. Then I watch them play videos. Then I watch them go on rides. Luckily, I brought my briefcase. Then as they eat greasy pizza, I think about Ray, who is undoubtedly, after a satisfying day of work, eating dinner (salad, chicken breast, new potatoes) alone, in a quiet restaurant.

"One-hundred and forty-thousand a year," my mother says. We're sitting in my family room, looking out the bay window to the back yard. The back yard is bordered by tall pines and lilac bushes. Earlier my mother remarked that pines reminded her of the old house, and I took this as a minor concession. This is also their last night so I indulge in a beer, and we have our annual argument on abortion. We know beforehand that neither of us will change our positions.

"Nobody wants to get an abortion, Mom."

"This one abortionist botched it, and the woman ended up with a baby without one arm."

"Totally unsubstantiated, Mom," I say, my voice raised.

"Is that the beer doing that?" my father says. He laughs, and the baby starts crying.

"Here, Dad." I hold out something I found on a computer search, *The Perfect Tomato*. Snatching the computer printout from my hands, he mutters, then goes outside to smoke a cigarette.

The back door slaps twice. The girls hurriedly put on their sneakers, and the back door slaps twice more. They get him to push them on the swing set.

"He's in his antagonistic mood," my mother says, her voice now quiet. She's on my chair, rocking back and forth. "He gets unhappy when he's not working on something." I look at the clock, and at my gargantuan pile of untouched computer printouts on the dining room table. "If I didn't push him, he'd be like his Aunt Ruth who rocked and rocked and pulled out her hair, saying the communists were after her."

Then together we look outside to where the children are swinging happily. The sun has fallen, the stars are bright, and the full moon lights up the back yard and its perimeter of tall pines. Startled, I look again, feeling myself on the swing, my hair flying, and my body escaping the pull of gravity.

My mother's dogmatic tone of voice returns. "It's a business, Kate. Abortion clinics don't present all sides."

"They're only trying to help people—to give choices, Mom."

"Choices! I don't like what's happened to that word." She throws up her hands then rocks more vigorously. "Choices, but no direction, and no thought of the final outcome. What are choices without responsibility?"

"That's why the woman has an abortion."

Then we look outside. My father stands beside the swing set, pushing one child, then the other, the moonlight glinting on his glasses. Chains squeak and the girls cry, "Higher! Higher, Mr. Gerk!"

"Mom, listen to science, the voice of reason. It's a fetus." I watch her cringe. "A few cells. You lose cells every day. It's more cells vs. less cells. A numbers issue."

"You know what they do in China with ultrasounds?" my mother says. "They want boys." For the first time, her face sags. "People think they're taking the easy way. In twenty years, when the experts look back on us, and see what was good and what was bad, will they say: It was a harsh time? The experts have all these studies, so they know something, but soon they begin to think they know everything. Who knows everything?"

My mother looks woefully around the room at the big-screen TV, the complicated telephone answering machine. "I almost forgot." She reaches into her purse, and pulls out The Book, holding it out to me. "I bought this for you."

"14,000. Yeah. Right. I don't need that." I try not to sneer. She's still holding out the book, so I take it and thwack it down beside my computer printouts.

"I know you like to read," she says, her eyes hopeful, latched onto the injured book.

"I don't have time, Mom. I work. I'm a working woman!"

The back door slaps, and everybody comes in. Then backs bent, my parents gather the clothes they've shed. They pick up their dripping, sticky bottles of suntan lotion, their crumpled tourist brochures they left in the bathroom. Who knows what they'll do with them! Then with plastic bags hanging from their hands, they lower themselves into my car and race off—in low gear—to their hotel.

They ignore the car's computer command to switch gears, so all the way to the next street over, I hear my poor car whine. It's like a baby: You have to listen to it, take care of it. But tomorrow morning I'll take them to the airport. The Gerks will be gone! They will be history until next year!

After I get everyone to sleep—and it's not easy with all the Coke they've been drinking—I run down to my office. I slump in my chair and count backward from ten, then call Ray on the phone.

"Ray?" I say. "It's me."

"Why are you using the phone?"

"My mother was on the computer trying to draw a picture, and she wiped out the communication program's exec file."

"Typical."

"How's everything going?"

"The data I'm getting are great."

"Ray, I know about the beauty of numbers. Listen: I miss you. I love you. I know how important work is, but how much longer are you going to be away? The baby smiled. You should have seen him."

"They want me to set up some other labs around the country."

I don't say anything.

"Kate, it's an invaluable opportunity. And we can talk every day."

"Ray, the baby smiled. Do you hear me, Ray? He smiled at my crazy mother."

"The TIDs!" he laughs. "The city will never be the same."

"Ray, I don't like you calling them that."

"Okay, I'm sorry. Have them stay longer. They're there for you, Kate. For you, alone." His voice is softer. "They're doing it all for you."

That night I have nightmares about limbless babies, babies with big heads or no heads, babies crying for their mothers. And me: I've been vaporized.

I'm floating like stardust, and I'm trying to catch the pieces of myself, but I'm no bigger than a speck of dust. In fact, I'm almost nothing! I'm a speck that came from the speck before me, which came from the speck before it. "Specks!" I scream, "We are all specks! We were all born from the same speck, so we must all be each other!" I'm screaming, trying to find my mother, trying to get her to understand, trying to gather my specks together, but I start sinking, falling faster, the pieces coalescing, then I hear terrible, insistent screaming, but I can't open my eyes. I wake up. It's the baby. I nurse him, and no sooner do I fall asleep, than I'm vaporized again. Gail's screaming. I get up and comfort her. Just as I fall back asleep, my alarm goes off.

The next morning, I drive my parents to the airport in the rain, during rush hour. My parents' silences, so rare, say: "We're sorry—we didn't mean to be pests." They're huddled together in the small back seat (a girl on each lap), which makes them seem even meeker, as if I am the parent. Traffic slows, and Gail starts crying. Then the baby starts crying.

"Who has the baby's pacifier?" I look back at the girls, then wildly, at my parents. Moving their squished shoulders, my parents make an attempt to feel around for the pacifier. Then my mother starts doing Itsy Bitsy Spider. My father warble-whistles along. The crying stops instantly. We creep forward, almost getting somewhere.

"What did you think about that article, Dad? *The Perfect Tomato*. Isn't that incredible what technology can do?" I smile into the rearview mirror.

"Incredible," he says, deadpan.

"Dad, the genetic engineers can make any kind of tomato you want. Juicy, not juicy. Seeds, no seeds. Green, pink or blue."

"But if it's tasteless," he says, "they said you might as well eat plastic."

"The engineers can do it. They can even make it rigid, so it will have a longer shelf-life." I honk at the car in front of me that's taking too much time." So it won't _give_ when you _move_ it across the country." Gritting my teeth, I smile into the rearview mirror. My parents look at me, as if I haven't understood a thing.

"The article also said they spliced a human gene into a pig," my father says. "A pig," he says, like it's a crime. "It gave the pig wrinkles and arthritis. Did you see that?"

"Poor pig," my mother says.

"I can't read everything," I tell him. "You can't know everything."

"Oh the poor pig," my mother laments.

"Look, the airport," I say casually, as the airport signs greet us, and I try hard not to show my profound relief. My parents look bewildered. They start crying, big tears that they don't even bother to wipe away.

"I'm sorry we never made it to Cafe Latte," I tell my mother. As we say good-bye, and I love you, I give them back to the land of sun. When I look in the rearview mirror for one last time, they're gone. I almost can't believe it. There's a profound silence. There's so much empty space in the car that I feel chilled.

Getting back on the highway, I tell the girls: "If I speed, we can make it back in time for the sitter."

Jean is in front beside me, and the other two are in back, strapped in like machine-packaged dolls. They look stunned.

"What are we going to do today, Mommy?" Jean says.

"We're going to do what we always do: Play, eat lunch at noon, take a nap at two, eat dinner at six—"

"But what are we going to <u>do</u>?" she asks, insistent. "It's going to be boring without them."

"Boring, I'll say. Huh, what's wrong with a little boredom?"

It starts to pour. Suddenly the highway becomes lines of brake lights.

"What happened to The Gerks?" Gail says suddenly. "The Gerks! The Gerks!" Jean repeats the chant, then starts heaving. Her face contorts; the baby's face contorts. They start whimpering.

We're at a standstill. From the radio I hear there's been a twenty-car accident a mile up—no injuries—but a semi spilled a load of soap. I turn off the engine. There's nowhere to go, nothing to do, nothing to read—except my mother's book on the floor. The kids are screaming, so I hold out The Book, fanning its rainbow-colored pages. "Look, Mrs. Gerk forgot her bible."

"You didn't read it," Jean screams at me. Arms folded across her chest, her eyes tighten into the accusatory stare. "And she's your mother."

I look at Jean, at the wailing baby, at Gail who's chanting and rocking. Cars are honking behind us, and cars are honking in front of us. "Goddamn traffic," I murmur. A burly guy a few cars up gets out and screams. Then he starts pounding on the hood of his BMW. A woman in high heels and a black raincoat gets out and walks along the shoulder, head bent against the rain.

"Why are they doing that?" Gail says between whimpers.

"That's modern life." Then I look at Jean, who's sneering at me. So I find the book's dedication page and read it aloud. 'To all Fools. Be a Fool, don't be uptight. You could be dead tomorrow, or even today. Yes?' Pretty optimistic stuff, huh?' Do you think that was written for me? Do you think The Book (I pause, emphasizing that term), has 'How to be happy in a traffic jam with three screaming kids?'"

Eyes tear-filled and glazed, the girls rock, chanting softly: "We want The Gerks. We want The Gerks." I skim the Table of Contents. Then I stop.

"Look!" I look again to make sure. "There's a page titled 'Traffic jams on the thruway in the rain with screaming kids.' Do you believe that?" I hold up the book. "I don't believe it." I turn to the indicated page: "'We all know life is not a rose garden. It's more of a bug-infested vegetable garden.' Ha! You can say that again. 'You can either give up and rot, or you can rise above it all. To rise above it, start by doing Itsy Bitsy Spider. Start slowly so you don't screw up. Ask the screaming kids to help. Don't forget to sing the words and move your eyes.'"

"Don't forget to sing!" I say sarcastically. "This is ridiculous." More cars are honking. More people are abandoning their cars. It's a hell of a jam, a jam to beat all jams.

Sirens are coming from several directions and the people from abandoned cars are walking to the next exit. Some are climbing the chain-link fence that separates the highway from the neighborhoods. Those in cars are screaming at those out of cars. I look up the highway and behold a sea of approaching soap bubbles. The bubbles keep coming. The kids are chanting and crying, so I start singing, slowly, just like the book says: "'Itsy Bitsy Spider went up the water spout.'" I crack open my window, and the rain, beating all around us like millions of tiny drums, has a sudden, fresh timbre. "Down came the rain and washed the spider out, out came the sun, and dried up all the rain—...."

They're not crying anymore, merely hoarsely chanting: "We want The Gerks. We want The Gerks." They're watching me, watching me closely with surprise, maybe alarm, and I start making faces. I do Itsy Bitsy Spider with the hand movements, faster and faster, and I do it for them (they've stopped chanting, their hands are moving in circles, following mine), and I do it for the car next to us, and then I get out of the car, the soap bubbles surrounding me, and I start doing it in the rain and the bubbles because I feel that white heat, that uncontrollable energy that overwhelms me, and takes me by surprise.

225

The Family of Camden High

"I told myself I would never come back!" I just about screamed, and luckily the door was closed or there might have been a visit by a security guard. I had practiced the statement several times: not only does practice make perfect, but practice make brave because I had never been brave, no, having been the kind of student who never raised a hand to ask a question—in 16 years of grueling classes—lest I appear stupid, or god forbid, to be daydreaming. Today they would say you were not *on task*. Courage was most certainly not my mien: I let others fight the battles, and when a confrontation loomed, I hid, scurrying for the quickest, safest haven.

Looking across the expanse of the new Principal's desk, already overflowing with paperwork, I saw that he was listening, so I described my perception of the altercation between my son, Bob (poor Bob) , and Dora Romona.

Dora Romona! The fact that cell phones were permitted in the cafeteria, that the snap of another student's photo was not forbidden — and so many things were forbidden! — was a big problem for Dora Romona. Dora Romona, from my perspective, was a vast incubator of problems, a messy bundle of neurotic insecurities, a bastion of evil thoughts, a ship of blubber listing in the throes of an Atlantic hurricane. Not my friend, Dora! And in my mind's eye I witnessed the struggle for Bob's cell: in one corner: -six-foot-two, sixteen-year-old Bob; the other: five-foot-two, fat-and-fifty Dora Romona. Dora Romona in all her abundant glory! I imagined the phone's lid snapping open-and-close, an excited beep of *help!* and the aggressive touching. Dora Romona. Of all people, Dora Romona should know better than to touch a student. Shame, shame. Hanging in the air in that new Principal's office was the clear hint of a lawsuit.

I had learned the game, too late for me, but not for Bob.

The Principal summoned Bob. Bob appeared, loose-limbed, his dark hair shining and hanging into his eyes, large beautiful brown eyes. What mother would not be proud!

He had refused to surrender his phone citing issues of privacy. He did not trust Dora Romona, and pray tell: who in his right mind would! Beforehand, I had talked to Bob: *Whatever you say, it must be the truth. Listen to your conscience. Face your fears.* Another discussion ensued and a consequence levied in such a way as to preclude feelings of resentment. In the end, I thanked the new Principal, Matt Bond. He had spent an hour with us. Unbelievable.

As I shook his strong hand, I realized I needed to leave Camden High without being seen; thus my sandals clattered like rocks on glass as I trotted away from the hopeful smell of brewing coffee, past the fresh donuts from the Swiss bakery — all part of the newly-installed regime's efforts to inspire confidence and hope. And it did.

My head was bent down to avoid potential eye contact, although Mr. Turner, with his big glasses and missing teeth, a

Native American who'd experienced hard times, moved into my line of sight. An aide, he was not part of the elite, vested with a generous retirement plan, health benefits galore. We nodded hello. Mr. Turner had been the aide of Jimi Agee, a former student (Sudanese) of mine. Jimi, with his familiar tropical-colored shirts - reminiscent of exotic African vistas — and sorrowful eyes, was no longer in the school system.

He was no longer.

Once outside the Main Office, and this seemed to take forever, I picked up the pace, fast walking, my arms in full stride as if I were one of those race-walker-women: sinewy arms pumping, big jaw jutted permanently forward—get out of my way! Here I come! I have one thing in mind and I'm going to get it! I'm an All-Purpose Woman.

Thus I strode down the long, empty hallway (thank god classes were in session!) to the parking lot. Then from the corner of my eye, one of my informants, Lenore Groat slithered into my field of vision, her rigid blue eyes registering surprise, her mouth opening into a crafty smile.

I ran. I shot across that parking lot of broken down, rusted student vehicles like an ignited cannon ball.

Once outside and beyond the school property, beyond Every Good Boy Does Fine and My Very Energetic Mother's Juicy Spicy Unusual Nice Pizza, I closed my eyes and breathed deeply.

Safe.

It seemed sensible at the time: a 44-year-old mother

returning to school because she'd wanted to teach. Always wanted to teach. The prospect of new ideas floating through my mind, new challenges was invigorating: I could almost feel the synapses in my brain firing and growing.

Boredom was the greatest evil – or so I thought — and boredom was my greatest fear. The half-dead looks that I saw on the Florida retirees (when I visited my favorite aunt) confirmed this chief fear, yet moving around the country every few years made it certain that no teaching degree would ever be completed, not until I divorced and set down roots. I never expected to be divorced: I expected to be married for life. *Until Death Do Us Part.* Thus, newly divorced I enrolled in the adolescent psychology, classroom discipline, science methods courses. I participated in the Saturday morning workshops on abuse and harassment. I would do just about anything to teach and that was how I found myself, starting in September, driving each morning an hour into the north country to work with actual living, breathing, unpredictable, hormone-driven teenagers. Everything about them terrified me: their grating speech, their hyperbolic gesticulations, their nightmarishly white teeth endlessly laughing. Laughing at whom? Me!

Initially I had requested a geographically closer assignment, but the student teacher coordinator, a scrawny middle-aged woman, her mousey brown hair stiff as a wig, half of it plastered to the side of her face, shot back: "You should be grateful you even got a placement! Just who do you think you are? Just who?"

Obviously not Dora Romona, although at that time, I had no knowledge of the Camden High Titan.

The drive to my placement took me along the west side of Seneca Lake, past fields of ripe corn, peach and apple orchards, and hillsides of grape vines, the concords still green in early September. I often brought home corn-on-the-cob—a treat—for the kids. I had three kids. When I brought home the corn-on-the-cob, then and only then did the kids forgive my inability to be home when they exited the school bus. I became more adventuresome as I drove these roads (once or twice, getting lost) and often stopped at a Amish stand where you could buy blue Hubbard and acorn squash for 20 cents a pound, zucchinis for a quarter. A trace element in the Finger Lakes soil produced especially delicious squash. We ate healthfully back then.

I passed through a handful of small towns whose main streets had once been grand, but you could see the wealth had gone elsewhere. The windows of once magnificent brick buildings were boarded up with plywood and speckled with mold. Ragged curtains blew in the breeze. The pavilions of small parks where bands had played were now littered with trash and bundles of the poor and homeless. They, no doubt, slept there.

In October the maples turned a velvet red, and the birch leaves, that yellow that makes your pupils contract. I'd roller coaster up and down hills, a cornucopia of rich colors, and reach a precipice and never ceased to be astonished by the vista of velvet glacial hills before me.

The first strong frost came in mid October, the snow in

November. When the roads were icy, it was an hour-and-a-half, sometimes two to my high school placement. Storms would come off the lake with winds that carried vast amounts of snow.

It was treacherous driving and I would not arrive home until after dark, and the kids would be crying. One night in December, I did not get home until nearly 8.

"Mom, where were you?" Amy said. At 14, she was in charge of her two siblings: Lynn, who was 11, and Bob, who was 9.

"I was teaching," I said, calmly, trying to sound as if it was the love of my life. Wasn't there an easier way to make a living? I cruised up-and-down snow-covered hills, then upon my arrival I was not heralded as the science teacher with tricks up her sleeve, but as the crasher of multiple teenage-talk-a-thons. It was not an easy life making enemies all day long.

"We were worried about you," Amy said.

"Yeah, Mom!" Lynn chimed in.

"Me too!" Bob said.

"What happened, Mom?" Amy examined the rip in my coat. "Why are you so late?"

"I got stuck in a snow bank, but I'm okay."

"You're shaking, Mom."

"That's because I'm hungry. Whoa... what do I smell?"

"Mac and cheese!" the kids chorused.

I removed my ripped coat and wet boots; had I worn my heels they would have been ruined and digging out the car would not have been so fun. Fun. That was what teaching was all about:

having fun!

Driving home from my country placement, the snow had been thick and coming down so rapidly that the road ahead of me completely disappeared. Luckily, a truck emerging from Timmy's Tavern pulled out right in front me, and I say luckily because I was able to follow the glow of his tail lights.

Although the small towns up north had lost most of their businesses, the taverns survived. On this stretch of road beside the lake, in no-man's land, the disappearing towns had no regular road patrol.

It was not easy keeping up with the trucker: he was going faster than I wanted to work my rusted Honda — but fearing veering off the road and plunging into the lake, I kept up with the truck.

The snow came down faster and it was so thick I could not make out the truck's color. For several miles I followed, my eyes glued to the brake lights, and just as another car joined our caravan, the truck's red lights suddenly glowed twice as bright. A split second later I saw the most incredible image: a full-grown deer — a buck with a three-foot antler span — flying through the air, headed right for my little Honda.

"Mom, there's blood on your coat."

"Don't worry: it's not mine."

We ate mac-and-cheese with peas and tuna, then I heated up milk for hot chocolate. We talked about their classes, completing homework in a timely manner, following their conscience when decisions of a moral nature transpired.

"What is that?" Bob said.

"The part of you that says what is right and wrong. Like not looking at someone else's paper when you're taking a test."

Bob nodded. Even at such a young age they knew. Why didn't adults? Or they knew, but chose to ignore.

It was 9 o'clock, and I still had not graded papers or prepared for classes tomorrow. At best, I would sleep two or three hours. I was setting my work out on the dining room table when Amy said, "Mommy: you don't do things with us anymore. We used to have a lot of fun together. "

This was true.

"I'll be finished student teaching in May," I told her. "Then I'll have time to have fun. We'll go to New York City. We'll bike. We'll drive out to the country and pick apples and blueberries."

So I imagined.

For the next two years I substitute taught, but raising three kids on 80 dollars a day was not easy, thus, I worked nights and weekends at a convenience store.

Most of my teaching assignments were at Camden High where I'd earned the reputation of being reliable, on-time, efficient, responsible, intelligent, obedient –obedient because I took roll call, left detailed notes, and followed lessons plans.

I was in demand. I successfully completed four science certifications because the schools recommended multiple certifications. Anything the schools recommended, I did. They didn't even have to snap their fingers: I was there, just like a dog, tail wagging away, tongue out, eager to please.

I met Dora Romona, then a biology teacher at Camden High, a few months after I'd started substitute teaching.

"I'm so happy it's you subbing for me!" Dora Romona said, her loaf-like arms moving to encase me. It was an exaggerated embrace that I allowed because to be loved by any teacher at Camden High would only bring me closer to becoming Ms. Full-Fledged Science Teacher.

There was a strategy to getting hired at Camden High. Camden High, a gem of a high school, highly respected for its academic rigor, and only a mere three miles from my abode. Camden High: where Amy was a freshman. Imagine teaching in the same school where my children went, where I could watch over them!

Their Dad lived 20 miles outside of town, in a remote rental near the lake, hidden by tall constantly creaking trees. Stan was not the most sociable person in the world: I treated him as if he had a permanent case of PMS. Nothing more. The house with its uneven corners and missing porch floorboards initially scared the kids. "It's okay, kids!" I'd say, but it really wasn't. Visits were court-ordered, there wasn't much I could do.

Today I was to give an exam to Dora Romona's students. The exam was on the human skeleton's 205 bones.

"Here it is!" Dora said, her pudgy hand shoved over a sheet of paper that showed a crudely drawn human skeleton, wobbly lines emerging from the various bones. Her elf-like ears seemed to twitch.

"Oh Darn!" Dora Romona said, pouting. "I forgot to copy the exam! Do you mind terribly? I have to run....see I have an appointment. It's rather personal."

She grabbed her large pink-and-green purse and waddled out of the room, her gray-brown dome (bad dye job!) bobbing down the empty hallway which soon would be packed with gangly teenagers with neon blue coifs.

Ten minutes exactly. The blood rushed to my face as I fled with the sheet, the heavy classroom door slamming alarmingly behind me — I paused to shrug at a frowning teacher — then I frantically raced from one duplicating machine to another, finding a 4-person line at the most popular machine (popular because it only broke down Monday mornings), past other machines, their plastic doors ajar, hastily scribbled notes on them: "Out of Order!"

Luckily —yes I do believe in luck—just last week I'd subbed in Languages, K Wing, where I'd shown a French film to students. I recalled an ancient copier hidden in a remote corner of K Wing.

Teachers were supposed to have all necessary materials: books, duplicates, roll call sheets ready for the sub, but theory and practice were often at odds with one another. It was frowned upon — substitutes operating duplicating machines — delicate machines with many moving parts, so expensive to clean those moving parts and make them move at the required split second-and- in-sequence.

Duplicating machine operation was an art—one for experienced professionals. Not substitutes. Please! How many substitutes had gotten papers stuck in the rollers then walked away hoping no one associated her with the carnage? It would come back to haunt you in one way or another, the consequences marking you forever. There was no room for error, not in a school where 50 would-be teachers applied for every position. So Dora Romona had told me.

I got my 113 copies, raced back to my room – huh—my room! – and taught the six required classes.

Through lunch and prep period I worked, diligently, even turning off the radio to achieve maximum concentration, correcting their exams, straining my eyes over the barely legible crabbed answers.

Where did these teenagers learn to write! They needed a class in penmanship! Yet I knew Dora Romona would appreciate it if I corrected her exams, all 113. This would bump up karma.

I had to push myself to finish the exams before 3:34 when school ended—loitering after hours was discouraged—thus did I finish—at 3:32—feeling enormously satisfied. Dora Ramona would certainly appreciate this gargantuan effort. Never, never would she forget me. This I felt certain.

Everything I did correctly (correctly: you tried, but the rules were nebulous, and they mysteriously changed from teacher to teacher) was a notch up the totem pole, and at the top was a full-fledged, fulltime job with health benefits and a pension.

Along the totem pole climb it was essential to impress the privileged and established: the teachers, the Associate Principals, The Principal; however the teachers were most important — and some more so than others — as they interacted daily with the substitutes. After every teaching activity they evaluated and sorted us. Thus, we tried. We tried our best. Still we required directions to the bathrooms, keys to unlock our doors. We substitutes were work. And in the advent of a school-wide assembly, we did not know where our classes were to sit, nor if it was illegal to shout: "Go Red Go!" Or throw confetti. Answer: shouting "Go Red Go" was okay if prompted by a teacher of power — Dora Romona. Throwing confetti? Never! How stupid are you?

Furthermore, if a teacher next door called you during your lunch asking for help cleaning up a demo, you damn well better put down your PB & J and help mop up the acid and metal shavings. And don't expect a thank you. You were a substitute.

They would lean on the newly-cleaned walls outside their rooms, chatting about the troubled lives of their students, and how their infinite wisdom saved students influenced by media-malfeasance, students involved in daily near-death choices. These teachers were something else! Wise sages, resourceful, infinitely kind, always willing to extend a hand: they would change the lives of their students. For the better of course! They were individuals you'd want to befriend, yet the friend quota seemed filled; to have joined in the chat would have been a suggestion of equality, a claim of membership in a finely cultured, knowledgeable and select group. I did not interfere. I honored the unspoken requests and did not over-step my bounds: if I could avoid the fatal error — whatever that error might be — then I too, would be part of the Family of Camden High. I had to be careful. I had to think ahead.

It was like being married.

It was essential that they remember you and think you were intelligent and well-read, and thus, I'd initiate conversations.

With a bio teacher I'd subbed for I mentioned genetic research as described in a New Yorker article on Richard Reeves, Superman of the 80s — prior to his horse riding accident that rendered him a paraplegic. What a compelling story! In my eyes, he was more than ever, Superman. "Oh, well," the teacher said, avoiding eye contact, "that's good." She then hurried off as if I had BO! It was true that at least on one occasion I'd been in such a hurry that I did forget the quick swab of Arid, but after that, I kept deodorant in my backpack. Breath freshener too. You didn't want to be or do anything that could mobilize a teacher against you. Teachers were not typically practitioners of reflection. They had no time for such foolishness.

I had other sub positions — some long term, and once you taught 20 consecutive days, you earned double pay. Long term meant you could develop a rapport with the students.

A teacher once bestowed upon me a plastic coffee mug — with a cap that actually fit — and not some chewed-up, cast-off mug! Unbelievable. This was because I had taught her class for a month while she recovered from a stillborn.

The gesture so moved me that I almost cried. But long-term subbing required correcting exams and homework at night, inputting grades before the day started, and when I worked it all out, I made below minimum wage. Hmmm... Yet in the universe of Teaching and Connecting and Endowing Students with Knowledge, this was not illegal.

In every job, you had to pay your dues.

I kept applying for positions and building up karma. I went on interviews where, in a tiny room, 12 interrogators sat grimly around a long table asking me questions, many of which I had no answer for.

"Could I think about that?" I said. But the hard lines on their faces indicated they wanted answers now, and if I did not have the answers now, then I obviously was unsuitable for entry into The Family. I did not possess adequate experience for the job.

There were no second chances. No forgiveness for inane responses. Sweat dribbled down my back as they bent down to their papers and committed to eternity my responses, which I felt to be shallow and mundane.

A chem teacher who liked me (imagine that!) told me to get rid of the backpack, and use a book bag. "And now that you've been on the interviews, you know the questions, so practice them. Practice them with friends. Stage mock interviews in front of a mirror and video tape yourself. And don't forget to give them a PowerPoint of your best lesson plans."

I did as advised.

On a snowy March day during my third year of substitute teaching (and convenience store working), a 9th grade Environmental Science teacher suddenly walked out of her class. This was unprecedented, yet should the abandonment have come as a surprise? Ninth grade Environmental Science was the dumping ground for the disruptive, the dispossessed, the underachievers, the Ds and Fs of 8th grade Physical Science. The students corralled into 9th Grade Environmental Science fed off one another and formed one huge cohesive mass of subversive resistance. They congregated in the woods just beyond the school property and smoked cigarettes and pot and drank vodka from their water bottles. The thought they were invisible, but I saw the tell-tales wisps of smoke, I recognized the colors and shapes of their jackets. I knew who they were. They hosted drinking games at their houses after school. They had sex in a remote school bathroom until a camera caught a girl exiting from the boys' bathroom. Whenever they thought a teacher wasn't looking, they'd text one another, challenging their rivals and assembling allies for a confrontation and there would be fights in the cafeteria, and in the congested hallways. The 9th grade Environmental Science students were often the provocateurs. A teacher would call their parents, but these parents were out of work, or underemployed. Or they worked two jobs. Or they were drunks or meth addicts who "lived off the land" and sold their hormone-free eggs and free-range chickens at the Farmer's Market for 16-dollars-a-piece. They barely survived.

That day the Environmental Science teacher marched out of the classroom in the middle of a lesson on landfills — an exercise that tried hard to engage. Engaged was an important word at Camden High. It behooved one to know the important words and insert them in your cover letter or mention them three times during an interview or during the impromptu hallway chats. There were magic numbers too, just like magic words. Sixty-five was the most magic number. The Administration always wanted to know what was on your mind, and one false note could mean a swift end to your career.

So the students on this snowy March morning were loading gravel into industrial-sized mayonnaise jars and one kid threw a piece of gravel at another. A battle ensued, and despite the teacher's warnings, a window shattered. She marched out, cursing that she'd had enough. "Being in a boring bank teller is preferable to babysitting midget mental monsters who can barely put a sentence together!"

This transpired at 11:10 on a Tuesday.

That morning I happened to be at home — no sub jobs, a rarity — watching the snow fall heavily and reading Simic's poetry. I was called at 11:20. All I could think of was that if I got in before 12, I'd get paid for a whole day. An entire eighty dollars. A half week's worth of groceries for less than four hours of work.

Pay day!

I ended up staying in 9th Grade Environmental Science, teaching the rogues when they let me, yet maintaining my equanimity and sense of purpose. It was in that class that I met Jimi Agee. Jimi: a refugee from somewhere in Africa –he never did specify — that was not Jimi's way. The chem teacher (who liked me) and I thought he was from Sudan. A small, thin boy, quiet — very quiet — and you got the impression that he grew up missing major necessary nutrients and essential steps of the emotional development pathway. In that way, he was like Dora Romona, but there were other ways, in which they were unalike.

I was hired the following year for my dedication and perseverance — nothing more than that — so Dora Romona wanted me to understand. Not for my intelligence, creativity or god-forbid: teaching abilities. *Esther: you're a new teacher! What do you know? Hah, hah, hah.* I knew nothing: nothing about teaching, nothing about students, but I needed to preserve her facetious perception. Still, I could not believe my good luck: I was a woman with perpetual bad luck, a woman divorced from a husband who had become increasingly isolated and non-communicative toward his children. There had always been a secret side to Stan. Sometimes months would pass without a request to see the kids. Forget child support! Thus here I was, lurching through my 40s with three kids, with jobs that offered no benefits, and had no future. I had no soul mate, no confidante. Becoming a full-time science teacher at Camden High was a dream come true. I would have — no: *be part* — of a Family.

The Family of Camden High.

At last!

Tenure was the topic of the first weekly session that I and Dora Romona—temporary Science Chair—were to have. Camden High had only a very few tenure-track positions, most of which were reserved for spouses of college professors. Was I discouraged?

I understood what I was up against.

We were to have weekly sessions, Dora Romona and I, me sitting across from Dora, Dora eating cashews (she ate a lot!) and drinking coffee. She wanted me to know what a great privilege it was to teach at Camden High.

"We have 50 applicants for every position. We don't even like to announce openings because we get such an onslaught of applications. We are buried. Absolutely buried."

I imagined snowflakes as big as pillows descending upon Dora Ramona, covering her as she consumed gargantuan bowls of pistachio ice-cream or plate-sized chocolate chip cookies. She was always eating. Later it occurred to me she had some type of illness.

"Everyone," she momentarily stopped popping cashews into her mouth, so she could give me her undivided attention, "wants to work here."

She leaned forward, and the odor of masticated nuts reached my nostrils. I steeled myself and held my breath. It wouldn't be good to let on that I was offended. "The best students, the most rigorous courses. It's like a college. We take only the best. Only the best make the team."

She eased herself back, and cracked cashews on her back molars. I relaxed. I inhaled.

The Team. I'd been on a high school volleyball team once, but briefly. I had the reaction time of a turtle's yet the team was desperate: I had been their 6th player. An image floated through my mind of bright red blood dripping down my arm, down my ugly, sleeveless blue uniform to my ugly skirt whose purpose was to hide fat thighs and asses, yet amazingly exacerbated them. My skirt was speckled with bright red blood drips. My nose had been broken by an errant ball. *For christsakes Esther:* my teammates screamed *keep your freaking eyes on the ball!* You couldn't use the F-word back then, not in a Catholic school.

"I am both humbled and privileged to be part of The Team," I said with a deep solemnity intended to express gratitude to my new science chairperson. I would use Dora Romona's terminology—it was safer that way.

Dora Romona had tiny eyes encased in soft flesh. Those tiny eyes narrowed, her elf-ears came to attention then she smiled, her fulsome lips arching up like a comic book character's — The Joker's. "Do you know," she slowly enunciated, "how many teachers have Ph.D.s?"

I shook my head no.

She waited.

"How many?" I said.

"Thirty percent." Her eyes widened.

I nodded in a way that indicated I was impressed.

Then we talked about my "special students" whom from my subbing experience, I knew to be druggies, alcoholics, psychologically ill, and truant.

Half of my students would miss most of their classes, which would necessitate repeating material, essentially boring and alienating the other half who had initially found it worthwhile to come to class. They would soon dismiss the idea and begin to skip too when the urge struck, necessitating numerous phone calls and parent-counselor-student meetings. Time: where did it all go? My students comprised the school's bottom rung. I was warmed by the fact that things could only get better.

Dora Romona, in her bid to be the science chair, was taking courses at the local state college rather than the more demanding ivy league institution nearby. And who better to practice her developing skills on than me, the new teacher?

"We'll have a meeting every week to assess your progress. To help you out," she said. We sat in the retired chair's private office with the faux Persian rug and low lighting.

This was Dora Romona's room now. There was a coffee machine just outside the door. And a small refrigerator packed with comfort food. I know, because I peeked in early one morning when no one was around. Pudding, ice cream, cookie dough. Yes, and Dora Romona had an office door that actually closed. Dora Romona also let me know she had classes to teach (so what if it was the same bio class for the past 25 years?) and she didn't have time "to orient" me as she'd like to.

"The time to orient you about the school's unwritten but *important* policies," she emphasized.

.I told her I was fine with that, and I would seek enlightenment from other teachers.

The Camden High teachers — all of whom I had subbed for, and all of whom I'd imagined welcoming me into this special club, The Family of Camden High — did not at first comprehend that I was a full-fledged teacher.

Even as late as the third week of classes, they approached me in the crowded hallways of perspiring teenagers, or the stuffy teachers' café with its sticky, orange-colored food, their arms spilling over with half-corrected exams, inquiring if I was free to sub on such-and-such a date. Or.... would I like to help them correct their exams? To get some authentic experience? I wanted to say, "I'm just like you now!" but I knew they would hold that response against me. And it wasn't true that I was like them: I did not have my hair cut regularly — lack of time — nor did I wear the smocks and clogs! I looked like a mechanical baby doll in smocks, and when I wore clogs, my toes failed to get a grip, and I often walked right out of the damn things. I couldn't describe the wonders of my most recent vacation because I hadn't been on one. Vacation? Are you kidding? Most teachers were 5- or 6- year veterans of the school system, and they not only knew the content of the subjects in their sleep, but they were acutely aware of all the ways in which the students could manipulate them, and would undoubtedly manipulate me. I was not them.

Them.

I embraced my status, and was careful of what I said, and to whom. I knew that if I did not require their cooperation now I would in the future for I would need to borrow pipettes, or to log onto the free but convoluted Gradekeeper software. That much was clear.

I needed to keep on their good side, and ask for help only when absolutely necessary because every teacher was busy, busy, busy: busy teaching, grading, and busy attending long, irrelevant meetings. Overworked they were, and I was aware of it. And I was being admitted into a family — The Family of Camden High, The Family whose dynamics eluded me, yet if I focused my powers of observation and kept in mind who was successful (success: another magic word, along with standardization, lockstep) then I would take my rightful place in the Family of Camden High.

But wasn't lockstep a prison term? I did not have the nerve to ask. Having worked at home alone for many years, I found the workplace politics somewhat puzzling.

I sensed another layer of duties beyond the teaching, grading, disciplining, attending meetings, but for the life of me, I could not determine what those duties were.

When I entered the teacher's lunch room, they acted as though they weren't sure who I was, and when I did have a few minutes to eat, I ate with the aides, or subs. The real teachers were friends of long standing: they graded together, planned together and lunched together. They were acutely aware of who they were, and who they were not.

One day, the teachers' café was packed to the hilt: it was the once-a-year *Teacher Appreciation Luncheon*: all food and drink gratis of the PTA, and there was an abundance of chicken fillets, sushi, noodle salads, lettuce salads, beans and cookies and cakes. Whatever you wanted, and had I known, I would not have eaten breakfast. Or dinner the night before.

I wanted to fill my shirt pockets with chicken filets and take them back to the kids and feast with them. So overwhelmed was I by the abundance — and delectable smells, the cornucopia of meats and pastas — that I inadvertently sat down at *their* table! Talk about boo-boos! My mind was fully occupied with the rich Thai curry — a smoother coconut sauce never had my taste buds experienced — and spiced to perfection! After a scrumptious mouthful, I paused to look up and it was then that I discovered that I must have displaced someone important. The Family continued on with their conversation, as if I did not exist.

Even Dora Romona, mentor and goddess extraordinaire, who sat directly across from me inhaling spaghetti with garlic, then sushi, then pasta primavera, all the while the fingers of her left hand hovering over a plate of brownies, said not a word to me, yet she amazingly (this was a teacher talent, which I would learn to do) kept up a conversation with Lenore Groat.

Lenore Groat paused, and looked at me with her steely blue eyes. Little did I know how connected Lenore and I would become. Her big head of frizzy hair, a giant red lollipop, would be the first image that would pop into my mind as I awoke at 4 am. But back then, at the *Teacher Appreciation Luncheon*, I wanted to be like her. (Later, I would ask myself: what was the difference between a lunch and a luncheon?) I wanted her crisp PowerPoints. Her fine-tuned lessons. Her absolute command of the class. She always knew what she was doing. And she had an unusual classroom that was lined with quilts. The quilts I wasn't sure about. The overly-bright, multicolored and multi-patterned quilts were significant in some elusive way—like Dora Romona's constant eating. Even Lenore Groats' window blinds were quilted and that should have said something to me. It should have prepared me, but back then, being an innocent and an ignorant, I stuck the quilts into the bizarre category, the stay-away-from-this: quilts were her specialty, and everyone needed to have a specialty. That meant you were well-rounded. That meant you were a good teacher, hence, a good person.

    I ate quickly and left the *Teacher Appreciation Luncheon.*

    Later that day as I cleaned my white board, and sponged off the students' desks, I realized that to admit a stranger into The Family required a sensibility and generosity that few were called to. Such was my situation, and I had to deal with it. If empathy or camaraderie befell me, I would be ecstatic; otherwise, I would do my job and be damn happy that I had one.

    Dora Romona, in her bid to be renowned chairperson extraordinaire, initiated once-a-month community-building birthday celebrations at restaurants. By celebrating with the math department, we'd made our group a solid two dozen.

"That way we needn't buy birthday presents for everyone," Dora explained. Dora was always explaining The Family customs to me, as if I were a dolt. Maybe I was. Still, when was the last time I bought a birthday present for a forty-something individual? I could not remember. I don't think I ever did.

"It's not always easy to find the right present," she said during our weekly meeting. She was eating almond crescents (the ends dipped in rich Swiss chocolate—I had had one once, while married) which went for $3.50-a-piece at the local bakery. I could not imagine myself ever being wealthy enough to afford such a treat.

I nodded affirmative.

"We meet at a restaurant on one of the Finger Lakes," she stopped to chew and swallow. "A nice restaurant where you dress up. You know, Esther?" Bite, chew, swallow. Then her eyes focused on my slightly-faded tee-shirt which had a smudge of dirt on the left breast. Today we chopped up old broccoli for our compost buckets. We added partially decomposed leaves and bacteria-laden dirt and a squirt of water. In the spring, we would examine the critters that would magically appear beneath a binocular scope. Magically appear? One tried to demonstrate to the little devils that science was about logic and sense. Facts. Science made sense – just like the venerated institution of school!

I nodded again.

The restaurants typically had sauces and gravies and rich fattening desserts, food that initiated a biochemical reaction that produced the kind of laughter and giggling that you associate with high school cheerleaders. Relieved from the burden of my disruptive and distraught students, I should have laughed too, but all I could think of was the pile of uncorrected exams in my bookbag, my kids walking into an empty house and wondering where I was, perhaps being frightened by the house's emptiness. I had not anticipated being late, and had not mentioned this to them. Gee, was I a worrywart! Several times during the first birthday celebration I had risen from my cushioned chair only to be halted midrise by Dora Ramona's opaque eyes and mouth-in-motion. It was at that celebration that I took a long and hard look at her pointed elf-like ears, so delicate and in such contrast to her fleshy face.

"Have a piece of cheese cake," she said coolly.

Then: "More pasta?"

I ate, and I ate: chicken tetrazzini, noodle salads swimming in sauces, vegetable swimming in sauces, lo mein and hi mein, cheese cake and brownies with buttery frostings. I ate to calm anxiety, and I ate to stifle boredom. I ate to please, and I ate to hide. Such a coward I was! And when I ate in the afternoon like that, the mountains of quickly fermenting food drugged me.

I would fall asleep, and not even the robust singing of *Happy Birthday* could rouse me from my torpor.

Every morning I woke at 4 a.m. to write lesson plans and make colorful overheads. I was especially careful to be neat and put funny pictures in them: cows farting to demonstrate global warming, or even a small stream of water dribbling down the once magnificent Niagara Falls to demonstrate resource shortage.

The students appreciated a sense of humor and even if they wouldn't listen to the lecture, they listened to the jokes, so they got something from the 44-minute period. And then there was the image of the hundreds of snowmen protesting building of a coal plant: what did it mean? — I would ask my students. The overheads were something tangible. They made me feel good: they gave me a sense of progress.

I had created a stack of overheads, which I carefully filed away with sheets of blank paper between them for protection. Next year, I thought, I will be ahead of the game, and being ahead of the game meant I'd have more time for my own kids. And I needed time.

I needed to sit back and reflect.

At 6:30, I'd stop working and make the kids eggs or oatmeal, so I could arrive at Camden High well before anyone else, assuring myself access to a functioning duplicating machine. To be successful, one required strategies.

I worked hard with my students—I wanted to like all of them, and I did, even the Sudanese student, Jimi Agee, who sadly, would be on my list of failures and make a startling appearance in another class of mine the two years hence. He couldn't read. I did not understand why he was in my class, but I did not question. He was openly hostile to other students and would sit in his seat and hold his arms over his malnutritioned chest and when I would request his classwork or homework, he would snarl and say he didn't do it. His parents missed meetings and never returned phone calls. I wasn't even sure he had parents. Initially, I suggested psychological testing, but the year's end was near, and I dropped the issue. I knew Dora Romona would not be supportive of such a venture.

Initially Dora Romona liked me. She just loved sitting at her big crumb-laden desk and grinning at me and telling me what I should do and how I should do it. How I should think, how I should be.

A family is a close-knit group, she often reminded me. With an abundance of neuroses, I thought, but did not vociferate. Her elf ears would twitch. I was her first *teacher*, her protégé, who she reveled in exhibiting to Merriweather Snorton, the then Principal of Camden High Principal. And me? I was a suckup, a brownie point collector of unimaginable tenacity and verve. Merriweather Snorton? He was not much of an educator: he was a numbers and standardization guy, a proponent of lockstep (indeed, it was a prison word!) who'd never really been in a classroom except for a year-long stint as a gym teacher. A gym teacher as the Principal! Whoever would have imagined?! Especially in our college town—it was something unexpected. How had the school board chosen this bean counter? He'd never heard the phrase *critical thinking,* much less understood its importance. But whatever directive was given, I obeyed with the blindness of a creature that survives the deepest, darkest oceanic trenches. I adapted. Did I want to be on the Sophomore Dance Committee? Got it in my date book. How about Avid? Sure, what's one or two afternoons a week! How about the 10th grade initiative? I love initiatives. Initiatives are the best because they accomplish so much. It's not all bureaucratic drivel on paper, for godsake!

I did as they requested. I made sure all my lesson plans covered the 5 Es (encourage, explore, expound, explain, evaluate) and 3 Ps (polite, punctual, peppy). I attended the faculty meetings and the department meetings, but I never spoke up: I listened ...well, sort of, as I loaded up on chocolate chip cookies and sugary sodas. The other teachers always had enough to say anyway. I practiced the *Zen of Listening,* a book I was reading when I had a moment here and there. My kids complained that I wasn't listening to them, and I sought to rectify the situation.

At the faculty meetings, I sat alone. It was not by choice: I understood the risks of befriending an unproven entity, a teacher who could be potentially held in disfavor. You didn't want it to rub off on you.

The school had ways to dismiss even tenured teachers; for instance, you could be assigned a duty so unappealing: three preps — running around from room to room, dragging your expensive and fragile Erlenmeyer flasks and heavy textbooks in a wobbly cart — that you'd quit. They'd take classes from you—classes that you developed – that you spent days on: looking up facts, assessing videos, planning homework and tests — and then assign you to a new class that had no developed homework or tests. The Administration had all the cards, and that was always in the back of my mind. Although I tried to focus on the words of the knowledgeable teachers, and concentrate on their descriptions of curriculum planning, PLC planning, lesson planning, my eyelids would descend.

"Mom!" my eldest, Amy looked at me, her bottom lip quivering. She burst into tears.

Kids—my own kids: we never talked. I'd heat a frozen pizza for dinner then would cry out: "Come and get it!" then I would bury myself in homework that required correcting.

I had 115 students and usually took home as many papers every night, and wrote comments on all of them. That's what a good teacher did.

Amy, who was a senior, was not part of a group of girls at school: she had never been that kind of person, a bright and energetic 17-year-old, she did not usually define herself by others. She felt friendless, and lonely.

"Today's just a bad day," I told her, "but tomorrow will be better. You have to keep that in mind: tomorrow will be better. There are some things that you just can't control. But you face your fears—what you can't control – and your life will get better, I promise. You have to believe me. And you know what, Amy? It's okay to do things by yourself."

She looked utterly disconsolate, as if she'd never ever in her life had a friend—that wasn't true of course. My high school years too, had been times of misery. In fact, they still were.

"It's a trick to find the good in a bad situation. But you can do it. I know you can."

At the year's end, I passed the required classroom observations. There was a curious moment during which Dora Romona and Merriweather Snorton examined my grades—remarking on the large number of Ds and Fs. Apparently failure rate was a big deal. *Look at the students you gave me,* I wanted to say: *Joe Blackwell who couldn't read beyond a second grade level, and never tried, giving up the second day of class, and Marcy Alvarez, who put her head down and never did a stitch of work. (I was convinced she was mentally ill.) Did they deserve to pass?* They didn't even deserve an F: I would have given them a G for Go back and do not collect $200.

"You don't want everyone to fail, do you?" Meriweather said. He had this way of remaining perfectly stiff and still. Creepy he was, as in Edgar Allen Poe creepy, as if he were deciding how to dismember me without spilling a drop of blood and where to stash the body parts.

I wanted to protest, to state my case—how in the end students would not be served by merely passing them to make the numbers look good—but he stared at me with his pale brown dead eyes, and I knew contradicting him would not advance my cause. With dread, I watched the way his eyebrows closed in, as if he knew my deepest thoughts: *He's a fool! He couldn't do math in his head if he tried! He has no idea what silicon is! And he left his zipper open! And look — hah, hah — at the corner of his mouth, dried toothpaste!* His eyes, like those of brown bears that suddenly and viciously attack you for the pure fun of it, stopped me cold.

"No."

"Don't you think everyone should pass? That every student deserves that right?"

So what was a little fudging anyway? Didn't all tests have a subjective quality to them? How much different, really, was a 63 from a 65? Or a 55 from a 65? Or a 50 from a 65? Or a 30? Come on! And why add to the fray? The local newspaper was hounding the school, pressing this matter of the extraordinary minority failure rate.

Snorton and Romona smiled warmly at me. I smiled back. Two happy administrators. That was the thing: to keep the administrators happy. Everything else was icing on the cake.

The next morning I found a little card in my mail box. *We want you to be part of The Team.* The Team. The Family of Camden High. I closed my eyes in homage, savoring the moment as other teachers pulled mail from their mailboxes and chattered and cackled. Maybe I could buy the clogs, and wear the denim pinafore! I was so thrilled that I found Dora Romona immediately. In her comfy office, she was, rifling through a pile of student infractions. For once, she was not eating. Maybe her mouth needed an occasional rest now and then?

"No more sleeping during faculty meetings," she said. As if my soft snoring was a personal affront to all. "It is extremely important to set a good example." Then she picked up a Pop Tart.

So there was food! Well....of a sort. The purple sugar inside and white sugar outside had somehow been successfully marketed to people as breakfast food. Imagine! Carbs, fat, protein: lo-and-behold: food. And in such a nice shiny (inside) package! Her opaque eyes bugged open as she peeled away the wrapper and the ears that had been at half-mast straightened to full attention. Suddenly the true meaning of break-fast occurred to me, and I wondered how I could use that tidbit in a lesson plan. Of course I wouldn't mention Dora Romona.

"May I have a piece?" I asked.

The kids and I had a spectacular summer: we swam at the falls, picked blueberries, made plum jam, hiked trails, biked into the country, and even took the bus to New York City to watch the street performers and gymnasts in Washington Park Square.

I reconnected with my kids, and we became a family again. It would be the last time that we would be all together as Amy would be starting college in late August. She would study chemistry. As we watched the gymnast in Washington Park Square, Amy said, "Mom, this is fun!" She had made it though senior year, and had become a stronger person.

"Mom, we can talk to you again!"

"We thought we lost you, Mom."

"I have been found," I said. "Saved by season and sun."

"What's that, Mom?'

I hugged Amy. I hugged Lynn and Bob.

"What would I do without you all!!"

They beamed at me, three circular faces, large brown eyes, waiting for what was next.

"But what happens when the school year starts?" Lynn said.

"Never fear: my prep is done. Complete. An entire 180 sheets of overheads. I rewrote all the labs. All 50. That's why I was working so hard so that the next year, I wouldn't have to work so hard this year. I'll have time! Lots of time! Well... maybe not lots. But some. More."

I walked and ran and biked so much that I lost the weight I had gained from eating confections and sugary sodas while employed by the Camden Public School System. I was eating healthfully again, and I was able to stay awake.

But all too soon, the summer was over.

A week before school commenced, I was told that no longer was I to teach Environmental Science; oh, no: that would have been too easy to have the same prep for two years! Oh come on! No challenge to that, Esther. Where's your brain?

"And we like to challenge our teachers, just as we like to challenge our students."

"Thank-you, Dora Romona, for thinking so highly of me."

Her eyes narrowed, and her lips downturned unpleasantly—but only for a moment, doubting my sincerity.

"You'll be teaching Chemistry, and with Lenore and Marrianne Jo." She smiled, her large lips turning up.

Lenore Groat and Marrianne Jo Smith. I knew of them. It was Lenore's seat I had appropriated during the *Teacher*

Appreciation Lunch. Lenore who had given me a savage look, as if I had taken something vital and precious from her. After that, I avoided her.

"They are tenured teachers of many years experience. Master Teachers," Dora Romona added.

The phrase brought to mind Gregorian chants and incense. Chalk boards filled with incomprehensible formulas and the perpetually downcast eyes from the lesser teachers— yours truly. Master Teachers had mysterious privileges. They were allowed to cut ahead in the cafeteria line. They could call in sick days on Fridays without a scolding on Monday, and thus spend a long weekend skiing or sleeping. Or sleeping and skiing. Sleeping, skiing and smelling the roses. Imagine!

"You will all give the same homework, the same classwork, and the same exams," Dora Romona said.

"Huh?" I said, not sure I'd heard correctly.

She repeated the declaration. I sat in silence, cogitating. Same. Same lessons, homeworks, classworks? What was going on here? Same was insane! Wasn't it? What was the point of teaching if you couldn't use your own lesson plans? Why not just hire a drone? Where was *choice* in this gulag of mental and moral imagination? This sounded like lockstep to me, but smart person that I had become, I kept my own counsel: for a non-tenured teacher to voice opposition was suicidal. Might as well return to the convenience store.

Later that day Lenore Groat halted me in a hallway stuffed

to the tiled, graffiti-strewn walls with teenagers and smelling of Axe and greasy French fries. "We plan every day at lunch," she told me, leaving a lingering glance on my blouse.

I had worn a blouse. I occasionally did this. I had a few blouses: none of them fancy or expensive, but nice serviceable non-offending non-promiscuous blouses. Lenore wore blouses that mimicked her quilts. Looking at them made me dizzy and I wanted to vomit. But it was nothing personal.

"Well...I...ah ...lunch." Lunch! Lunch: my time to sit back, close my eyes and take a 10-minute snooze, then meditate for 20 minutes in preparation for dealing with the next three hours of testosterone, high-pitched screaming, chain rattlings and pleas to hideout in the restroom.

"That's the only time all three of us are free!" she snapped. "We need to work as a Team." Her thin lips closed tightly and her blue eyes stared at me. It was not a friendly gesture and I knew then that dealing with Lenore Groat would be a constant struggle, like trying to plug a leak in the Hoover dam with a rubber cork from a wine bottle. A Team: with Lenore Groat as the Team Leader!

"Dora Ramona specifically tweaked the schedules so the three of us could plan during a common period. It was not an easy accomplishment. Scheduling is so complicated! To-ge-ther," she emphasized, as if aware of my anti-group predilections. Could she see the alarm in my eyes? I tried hard to neutralize whatever thoughts were scuttling across my frontal lobe. Lenore smiled, exposing shark-sharp teeth. There was a smirk in her smile and I felt sure she'd listened in on my students' conversation about her quilts. I tried to keep out of such conversations. *That's not nice*, I'd tell my students, as the room broke into guffaws, when they called her quilts elephant blankets. What elephants wore blankets anyway?

"Dora Romona thinks of everything!" she said. Then her big red head of frizzy hair disappeared into the crowd of bare arms and legs.

Dora Romona. Making sure I had teammates. Pals. Friends. Here were the friends I'd always longed for. Dora Romona: always watching out for me! To do what was best for me.

"Ah… by the way, Esther." She looked at me pointedly, focusing on my right shoulder. I had a habit of raising my right shoulder when I got excited or nervous. When I was a tyke, my piano teacher would sit on the piano bench beside me and push down my shoulder as I would get going on a particularly rousing Chopin waltz.

"What?" I asked. I looked at my shoulder to see if it had risen.

"Your blouse is on inside-out."

I ended up eating lunch every day with Lenore Groat and Marianne Jo Smith in Lenore's room. The room was adorned with crazy quilts push-pinned into corners where the treasures could not be reached by exploding chemicals. Some of the more valuable brightly-colored quilts were covered with clear plastic.

The room made me dizzy and I had to close my eyes frequently. Chemicals did have a tendency to unite and explode in chemistry rooms when the teacher's back was turned.

This had not been an issue in Environmental Science – our main commodity was compost, not chemicals – but I was taking it all in, getting used to the differences between what I had taught, and what I would teach, and because Lenore and Marianne Jo had been teaching chemistry for many, many years, they knew exactly what was needed to be taught and how.

They led the way. At nearly 50 years of age, I was the doting follower. They were to give me lesson plans during the convivial female-with-secrets lunch, yet more often than not, the lesson plans were not ready—there was always something they had to fix—and I'd leave empty-handed and stomach-bloated, which did not position me favorably for dealing with the afternoon teenage masses.

Maybe it was the student rumble tumble out in the halls compelling me to eat, and so I ate, and ate: potato salad, eggs rolls, and irresistible chocolate fudge that I snuck when their heads were nearly touching in some passionate discussion on student gossip. Or during the heated conversation between Lenore and Marianne about the worth of Lenore's quilts. Marianne, I gathered, was jealous of Lenore's quilting talents. If I got any lesson plans, I got them at the last minute, with no time to review them; consequently I made my own plans. How could I use their plans with no forewarning of what was to be taught? I had to learn the material! I needed the right chemicals, the correct formulation of hydrochloric acid! It wasn't something you could produce in 5 minutes. Furthermore, my logic dictated a different sequence of lectures and labs from theirs. My thinking process was fundamentally different from theirs. Yet they discussed quilts, or singing in two-part harmony. They regularly sang for their church and the Salvation Army. When five minutes remained of the hallowed lunch, Marianne and Lenore would finally mention lesson plans.

"Next lunch," they'd say.

Consequently, I was compelled to modify Lenore's and Marianne's exams.

"Everyone must give the same exams." Dora Romona had called me into her office following the first exam. Someone had told her that I'd given a different exam. Kids talk. Teachers talk. Apparently mine had been easier—because the scores were higher—and this made me look better, and a new teacher was never to look better than a Master Teacher. Oh no. Lenore and Marianne had also been invited to the meeting in the small office with its faux Persian rug, soft lighting and faint classical music and pervasive smell of Kentucky Fried Chicken.

"We all need to be on the same page," Dora Romona said.

"But how can I test them on material I haven't gone over?"

Three sets of cold eyes stared at me. Obviously none of them had read the *Zen of Listening*.

It stands to reason that when a teacher gives exams to students on material that hasn't been taught, that the trust carefully developed between the students and teacher over several months suddenly vanishes. Students understood justice and fairness. How could they be prepared for exams when I acquired copies of the exam only on exam day? It was pointless to appeal to Lenore and Marianne. And the teacher's union? The union was in cahoots with the administration. In Camden, everything was nice on the surface and bringing up such an issue to the School Board would have meant never teaching again. Thus, my students rather than exclaiming, "Hello Ms. Deetster—how are you?" ignored me and looked down at their feet. When I asked for volunteers to hand out papers, they stared blankly at me. Yeah, right!

I'd come home from school and open the refrigerator. I'd eat and tell the kids: "I need more help from you. When you get home, put away the dishes. Start the dinner. We're stronger if we work together. Remember TEAM?"

I looked at my son, whose baseball coach loved the acronym. Together Everyone Achieves More. He gave me a sad look: coach Ike was long gone because I had no time to cart kids around to activities.

There was TEAM, and there was AWEB: Apart We Battle.

A student once came in after lunch stoned and screamed "Fucking Bitch" at me when I told him to leave the room; another: "I hate you, Ms. Deetster!"

Yet I set boundaries, I reserved judgment because I knew

their lives were not perfect. A parent had died, there was a mentally-ill sibling.

The Administration was too busy eating junk food and calculating their retirement benefits to acknowledge a student's inner life. My students required encouragement, patience and firmness. Boundaries. I was aware of my failings: I made mistakes, the exams were flawed, I didn't always have a quick comeback to a remark and I was never as prepared as I wanted to be, but as long as my students trusted me, they forgave me, they stopped calling names. They apologized. There was a willingness on their and my part to wipe the slate clean: every day we started clean.

One thing I that fully understood about teenagers was that they not only had the capacity to change, but they wanted to. They knew when they crossed the line, yet they also knew that a new quadrant of relationship could be initiated at any time.

They had a conscience. They could change their attitudes. But for Lenore, Marianne, and Dora Romona: high school had been a long time ago. They lacked the imagination and the openness that makes new ideas possible.

People of position and power are deadly opposed to change; that is, of course, how they stay in power. They were, in the strongest sense of the word, rigid. They did not wish to like me and what I stood for, and so I could never win them over: I could only avoid them, and try to minimize their dislike of me, and the suffering they caused me.

One morning as I was correcting homework—homework

created by Marianne and Lenore—the loathing in me welled up. Every time I saw them, my head started throbbing, and pain radiated from my gut: pain for exams I was forced to give, pain for the moments in which I had to smile and pretend to be like them. This was not good! Once they realized my intent to minimize contact with them, they positioned themselves for even more contact with me. They convinced Dora Romona that I needed to sit in their classes once a week! Like my ex, they reveled in discovering new ways to punish me, and they were relentless in this respect. They all had to have some part of me.

Once again the traumatized Sudanese student, Jimi Agee, was in my class. This time it was Chemistry class, a more demanding science: you couldn't bluff your way into a C like you could in Environmental Science. Jimi couldn't even read the Chemistry text. He failed every test, even the confidence-building quizzes. He was even more hostile than in previous years, and when I wasn't looking, he tried to sabotage the other students' labs. He was a constant danger in a space filled with flammable materials, and Bunsen burners fueled with methane. I tried all sorts of strategies, but I knew my limits: I was not a therapist. Jimi, a confused and sorrowful soul desperately needed professional help. Once again I requested psychological testing—going all the way to the head social worker this time. I demanded placement in a lower-level chemistry class. I demanded psychological testing. This time, I did not give up.

"He's in the appropriate level, and he doesn't need testing." Dora Romona fastened her stern eyes on me as she plopped low-calorie chocolates into her mouth.

Her doctor had put her on a diet, I'd heard. She had high blood pressure, was a borderline-diabetic and could possibly get a stroke or lose her legs. What a mess she was! You heard about everything in the school: whose daughter was pregnant or whose son was in dry out. Dora Romona, for instance, bought her billowing clothes and extra-wide shoes at a special shop in Syracuse. Forget about a coat — what piece of apparel could button over her excessive portraiture? She wore ponchos that looked alarmingly like quilts, and when she walked, from afar she resembled a giant poisonous mushroom, hobbling on two thick stalks, that gray-brown dome of her bobbing from side to side.

"Aren't you aware of the school's record on minorities?" she asked me.

"After 3 months, he still has no clue what the Periodic Table is!"

Dora Romona's eyes narrowed, as if she'd just discovered something unknown and unacceptable about me.

Her line of questioning, which further unearthed my subversive side, also answered my undying question: how had Jimi passed Biology last year?

"Lenore, who is a certified Bio teacher, spent an hour every day after regular school hours tutoring."

" Unbelievable!" I said — in apparent celebration of Lenore's and Dora's strategy. What a fool, I thought. Who had such time?

"As you know, he passed the Regents exam," Dora Romona said. "That was a feather in her cap."

I wanted no feathers in my cap, I didn't even want a cap: I just wanted to be left alone, to teach unimpeded. I knew that Lenore and Dora re-graded all exams that were "close." I was sure that Jimi's Bio exam was re-graded. Thus, I tried appealing to Dora Romona's humane side. Everyone has that side, right? The side that says here's a poor starving kid who'd been through unimaginable horrors in deepest Africa: marching, living on drugs, hiding in the bush, being forced to kill his countrymen. We *need* to bend our civilized rules. We *need* to genuinely help this lost soul. Yes?

"We're not giving Jimi a fair chance," I said softly. "We're bullying him. The system is...bullying him," I corrected myself so as not to cast blame on the great and all-knowing Dora Romona.

Dora Romona looked at me in silence, the edges of her mouth curving down, her eyes flattening in an unflattering way, and I understood I'd gone too far with the humane side. This was a school, of course — not some social service agency. What an idiot I could be! Where was my brain! This was one conversation that she would undoubtedly remember.

Then Dora struggled to rise from her chair, and I reached out to help her, and I felt her sweaty, chocolatey-sticky hand on my hand, and I pulled her up and she seemed grateful — ooh, the beginnings of a genuine smile — but then something settled in her face, and when fully erect, I saw the moment of honest contact had vanished. The elf ears were at attention and she was once again, fully and overwhelmingly Dora Romona: rising Science Chair not to be messed with.

After that, Dora Romona, Meriweather Snorton and the other APs, and even Lenore and Marianne, came in my room regularly and would sit in back, their dark shoulders hunched like vultures, waiting for the living to become the dead. They scribbled away and they chatted—and not always in the hushed reverent decibels befitting a serious classroom situation. Sometimes, it was like a circus back there, as if they intentionally wanted to disrupt my classroom. Imagine that! Purveyors of education trying to discredit a sincere and earnest teacher!

Later, they would quote what I had said to my students, but the quotes were out of context, or missing appropriate adjectives. As if they knew what adjectives were!

I could hear their pages rustling from the front of the room as I gave instructions, and when I saw them like that, staring at me, two or three of them hunkered down, their noses twitching in unison, I would freeze.

Their notes became official *Observations* which went into my personnel folder where they would stay forever. This was an indelible record, its weight Biblical and undisputable. Into the *Observations* went the student talking during my 10-minute presentation, the one illegible word on my overhead, the sentence that was too small, the questions I asked that they determined not to be of *higher order thinking*. As if *they* ever thought! I was advised (I love that word: advised) to sit in on Lenore's and Marianne's classes and replicate their lesson plans. And I would, although emerging from Lenore's room I'd have a massive headache exacerbated by the quilted walls and ceiling.

And then when they weren't in my room, Lenore would listen in on my classes.

We shared a prep room which opened up to both of our classrooms, and Lenore could easily hear what went on in my classroom.

Once, during a particularly long class — a review session — a student made some castigating remark about the quilts: my students, for some reason, could not come to terms with those quilts. It was a rare moment of mirth in the class, and I went along with it. Too late, alas, did I hear test tubes rattling with an angry warning in the prep room.

The vultures refused to recognize any of my good teaching techniques — such as involving students in demonstrations or having them work together on problems at the front board. Such practices never appeared in the *Observations*.

Thus, was I advised to enroll in special classes for new teachers, which occurred after regular school hours; all extra work and workshops being *voluntary*. This was because I had too many Ds and Fs:

I did not have the Ds and Fs, I tried to tell Dora Romona: my *students* had the Ds and Fs. Look what you gave me!

Kids whose brains had more holes than matter because of all the pot they smoked. Kids who drank to excess every weekend.

Kids who slept a few hours a night because they played video games until four a.m.. Kids who never had a square meal. Kids whose parents didn't give a damn about what happened to them. How about helping the kids? Designing the curriculum to help them succeed? And not just succeed as in C versus F (or G), but to succeed in life?

    I arrived at school early, I left late. I never had a free period. I was made to look inadequate as a teacher, and finally, insubordinate.

    Slowly, I became what they accused me of.

    Time: it's a funny thing. Sometimes I wanted it to go very fast—like during the 80-minute Core Chemistry classes where a bottom-rung student would light a can of hair spray whenever I turned my back, or when Romona and cronies sat in on my classes.

    But then at night, at last home and safe, at the kitchen table with my kids eating macaroni-and-cheese, I'd want time to slow down so I could hear how my remaining kids (Amy being in college) spent the day. *How was your day? How are you feeling? How was the bus ride? What class did you enjoy most? What do you want to talk about?* I wanted to have a real conversation with them but there was always too much to do. Both Lynn and Bob were having trouble in school, but it never registered with me. Bob couldn't focus, and wanted to make sure others did not focus. He became the class clown, and his grades plummeted. Lynn, a sophomore, started hanging out with a group who drank and smoked pot.

And so the laundry piled up, the dishes became encrusted with leftover food. Floors remained unswept. I needed time to sort through the school politics and assure myself of job security: if I had job security—tenure—then I could stop worrying. But time was the one commodity I lacked.

I began to fall asleep once again at the faculty meetings. It was nothing I could control. Exhausted after seven hours of teaching, and saying no and yes, I was tempted by the chocolate-chip cookies and sugary sodas and the sedating murmuring of numerous teachers. Requiring comfort, I'd eat, and my eyelids would descend. It was pure Pavlovian response. I vaguely heard the last meeting's topic: we were all akin to marketers in a fish market, and we needed to smile over the bins of smelly fish and expatiate about all the fun we were having.

Should it have come as a surprise to me that during my pre-tenure meeting in April, after four-plus years of hard work (two subbing, two-and-a-half authentic teaching), that I was told my services were no longer needed?

"We don't want to put any more effort into you," Merriweather Snorton said, his dead eyes fastened on me.

Dora Romona, who had been sitting beside me in one of her flowery ensembles, with neither drink nor food nearby (a highly unusual situation for her!) reached out and squeezed my thigh.

"Get your fucking hand off of me," I said. I walked out of the Principal's room fully imagining that I would never return.

Every morning thereafter, I awoke in a deep gloom. I slept poorly and barely ate. Never had I been fired from a job and the experience's novelty discombobulated me. Everything was off: I tipped over cups of hot coffee and hit my head on opened cupboard doors. I couldn't get the fitted sheets to fit on my bed. Whereas I at one time derived pleasure from the chirping of birds — it was April, the snow had melted — I now found birdsong an intrusion into my gloom. It was essential to have a solid, deep gloom because by immersing myself so totally, my emotions, I believed, would reset.

I agreed to stay until the year's end: I had no other job prospects, and I had bills to pay.

At Camden High, a crescendo of whispers followed me after I left the duplicating machines, or when I entered the main office to check my mail. Whispers followed, yet the teachers avoided me, as if my failure was contagious. As if I was the irresponsible kid who failed to complete her homework. I lacked some necessary trait that made me a complete teacher: I was only half a teacher, and the missing half failed to foresee the consequences of my actions. Yet miraculously, I completed the school year, despite increased harassment from Dora Romona and Merriweather Snorton; had I quit, the school district would not be required to pay unemployment and I would have had nothing to live on.

That August, I found myself in a stuffy room interviewing for a science position with a charter school: only a charter school would consider hiring someone my age. Everything was going well—the group assembled—teachers, parents and a student—listened eagerly and smiled at my responses.

They loved my demo with the dollar bill: churning it up in water then collecting the iron with a strong magnet. They applauded my grasp of think-pair-share, chunking and jig-saw. But then the student on the committee asked me: "How would you make class fun?" Fun? What a privilege it was, I thought, for the students to be in this magnificent downtown building with extraordinarily small classes and dedicated teachers. Teachers who took students on expeditions to goat farms, yoga studios and compost facilities. This would have been impossible for my own students, or even my kids: they would have been the ones shoveling the goat poop or polishing the yoga studios' wood floors. Fun? Something inside me broke, and I collected the binders of lessons plans that I had brought with me. I left the room.

I still had five months of Unemployment, but it didn't pay enough to live on, and I job-hunted in earnest.

The schools wouldn't hire anyone my age, so I took whatever I could get, low-paying jobs sans benefits, and even those jobs became rarer as the country slid deeper into a recession. With unemployment rates above 25 percent in some parts of the country, the recession was more like a depression.

I worked side-by-side with poor people, people who grew vegetables not to put the prize tomato on the kitchen table, but to grow enough beans and corn so they could freeze or can them. They lived in trailer homes surrounded by mud. Their water supplies were dubious. They wore crappy boots and smoked cigarettes. They fixed their own cars and bought all their clothes at resale shops. There was all manner of junk outside their homes because they lacked the money and time to haul it to the dump. It was an uncomfortable, disorganized life—a life I was trying to avoid.

    I still could not drive past the high school without imagining my classroom with its giant Periodic Table, and my students crying out: "Hi Ms. Deetster! How's life? What's happening?"

    I grieved.

    I vowed never to return to Camden High, yet four years later there I was, talking to the new Principal about Bob and his apparently illicit cell phone behavior. After the meeting, even though I was agitated, I returned to work: for an hourly worker, every hour counted, every hour away was a ten dollar loss. I ran tests in a lab at a high-tech company for an abusive, insane boss who we hypothesized had been poisoned by the mercury vapors inside his permeability machines.

    When I got home that night, I fell into bed and fell asleep. I slept and slept until awakened by Lynn.

    "Mom," she said looking intensely into my eyes. "What are you doing?"

    "Sleeping."

"But it's only seven. And there's no dinner."

Bob came in the room too, and stood by the bed, and they both stared at me.

"Oh...I'm sorry." Tears began to well up behind my eyelids.

"Mom." Lynn sat down on the bed beside me. She had become a young woman, I realized. She would be going off to college in the fall. I had missed a part of her growing up.

"What's wrong?"

I briefly considered my 8-hour shift on the porosity machine, how I sometimes fell asleep sitting at the stool. I missed the intellectual stimulation of the classroom. My current assembly-line job had not been part of my naive 27-year-old career path, but I couldn't tell Lynn that.

"Remember, Mom, that you used to say that there was something good in every bad situation? That it's up to you to find it? That if you guard anger like a present, that it becomes a part of you?" She waited a moment. "That you have to know your fears, and face them?"

"I said that?"

Lynn's round brown eyes stared at me.

The next day, as I waited for my Parameter 110 to pressure up, it occurred to me that although I worked alongside disgruntled people who were perpetually in debt, I was not yet in debt. I recently re-read *Zen and the Art of Listening*, and as I recorded my data, I worked through my humiliations and disappointments. I started to listen to my co-workers who had spent years and years in a feudal relationship with greedy employers who denied them full-time labor, sick time, even paid holidays. We began to exchange websites, and books. I started to listen to radio shows I hadn't realized existed. We went to Washington together and marched for rights: rights to a Living Wage. Rights to Health Care. Rights to Healthful Food. What could be more basic than a right to healthful food? .I became involved in their struggle, because it had become my struggle.

A few years later on a beautiful July morning, I was biking into town for a meeting on vegetable gardens. I was early so I bought a cup of coffee and was about to sit down on a stool facing the street when who did I see but Dora Romona. Dora Romona!

I had not seen the mini- massive warehouse for five years! Imagine my surprise. There she was at a back table, partially obscured by a booth, and I was unable to determine if she was in all of her splendid glory, but I would have recognized that dome of brown (and now gray) hair anywhere although the dome was more scraggy and greasy than I recalled.

Her thick neck swiveled — she always seemed to have some sixth sense of when I was around — exposing the iconic pasty and puffy face. The smile she gave was not the triumphant one I so fondly remembered, no, it was rather asymmetric, as if she'd been hit by a bus.

She had a companion with her, but it wasn't Merriweather Snorton. A companion! Imagine Dora Romona with a pal! And not a school pal — my intuition told me that — this was a professional companion — one you paid for. I recalled just then reading a newspaper article about Dora Romona: *Acclaimed Science Chairperson Retires*. There had been a small photo of her: dark circles beneath the eyes, a shiny face, the rag like gray-brown hair, lifeless. She was retiring because she wanted to spend time with family — so the reporter quoted. What family, I wondered? The Family of Camden High? But clearly, even to those not so familiar with the legendary Dora Romona, you could tell she was not the same person.

She was ill.

She beckoned me over, and curious, I walked back into the dark corner of the coffee shop where she had stationed herself. She was in a wheel chair, and I noticed that one side of her listed, as if she'd had a stroke, which I found later to be true. She motioned to me to sit down.

"You always had to do things your way," she said, wheezing dramatically, as if her lungs had shrunk. A 20-something year-old pecking away on an incredibly small computer glanced at us, then turned up her IPod.

I looked at Dora Romona, her brown eyes swimming in flab, the elf-like ears – not so pointed anymore. I said nothing. My way? Of course: Dora Ramona had never had a conscience — not one that worked well anyway — it wasn't part of who she was. I noticed then how dull her eyes were, and I felt a pang of sorrow for her, former renowned Titan now an amorphous, protoplasmic blob. She reminded me of the insane homeless people who lumbered along The Commons, talking to imaginary gods and smacking on pizza crusts left in empty boxes, out on the black wire tables.

"You too," I said. "You always did things your way."

"But I was the boss." She grinned sickly, and I saw that some of her teeth were missing. It must be hard to eat without the essential teeth, I thought. But then Dora Romona had always preferred the soft foods: the Pop Tarts, the cookies. The ice-cream. There had always been little cartons of chocolate pudding in her personal refrigerator. I took one once. Or twice.

"That was my job," she said.

I shrugged, and thought of the line from *Cool Hand Luke* that I liked: *Calling it a job don't make it right, Boss.* I'd recently watched the video with Bob.

"They were all against you," she went on. "Anything you did Marianne and Lenore reported to me. You had your own ideas and that doesn't work in a school system. You either please the administration, or you're out. You never understood that." She cackled: *Eh, eh, eh,* then she wheezed — wheezed and cackled — like a broken washing machine. This went on for the longest time, although it was likely less than 10 seconds. I worried that Dora Romona would expire right in front of me — and perhaps in the final death rattle — lunge for me — so I said nothing, and I waited.

I tried not to inhale.

"Right?" she finally said. She was breathing normally again...well normally for Dora Romona.

"Do you remember Jimi?" I said. "Jimi Agee from Sudan?"

"Jimi?" I saw her face muscles loosen, and for a moment, she looked 80, not 60. So she knew.

"Jimi Agee," I repeated. "He was one of my students. I had him twice—once in ninth grade, and once in eleventh."

"How am I supposed to remember one kid out of thousands?" Her voice shook a little.

"You don't remember students who kill themselves?"

She was sweating, large drops of moisture popping out on her low forehead. She closed her eyes and her ears seemed to shrink.

"That happens. It happens every year."

Did she ever think about all the misery she caused? The lessons she taught—not of compassion or kindness, but of humiliation and cruelty.

There were thousands of students over the years that she and Snorton graduated, 18 year-olds without the slightest notion on how to get a job, how to cook a frugal dinner, or even how to make a friend.

I could have told her how Jimi did it, and the others lives he destroyed, and given her an image to haunt her the rest of her sorry life, but she already had a sorry life. What was the point?

"There are millions of reasons why students kill themselves," she said, her voice barely a whisper.

"Sure." I said to her, narrowing my eyes. "Sure.... You know what, Dora? Maybe I never appreciated the difference between the administrators and the teachers, but I've always known the difference between right and wrong."

I turned my back and started walking out.

"Right and wrong," she said with great indignation, and I kept walking, and she went on about the high school, how it was a family, how everyone had to give, and that was the way it was, the way it had always been and had to be, because there were many people to please, almost screaming now, and everyone was watching her, this little gnome stuck forever in a chair, a shrink-wrap version of her former indomitable self.

When I got outside, I scurried around to the building's back corner, to get one more peek at Dora Romona. Dora Romona! There was the familiar harsh face, exhausted but it brightened considerably when her companion returned and placed a soft cookie on a saucer before Dora Romona. Dora Romona! Had to have her sweets! She took the cookie in her bird-like hand and without even a thank-you, or the slightest glance to her companion, she began to chip away at the confection. This was her life now. Her eyes were totally opaque, like the eyes of a slug.

I spent the next couple of hours with some of my co-workers deciding how to orient a vegetable garden on some vacant land beside their apartment complex.

Where should we site the compost, the lean to? What tools did we really need? We hoped to plant the fall lettuce and beets once we got the raised beds built. Next year we'd plant perennials: rhubarb, asparagus and lovage, which is similar to celery. There would be corn, squash and beans, The Three Sisters — which worked together — and onions, because they were good companion plants. And garlic. Garlic deterred slugs. Once slugs got into a garden—forget it! You had to use all kinds of strategies to eliminate the slugs: copper strips, beer, salt, but planting garlic was the best. And why not have lots of garlic? So many delicious dishes depended on the herb. What was Tuscan white bean soup or basil pesto or polenta and spinach without garlic? Tasteless and empty, devoid of the debonair and elegance one expects from good food. And who did I have to thank for giving me this appreciation for fine food? Dora, of course. (Dora Romona! Dora Romona!) How could I ever forget her?

The Big Burp

Every morning I would run before dawn with Gordon. Nothing in the world made me happier than a strenuous run through the university's arboretum at 5 am. As night gave way to day, the lake's molten surface would slowly came into existence and it was as if I experienced the birth of the world, and every morning it was it was new and fresh and thrilling.

I lived for those moments of transition, the emergence of world and my conscious mind. Back at the rental I'd shower and wipe up the spilled coffee, feed Gordon, then prepare myself for that all-American character-building activity: job hunting. At noon I'd break for a yogurt sandwich mixed with tuna. After lunch I'd read novels — there were only so many jobs to apply for. At four I'd switch to non-fiction — science — before starting dinner at six.

After dinner I'd read more because while reading, I learned that the language of pets was real, and that hot, spicy foods eaten in hot weather makes you sweat, and therefore cools you off. I experienced adventure and love. The risks I took were vicarious, yet I was going somewhere because while living at the rental, I never went out except to run. I had no money. I had no friends. Reading was my portal to knowledge and excitement. Such was my unemployed life back then, and although my life had its moments of inspiration and insight, I still wanted a job.

This was when I was in my twenties.

Brent and I had moved to a college town in the Midwest. After unpacking the essential boxes—we didn't have much, having accomplished our entire move from Houston with a small U-Haul—I job hunted.

The country was in a recession back then and we needed that second income as living on Brent's post-doc pay was impossible. *You should be lucky you're getting paid at all,* was the university's attitude toward Brent.

I applied to many jobs, but without success. No one called to interview me. I thought too much of myself and my education, I garnered, and these businesses knew me better than I knew myself.

Hence, day-after-day I spent in the company of Gordon—loyal running pal and soul mate—and the likes of Paul Auster, Joyce Carol Oates and John Steinbeck. After a few weeks I stopped applying for the good-paying professional jobs, and opted for any professional job. Then any job.

Could I manage a 20-unit apartment complex, or run a holiday store? It was September. The holiday store was gearing up to sell Halloween costumes—college kids really got into dressing up—Star Wars villains and heroes were popular in the 80s; after Halloween, the store would sell Thanksgiving and Christmas knick-knacks.

What about teaching 8th grade science? I did not have a teaching degree but I had enthusiasm and motivation. And I loved science. This was how I portrayed myself.

285

Perhaps it had been foolish to rent an artist's house rather than settle for a cheaper apartment, but Brent and I had had enough of the drunken students stumbling up-and-down metal stairways and blaring REM at four am. We wanted privacy and peace. I applied for just about everything.

One Saturday afternoon in October, while debating whether to rake up the fallen oak leaves or wait until they all fell — our lot was dominated by breathtaking oaks and maples that blotted out the sky — the phone rang. The stark ring echoed in the artist's old house. No one ever called except the landlord, the artist. Or my mother.

My mother called to ask how cold it was in the Midwest and if it had started snowing yet. *Cold doesn't really exist,* I told her: *there's only heat.* I refrained from describing the motion and excitation of millions upon billions and trillions of molecules.

She knew little about the Midwest: she was no reader, and never had been although she played Bridge like a maniac. Bridge kept her mind sharp and gave her the excuse to drink Coke and eat chips loaded with artery-clogging dip.

I thought at first it was Brent on the phone — who else knew our number? But calling for no particular reason was not his thing. He was too busy.

After establishing my identity, the man on the phone asked if I spoke any foreign languages.

"Some Spanish in high school. Who is this?"

"You sent us a resume. This is Dr. Mena, President of Flow Materials Inc, an international company on the cutting edge of porosity and permeability."

"Hello," I said. "Nice to meet you, Dr. Mena." It seemed very unusual to me that a company president would call a potential employee, especially on a Saturday.

"You have science background?"

"Two degrees."

"Can you come in next Sunday? 9:30? I'm out of town this coming week."

"Yes."

"Do you know where we are?"

"I know where you are."

Sunday, Monday or Tuesday: when you aren't working, all days are Sundays, Mondays or Tuesdays, or whatever day you want it to be. I was elated — an interview with a company! But I was also terrified: any job I had gotten in the past I attributed to desperation of a naive and uninformed employer. I had no plan, no strategy to convince anyone to hire me.

Every morning I woke at five and ran, and I ran with more energy after Dr. Mena's phone call. This was a six-mile run, not a hard run when you are twenty-six and full of ambition and in possession of knees that you can't imagine ever aching.

Running gave structure to my life and with structure came a semblance of meaning: no, I wasn't just a housewife following a young academic upstart around the country: I was a runner and a reader, an individual on a journey to a more fulfilling and rewarding life.

This was only chapter two. Starting the day with an accomplishment gave me focus, movement in a forward direction. Back at the artist's rental, I'd feed Gordon and drink coffee, initially with Brent, but more often alone as he would be pedaling off to the Chemistry Department where, after examining carbon atoms under extreme temperature and pressures, he'd report to Dr. Jenkins, and together, they'd devise more experiments. They never ran out of ideas: that's why they were the academicians, spending their lives tinkering and thinking, and getting paid for it. They were like two school boys, constantly in awe of what mischief they could cook up. There was always more work to do.

I kept running. Even if I felt lazy, I ran. And I ran in the freezing rain and snow. The early rising was a legacy inherited from my father, who never slept past six a day in his life, except for his last week of life, bedridden, dying from lung cancer. Having spent 25 years working in Bethlehem Steel's coke ovens, the microscopic coal particles he inhaled finally proved fatal.

A week later I was sitting in the front room, a hot cup of coffee warming my hands (waiting to hear from Dr. Mena), not yet dreading the grind of perusing the steadily diminishing possibilities in the *Classifieds*. Sunlight streamed in through the front room's windows, windows that rose from the floor to the ceiling. Beside an old radio murmuring with classical music was Gordon, stretched out on a rag rug that I had bought at the

Salvation Army on half-price Tuesdays. He chewed contentedly and farted, which was what he did all day. When I happened to look in his direction, he'd burp. "Gordon," I'd say, giving him a big hug: "I love you!"

This was my moment — all mine — when everything was under control: there were no grilled cheese sandwiches burning on the stove, and I had not left my checkbook at the grocery store. Life was working. This was a moment of peace that I knew would not last forever, but a moment that I enjoyed nonetheless. It would be a moment that I could call upon in the future when the need asserted itself.

Then the phone rang and I answered it.

"Hello, Marilyn?" It was my landlord. The artist. "I was hoping I'd catch you."

Where else would I be?

"How is everything?" she said.

"Everything is just fine and dandy." I knew her worries: the fragile, stained glass panels in the front door, the house's old timbers that could go up in flames should a rogue hot coal shoot out of the woodstove, yet I reassured her: we entered and exited through the back door avoiding potential calamity with the glass panels, and we hadn't fired-up the woodstove. Moreover, the upstairs bathroom had not flooded despite the old house's ancient, precarious plumbing, and the lights, supplied with electricity through electrical wiring nearing its useful lifespan, still worked. We hoped to extend our year's lease to two, as Brent's second year of funding had been approved. So I humored her.

"How's New York?" I said.

"Invigorating. Exhilarating. The ideal environment for an artist. And how is…. the dog?"

She could not bring herself to call Gordon by name. Previous renters had tracked in microscopic dog poop. Thus we'd given the artist a hefty security deposit, leaving us broke, and we'd made what Brent and I referred to as Over theres! "Over there!" we'd cry at Gordon, when we saw him crouching near the woodpile, or the tiny storage shed which housed the artist's larger art pieces. The south side of the storage shed was especially vulnerable because this was where the rhubarb would grow in April. But Gordon being Gordon, he'd look up at us as he was relieving himself, grin like dogs do, then trot happily away, tail wagging. And I picked up everything and this was before it became good citizenry to walk your dog with a plastic bag, yet I suspected my vigilance would wane, given a person's natural tendency toward sloth and the impending Midwest below-zero temperatures. I did my best to encourage Gordon to do his business in the arboretum where we ran, along with all other wild creatures of the world.

"Gordon is fine," I said. "He's keeping up his part of the bargain."

Upon hearing his name, Gordon looked up from his lamb bone and grinned. He would chew it down to nothing then lick up any powdery residue. He was a clean dog.

"Be careful of the floor," she said dryly. "His nails. The wood is very soft."

The following Sunday, after another surprisingly brief interview (10 minutes), Dr. Mena hired me. "Can you wear many hats?" he asked. A small man with a penguin-shaped body, the effect heightened by his white-and-black suits, he had wiry hair that sprang up from either side of his small head like a Mr. Potato Head. His was not the kind of head that could easily wear a hat, yet I assured him that *I* could wear as many hats as he had. He looked at me: which hats? So I told him I could write, I could do math, but I stopped short of explaining The Big Burp: millions of methane molecules in thousands of kilometers of muck at the bottoms of deep seas. When the Burp came, Earth would change forever.

"I have great plans for you," Dr. Mena said. He was a small man, and he kept staring at me, watching how I was interpreting this information. I was all ears. I couldn't believe what I was hearing.

"But...it's up to you. Maybe you will be just a technician, or maybe you will be Lab Manager, eh? Or travel around the world, calibrating machines?"

"I would love to travel," I said.

I felt so good that that afternoon that I treated myself to a pecan ice-cream cone at Michael's Ice-Cream, a half-mile walk from the artist's house. The pecans were crisp and fresh, the ice-cream made from milk produced from the university's cows.

As I surveyed the green-and-pink mini-ice-cream palace with the ease of someone who has life all figured out (for the moment happiness reigned, I was blessed), my compelling thought was: I am living the good life. What more could there be?

Then I saw a young couple fawning over an infant, a multicolored knit cap encasing its impossibly small head. Miniature mittens covered its paws. Its tiny eyes were closed, overlain by translucent eyelids. I left with a warm feeling in my stomach, and that surprised me.

The road I took to Dr. Mena's Flow Materials Inc. was long and straight, peppered by family-owned corn-and-cow farms, weatherworn red barns and silver silos. FMI was an R & D establishment on the cutting edge of porosity and flow. Even Brent—Dr. Nanotutbe of the future—was impressed. He couldn't understand why I was hired to do R & D.

My first day at FMI, I was met at the door and shown how to use a plastic card to gain building access. Then there was another door that required a punch-in code. This was all in the interests of protecting Flow Material's vital secrets.

"Make sure you read this," Vanessa, my mentor, instructed me.

Vanessa, a middle-aged woman in a jeans skirt that stopped short of her wobbly knees, was not the happiest person I'd ever met.

So what, I thought, that she doesn't like her job! You don't have to like your job! And she's not a scientist! So why should she like her job? I, on the other hand, was determined to love my job.

She fanned the pages of a haphazardly duplicated booklet. The words were barely legible, yet I thanked her all the same and took possession of Conduct and Code at FMI, and followed her as she led me at a brisk pace to a cubicle equipped with a phone and a computer.

Then I was left on my own.

So I read. I educated myself on the attributes of the *Flow Porometer*, the *Condensation Capillarity* and the *Oxygen-Nitrogen Permeameter*.

When I tired of pressure transducers and envelope surface area calculations, I read Conduct and Code at FMI and it went like this: *Do not gossip. Do not eat at your desk. Do not talk on the phone. Do not take long breaks – and remember to sign out! Do not use the restroom unnecessarily. Do not part the vertical blinds or take non-essential sick days. You are not paid to sit home and sleep in bed!* **A good employee is healthy and never sick. He works very hard.** This was in boldface type across the bottom of each page.

I read for hours without rising from my chair, a comfortable enough chair but its ripped plastic arms and squeaky coils announced its future: the chair had seen better days.

Still, I was getting paid for learning, and this was preferable to mindlessly entering data into a computer. As I read, I heard the echoes of soft shoes as other employees walked by, quietly, no greetings uttered.

An opaque corkboard wall separated me from the human traffic, preventing visual contact. This was to ensure that my important work was not disturbed.

The other employees must have seen my feet, encased in new black shoes which I bought just for this momentous occasion, along with a navy skirt and jacket—yet no one knocked on my corkboard partition, or even stood on their toes to glance over it. Behind my partition, I flipped pages robustly. I blew my nose with even more vigor than usual. Still, no one.

That night, Brent worked late, so I ate dinner with Gordon in the front room, watching the sun set: kibblets for Gordon, beans and rice for me, our usual Monday fare. No matter: so thrilled was I to have an economic identity and a viable place in society. Although it was not a place that moved me, it was a place. This is how you think when you are young.

After dinner, because it was an unusually warm October evening, I ventured out to a coffee shop along State Street with Gordon—who was always cheered by a walk—and I bought a coffee and a plain salt bagel. The coffee was one dollar and the warm salt bagel, 40 cents. I was living the high life.

My second day of work was much like the first, except that I took the liberty of strolling along FMI's main hall on the pretense of using the bathroom. As I passed other employees, they looked down at the worn carpet, and continued on at a glacial pace to their cubicles or the lab. No one spoke a word to me, not even, "Who are you? What are you doing here?" Or: "Are you a spy, trying to steal our technology?" Instead, they set their eyes straight ahead and silently paced the halls.

The third day, as I sat down to read FMI's <u>Porosimeter Manual</u>, the heart of FMI (according to Dr. Mena), I realized that I'd already read the manual. The more I read, the more my eyelids descended.

Thirty machines that measured in one way or another some aspect of permeability or porosity. Was I up to the task? Well ...I had to admit to myself that I hadn't absorbed much information. Was it the Continuous Porometer or the Condensation Porometer that used water vapor? Or did it use alcohol? Which alcohol? And how did it work?

There was no one to consult: everyone passed my corkboard partition without even a cursory greeting. Maybe they wanted me to be fired because they knew I was a fraud: I would be asked to leave, my shoulders sunk to the floor in disgrace. Never again would I have the disposable income to buy coffee and a warm salt bagel. As I sorted through the pile of manuals, internally debating what to do, wondering how damaging *Worked at Flow Materials – 3 Days,* would look on my resume, I suddenly heard a voice above me.

"You seem like a serious and sincere person."

Glancing up, I saw a man in a striped pink shirt and a blue tie. I had the impression that he had been trying to get my attention for several seconds. Of course he had seen the consternation on my face.

"I am!" I quipped. It felt odd speaking aloud in my cubicle, although it felt good to have someone finally talk to me. Vanessa, after our initial meeting, disappeared. I didn't even know where her office was.

"Serious, and sincere. Very sincere!" I added.

"You're sitting at the Desk of Death," the man said. He was 30 or so, an older man, a man of experience, someone I could learn from.

"Desk of Death?" It had a nice ring to it.

"The last seven people who've sat there have either been fired or left prior to firing. FMI has a Hire-and-Purge-Program: massive hiring along with the boss' pep talk: *I have great plans for you: but it's up to you. You could be the lab manager: I can see it! Or you can travel around the world, calibrating machines!* Four months later will be the terminal speech: *Your work has been very disappointing. You will need to be let go.*"

"Should I move?" There were three other cubicles nearby, all empty. Why had I chosen the Desk of Death?

"It won't make any difference."

"Oh."

"Come on. I'll show you around. I'm Jeff."

"Marilyn." We shook hands.

"Have you been in the lab yet?"

"Only briefly."

"I'll show you the machines."

We entered the lab through a door layered with notices in bold red lettering: *Hazardous Materials, No Eating or Drinking,* and

Protective Eyewear Must be Worn. Wear Booties. The vast room was a forest of floor-to-ceiling silver columns, veins and arteries of pipe gleaming in the overhead lighting, some of the piping emerging from the high ceiling. The expansive room gave off an electrical odor of diffuse activity, suggesting we'd entered a province of otherworldliness. I noticed multicolored lines — gas lines, I assumed, — of various dimensions emerging from the silver columns. Some were attached to machines. Everywhere you looked, there were machines and somewhere, I imagined, there must be a heart, the center of engineering, of creativity and logic.

"You see the machines?" Jeff said, gallantly bowing before one.

"Of course."

"Look closely. This one here."

I did. I shrugged.

"Panels are not on, in fact, there's not one machine with all of its panels installed."

"Because?"

"No."

"No?"

"This one right here." He stepped to the other side and indicated a machine with a sample chamber and a piston. I recognized it from one of the manuals I'd read. "It pulls a vacuum. The error of testing is very small, on the order of a torr. In other words, the noise must be less than a torr or the signal will be obliterated. That means one out of 760, being that atmospheric pressure is generally about 760." He waited.

"Of course," I said. "Atmospheric pressure is 760 torr! How had I forgotten that!" Finally, here was someone willing to talk to me, and I didn't want Jeff to think I didn't know about torr. Torrs?

"Now if readings are off by more than 1 torr per hour, then our signal to noise ratio diminishes."

"And the data," I raised my eyebrows, "are not good."

"Exactly." He raised his eyebrows.

"Ah."

"A little leak inviting in the atmosphere," he demonstrated with his thumb and forefinger, "and everything goes to hell. We're measuring flow here, but very *small* differences in flow. Small differences sometimes make all the difference."

I agreed.

The machines tested permeability: permeability of tents, brake pads, tires, bed sheets, diapers, artificial veins, GORE-TEX® clothing, in fact any membrane, powder or material you could imagine.

"Cool," I said, feeling proud that I worked for such an innovative and high-tech company. I considered myself lucky. So I hadn't made a mistake taking this job. This was the job, I reminded myself, that I would love.

"Most of the machines don't work. Almost all have been in various stages of disrepair for months. Years even. This one right here," he put his arm around a machine that had 6 thermos-sized tubes of water, air bubbles rising in the tubes and exploding near the top like some mad scientist's experiment, "has been in the works for over three years."

I looked around. Silver quick-connect lines — I would learn the term later along with swedgelock, pressure transducer, needle valve, vacuum pump — reached out into empty space. Every flat surface was covered with wrenches, tiny screwdrivers, valves, nuts, bolts, tubes of grease and Swack, black o-rings — some the diameter of your little finger. Dozens of motors ran, machines gurgled and spewed out vapors as valves clicked open, then closed, open, and so on. There was a monotone beep, a hum, the sound of a piston ascending then descending, a vacuum being released. There were flolocks, minute-adjustment needle valves, tanks of nitrogen and tanks of oxygen. Tanks of helium.

"It looks complicated, but don't let anyone fool you. The machines all basically work the same way: gas in and gas out. We're watching tiny flows. Recording tiny burps."

"Burps...hmmm." We sidestepped a puddle of clear viscous liquid. When I looked up at Jeff, he raised his eyebrows.

"Your guess is as good as mine. Just don't step in it. It might eat through your shoes."

Flow Materials Inc. had breaks. The breaks were at 10 and 3, and you knew it was break time because a harsh, metallic bell would ring out. The jarring noise was omnipresent and had the power to vibrate your breastbone. The first time I heard the bell I wanted to run out of the building. Yet strangely, yet no one else expressed such indignation; instead, all employees immediately dropped whatever they were doing — and it did not matter if they were in the middle of debugging a program or testing an expensive valve — and rose from their computers or machines, grabbed their worn hooded sweatshirts, their cigarettes and lighters, and moved zombie-like for the back door. Throwing on my light-weight jacket—we didn't have cash for a winter coat for me, and on principle, we never put anything on credit—I followed the zombies outside. There I stood in the cold October sunlight, trying not to shiver. They congregated in the parking lot among the stacked 55-gallon drums, several dozen, their bottoms rusted, stained red or green from which liquids continued to leak. A smell of sulfur hung in the air as if someone was boiling eggs in a giant cauldron. There were other chemical smells too, ones that I could not identify. I kept my distance from the drums.

I wasn't a smoker, but not joining my colleagues would say something unattractive about me. Thus I watched them, especially the women with their dyed hair up in buns. There were two women and they worked in the machine and assembly shop putting machines together and taking them apart. They owned their own tool set.

In the chilling morning air, the employees of FMI bent over and helped one another light cigarettes. No one offered me a cigarette, having concluded that someone who ate peanut butter on whole wheat bread was not the smoking type. I saw what they ate: microwaved sandwiches, cheese curls, Oreo cookies encased in cellophane, and later when I mentioned the limited nutritional value of such treasures to a burly machinist, he said: "You ain't gonna live forever, honey." Then he laughed.

I kept listening, and I learned from them.

"That Joe," a technician said. "His girlfriend had a ring. You know where."

"Yeah." Lenny: six-foot-two, thin, was so thin that he couldn't get his ratty jeans to hang anywhere on his body, and the jeans kept slipping down. He washed his hair monthly (so he told another technician) and hacked at it now and then with a pair of dull scissors while waiting around for a permeability test to finish. His eyes swam around in their sockets and his hands shook constantly.

He was FMI's chief technician.

"You know what a pain in the ass they can be sometimes. He had one too."

"Must have been hard getting it in."

"If you haven't tried it...Anyway, when they were doing it, he ripped it. Now she has three lips rather than two."

"That's crazy, man."

I quietly sidled a few feet to my left, so they could not see my red face, and eavesdropped on another equally intellectual conversation between two engineers.

"Fucking Mena."

"Fucking Mena. He's such a retard."

"A big fucking retard."

"Biggest retard I ever met. Can't even get his fucking passport together to go out of the country."

Then the two men who had been conversing looked up from their cigarettes, having just noticed me.

"A retard, eh?" I finally said. I left off the fucking as it wasn't part of my regular vernacular. Stupid comment, yet to fit in, I felt the need to say something.

The two men continued to smoke their cigarettes.

I quickly made for the back door which I could not open because I had neglected to bring my entry card with me. As I pulled again, hoping that the locking mechanism had screwed up—a realistic hope as most FMI machines did not work properly—Lenny's long fingers appeared right before my very eyes. His magnetic card swept the electric eye, and as it did, I glanced at the underside of his wrist. There was a black tattoo of a dog. Beneath it in red was BOO FOREVER.

Along with our heating bill from October came a phone call from my mother inquiring if it was cold.

Temperatures—temperature: a measure of heat, never cold— hovered near zero during the day and sunk below zero at night. When I got home from work, and it was just Gordon and me, I kept on my wool cap and put a sweatshirt on Gordon, which he appreciated. It was 20 below at night for a week, but I still ran at 5 a.m., I ran with double sweats, double socks, and double gloves. I put two sweatshirts on Gordon.

Cold. There really is no such thing as cold, there is only less heat. And what is heat but quickly moving molecules, molecules traveling from high to low concentration in an effort to reach equilibrium? It's like gas flow, flowing from high to low pressure, all systems attempt to move toward equilibrium.

Our rental was more window than wood, and although it was wonderfully full of light, the windows were a mere sheet of glass—no double panes with argon between to retain the fast moving molecules.

The argon-filled windows were expensive, and the artist never bought anything expensive. That was how she survived and still did her art. That was how she raised her kids alone. Thus, the fast-moving molecules escaped.

I locked all windows—there were 24—and caulked between the spaces. Searching the artist's dark moldy basement for storm widows turned up nothing but piles of old art magazines and tubes of oils, old canvases that should have been tossed out. Why would she save such things?

On the weekend, I called the artist and inquired about the woodstove's operation and where to procure wood. "Paul DeMarr," she told me. "He lives in a small cabin up the road." And she warned me about leaving the stove's bottom vent open.

"Beware of stray sparks," she said ominously. "One tiny stay spark can start an inferno. One spark is all it takes. You'd be surprised."

I went that afternoon to visit Paul DeMarr.

Smoke curly-cued from the cabin's chimney as Paul DeMarr stood outside stacking wood.

"Howdy," he said. He continued to stack wood. He wore thick gloves and a pea-green coat with the stuffing coming out around his left shoulder. His sculpted black eyebrows denoted him as a character of the world. His small cabin, which looked neat and tidy—the world always does after a snowfall — seemed attractive to me. It would be warm and toasty inside (unlike our house), and on the woodstove would be a thick meaty stew bubbling away. Frozen oak leaves crackled underfoot as I came closer to the woodcutter.

A huge pile of logs that had been dumped in his gravel driveway and that pile would be gone before nightfall. I followed him from pile to stack, and introduced myself as Ms. Reynold's renter, seeking a cord of wood.

"I'm listening," he said, as he continued to haul and stack wood, "I just got a lot of work to do before it snows again. One cord?"

"At least." A cord sounded good. "Maybe two or three." I had no idea how big a cord was.

"I could do that. Sometime early next week?"

He quoted a price which was cheaper than our last heating bill.

"We really appreciate it," I told him.

"We?"

"My husband and I."

"Oh." He stopped stacking wood. A snowflake fell on the tip of his nose. We both looked down the road at the artist's white farmhouse, which you could see clearly through the spindly tree branches, now that most of the leaves had fallen.

"He's not around much. He works hard. All post-docs do. He's a post-doc." I always felt proud to say that, as if Brent and I were in this together: he examined the carbon microscopically, and I examined the carbon macroscopically.

"Is that so?" The question was uttered in a way that suggested he knew something that I didn't.

I answered an affirmative.

"Anyone can chop wood, and stack it," Paul said. He returned to stacking. I imagined he did this all day, and when he had enough of stacking, he'd drive out to his woods, his 100 acres on a hill — so the artist mentioned — and chop down a few 40-foot trees and have it all chain-sawed up by nightfall.

"But you need a chain saw," I said. "And they're dangerous." Brent didn't even fix his own bike. He cut his face every time he shaved. Was that the kind of person you'd want to wield a 100-pound chain saw with the potential for whiplash?

"Dangerous they are," Paul said, going back to the pile, picking up more wood. "How about Tuesday?"

"Tuesday?"

"I'll have the cord by Tuesday. Where do you want it?"

"I haven't thought about it."

"Think about where you want it, because you'll have to stack it and eventually bring it in the house."

"By the front door."

"Not the back?"

"It's a longer walk to the stove."

"Whatever makes you happy." Then he grinned at me. Another snowflake landed on the tip of his nose.

Happy? I was happy enough to have a job.

I was eventually assigned a machine—most technicians had 4 or 5—mine was the CCFP: Capacity Condensation Flow Porometer. You obtained job security at FMI by becoming an expert on a two or three machines then hoarding your expertise; thus would the CCFP ensure my success at FMI. And I would have a title, and with the title would come prestige.

I was also beginning to understand why FMI employees disliked Dr. Mena. For instance, it was not unusual for a hose to pop out of a machine and spew out a noxious vapor, causing everyone in the lab squint and cough toward the emergency exit. Dr. Mena would stare at us severely, and even as he tried to stifle his own coughing, he'd admonish us: "What is all this? Where are you going?" Dr. Mena's arms would go every which way, like a Hindu deity, as if to enclose us, to bring us back to our abode, to our duty.

Daily, unless he was out of town, he'd approach Jess, one of the blonde-haired women, and chief machine assembler. "Where is the porometer? Why isn't it done? This machine must be shipped out tomorrow!"

"You didn't give me the specs until this morning," she'd retort. "It's only one o'clock."

"You don't understand the machines!" he'd say, emphasizing the word machines. His eyebrows would arch up, and rather than looking at her, he'd glance around the machine shop, to see who was listening. "This is a two-hour job!" he'd announce to all of the assemblers, who were at their stations, looking busy, screwing on panels or installing pressure transducers. When Mena wasn't on the floor, everyone left their machines to drink coffee and talk. They talked about football, large vegetable gardens and how the price of asphalt shingles had gone up.

"And you've taken the whole morning!" Mena said, then he'd laugh derisively and you'd start to worry that he'd see you standing by exchanging looks with the individual under attack, and then he'd tell you: *you* needed to be *let go*.

"After 5 years, you still don't know what you're doing!" He'd walk away, like a fat duck, his dress shoes clicking rhythmically on the cement floor. He always wore a black suit—the same one, day after day after day.

Next he'd accost a software programmer: "Why does it take you two weeks to write this program? I'm very disappointed in you." Mena didn't understand any of the problems that the programmer came up against such as valves opening when they were supposed to be closing. Why? Why did this happen? Because the wiring was all wrong. Why? Because the electrician had quit, but before he quit, he sabotaged the machine. They always did. Then Mena would fire the programmer, bring in another one, and in a week, the new programmer would have the same problems, but that was 2 weeks ago, and Dr. Mena had already forgotten about the previous programmer's problems.

Thus, at FMI, an organization on the cutting edge of permeability technology, where I still imagined I would someday shine, I kept a low profile.

By late November, I'd fallen into routines, one routine superseded the other, and although routines gave me comfort, they did not challenge me. I'd spend the morning in the lab, gathering data, then in the afternoon, I'd analyze the data with the research director, Dr. Datta, and input the data into a spreadsheet. Gathering the data meant recording three sets of rapidly moving numbers every 10 seconds. Once I knew the trend, I only had to record two sets of data, and then only three digits from each set. Still, after a few hours of this, my mind would reel with exhaustion. A simple computer program could have gathered the data, but we didn't have the code because the programmer who'd written it, not surprisingly, had had a disagreement with Mena. The programmer hadn't been paid. Mena never articulated his goals; if you asked for expectations in writing you could be *let off the job*. Many were. If you asked too many questions, or displayed opposition to Dr. Mena's counter-productive directives, you could be *let off the job;* similarly, if after your three months probation, you asked for the FMI Full Time Employee Letter that stated that you were a bona fide full-time employee, and therefore eligible for benefits, he could say: *You are let off the job. Bye-bye.*

Because we did not have the code, the software program I envisioned needed to be re-written from scratch; thus began the merry-go-round of potential programmers who would hang around for an hour or two as I demonstrated how my machine worked, and describe what I needed the software to do. The potential programmers would give me the required assurance: *I can do that.* During their next visit they might hear one of Mena's harangues *The job isn't done yet! You've had all morning! How can you call yourself an engineer!* Or maybe decide the hassle and uncertainty wasn't worth their effort because Mena never signed contracts. Never. Why should he? The recession that the country was in was deep. Anyone who quit was easily replaced then *let off the job.*

The programmers were all nice guys, many in tough situations. One who hadn't yet completed his college degree, had four young kids and his wife was pregnant with number five.

"What can you do," he said breezily, showing me photos of his angels. "We're Irish." Irish! I fawned over the photos (he had enough of them!) but secretly, I was envious: such happy little cherubs, who would no doubt adopt you as their god. I would not mind a smile of pure delight—adoring me! Me! But I knew how Brent felt about kids, and especially what a baby right now would do to our plans.

Like the others, the Irishman never returned.

In December Brent's professor, Dr. Jenkins, invited us to dinner. Brent was so excited that he went out and bought a new jacket. It was houndstooth with the faux corduroy elbow pads that had been popular in the early 70s, the color and texture resembling the rubber pads one employed to pry open pickle jars. He spent an hour preening in the bathroom and when he emerged, his black hair steaming, standing up like spikes on an iron fence, he sneered at me. "You're wearing that?"

"I am."

"You can't wear jeans. You should wear a dress. No, a skirt. Wool." He sighed. *You should know better,* that sigh said. He went off to polish his shoes.

A tee-shirt with a skirt would not work, I knew. I did own five blouses—one for each day of the week—but they were all in the basement, still cold and damp on the drying rack. The artist, with her limited income, did not own a dryer. Thank god she owned a washer. She did not own a television, but this was no hardship for a couple who read. I searched through the cardboard box where I kept my clothes looking for something suitable. It did not feel right putting my clothes in the artist's dresser, sensing that she'd find out, and disapprove. At the box's bottom I found a wrinkled turtleneck with little fur balls on the sleeve bottoms. It matched reasonably well with the wool skirt that I owned. The skirt was a little high schoolish, but it was solid, and it was pure wool.

Brent suggested makeup, and I complied.

We drove along a potholed road that curved up a steep hill. We missed Dr. Jenkins's house the first time, so well hidden was his small stone castle in the dense pines. And then Brent, who always drove when we ventured out, was a little jumpy, having drunk too much coffee. He always drank a lot of coffee whenever we did something new.

The Jenkins' stone house was surrounded by white snow, unlike our snow which was spotted yellow and brown (Gordon once again, ignoring our human rules) as if something beneath the snow were brewing, in practice for The Big Burp.

From my vast readings of science, I'd discovered a rogue theory: a gigantic burp of methane would suddenly outgass as sea bottoms warmed. Methane was CH_4, mostly carbon. And what was the mechanism for the warmer sea bottom? Warmer sea waters, warmed by increasing CO_2 output, CO_2 generated from combustion of gasoline: 20 pounds of CO2 per pound of gasoline. The Burp would burst from the ocean floor causing chemical and physical changes, great and small. There would be torrential rains in some parts of the world, devastating droughts in others. Thus the Burp would change the way people lived, and the way people thought about themselves.

You could not go back.

"Did you ever hear about the Big Burp?" I asked Brent, as I shivered. The Honda's heater was on the blink.

Brent snorted: he did not approve of activities that required time and energy, yet resulted in no present or future financial gain. His hair was still in spikes, his eyes wide with anticipation of the Jenkinses and in the green glow of our Honda, he looked like an alien.

As we walked from our car to the front doorstep, the view of the opposite ridge and valley wall stopped us in our tracks. The university's spires and its world-renown clock tower seemed to hold up the sky. It was a black sky with a smattering of tiny stars, and in the southeast quadrant, a bright half moon. Lights on the ridge and in the valley glittered ferociously. It was a breathtaking view, one that I could never imagine having from our backyard.

A tyke with big blue eyes greeted us at the front door as a wave of warm fragrant air, cherry-wood scented, wafted over us. The tyke called his parents, then walked off in knee-high rubber boots festooned with cartoon characters, boots clearly not intended for tromping around in mud.

Cautiously I entered, lest my boots which did tromp through mud and other unmentionables, leave an unsavory mark upon the hardwood floor. The artist's floors did not shine so, no, her floors, dark and dull, could have used a good stripping and polishing, and I gleaned that housekeeping was not one of her virtues, and in this way we were soul-mates.

At such moments I could forgive Ms. Reynolds for her misunderstanding of canines, that being there were no dogs inhabiting this house. Then I noticed Brent nodding, making a calculation, but I did not inquire as to his thoughts. There were bare table tops, and what books and reading materials did exist, I would discover later, were neatly shelved in topical and alphabetical order in the built-in book shelves that lined the walls of a library. Imagine a room of solely books and comfy reading chairs! This was a house where everything had a place and rooms had a name. Order and rule reigned. I was not such a keen organizer, but then the artist's house was too small for a library. I glanced at Brent, and he seemed to nod again. It was beneficial to know from time to time what he was thinking, so I could prepare myself.

"Please excuse the construction," Professor Jenkins' wife, Julia Jenkins said. She took our coats and placed them carefully on a stuffed chair next to a matching stuffed couch.

"We decided it was time to do something for ourselves, so we're putting on a wing, but it's taken longer than we anticipated. The first handy man came in hungover. That was not good."

I agreed.

"You could see it. The shoddy workmanship."

I agreed again. Brent had retired to a corner where he was talking excitedly with Dr. Jenkins, using his hands to explain something, then twirling a mobile in the air, to demonstrate the *beauty of mirror symmetry.*

"The second group never cleaned up after themselves. Then we finally connected with a contractor who uses good, reliable people, people who care. More experienced workers. You could tell."

I looked around, seeing nary a smidgen of powdered gypsum board. No half-empty spackle jars or tubes of caulk, their ends plugged with nails.

"But then, you get what you pay for."

"I wouldn't have guessed," I said, imitating her breezy style, flattering her, "that there was construction going on. It's so clean in here!" No dust balls. No dog hairs. No dog! How could anyone live without a dog?

Julia Jenkins was pleased. Brent glanced over at us, and relaxed. Julia Jenkins, even though she was a good 10 years older than I, was fashionably dressed. Her hair was frosted and cut in a way that brought out the best features of her face and her clear blue eyes. Someday, I thought, as I admired the display of colors in that amazing coif, I would have my hair cut like that. But not now.

We heard wispy violin playing a sonata.

"Timothy." She smiled contentedly. "He wants to play for the philharmonic."

We ate hors d'oeuvres of mushrooms and scallops, and perfect squares of expensive chewy breads topped with spicy dressings, food that belonged on the pages of a fancy cooking magazine.

Never had I had such food, and my taste buds, which previously found pleasure in plain bagels and cream cheese, roasted chicken (sometimes dry, sometimes burnt), were in ecstasy.

How much time it must have taken! The meticulously rolled up ham and cheese with a special sauce, stabbed with toothpicks with green flags on the end. This was the first time I had ever seen such things. And the ever perceptive Julia Jenkins responded: "It's all part of my routine. I know exactly what I need to get at the store, and which store I need to get it at. I've made these so many times, that I can prepare them in 40 or 45 minutes."

"Is that all?" I said, nodding. I shot Brent a look: 45 minutes on mushrooms! Brent turned back to Dr. Jenkins who was bringing out one of his son's soccer balls — there were many, apparently you needed many if you were to play soccer in a serious way. They were discussing carbon structure. Never had I seen Brent so happy.

We ate organic greens—none of the *utterly prosaic iceberg lettuce*, which according to Julia was not even very healthful—and feta cheese, carrot slivers and toasted pecans.

We ate by candlelight, which cast a soft glow over an already soft dining room that enveloped us in goldenness. The sense was that we had all arrived at our station in life, or would be shortly. We were lucky.

"You are what you eat, after all," Julia said expertly. "The little extra expense pays off in the long run."

"It's all about carbon!" I said. "With some hydrogen, a little oxygen." I'd had a little too much wine.

Brent frowned.

Julia smiled. "The greens are expensive, but especially for the youngsters, their growing bodies. What passes for *food* these days!"

"What they call food these days!" I cried out.

We smiled at each other.

"A little more wine?"

I held out my etched crystal goblet.

The youngsters sat nearby at a youngster table, eating with manners that I considered impeccable, so unlike the manners of the machinists at Flow Materials, Inc. whose nutrition was obtained from microwaved hot dogs and second-hand smoke.

Mentioning vegetables once to them, they'd guffawed, the

black teeth in the backs of their mouths visible. *We don't eat them! Hah hah hah!* They'd retorted. *You fool,* they'd say in so many different ways throughout the day! The junk food machines in the break room were emptied — completely — at least once-a-week.

Julia Jenkins' main course was flat green noodles with slivered carrots and beans in a cream sauce. "Fettuccini," Julia announced, as she brought the massive wooden bowl to the table. Surprisingly, there weren't a lot of noodles in the bowl. She gave each of us a small portion, and because no more was offered, a small glump was all I had of the rich creamy mass. Asking for more would have stepped over an invisible line.

Brent and Dr. Jenkins discussed carbon's valence electrons, how you could trick carbon into giving up more. It was not easy, Dr. Jenkins said. "What about the Big Burp?" I interjected. Both Dr. Jenkins and Brent glanced in my direction, then they moved on to gallium and silicon.

Before departing, we agreed to pose for a photograph. Julia was a photographer, her specialty being black and white photos of people, people together and people apart. The photos, all neatly framed and arranged in an interesting pattern, filled both sides of their cream-colored foyer. They were the kinds of photographs that you could stare at for hours: they were not the *we are happy and successful people*, which you often see, but rather people caught off-guard, and wanting to impart something wise and trenchant to the viewer. This was my second surprise of the night.

"I photograph everyone," she said. "You look at the photos later, and you find out who that person really is. I'll send you a print," she said to me, winking.

"That was a spectacular house," Brent said, as we made our way to our wonderful Honda. He stopped in the snow, to take one last look at the view. Even the view was organized and symmetrical: the spires on one side of the house, the clock tower on the other. We drove away in the snowy night, the Honda rattling down the isolated curvy road, back to our rental.

Brent drove a little too fast for me, so excited was he, as if driving faster could achieve his goals sooner. I could tell he was hatching a plan.

"What do you think?" He grinned at me.

"The food was good." Yet my stomach felt queasy. I kept tasting scallops—an ominous sign. I would spend the night retching, but it wouldn't happen until I got nice and warm, in bed with Brent.

"The food was good!" he cried. "Is that all?" He swerved on the icy road.

I tried harder. "Well... their kids—their boys," I ventured. "They were ...adorable. The way they cuddled together to watch *Snow White*?"

Brent looked at me: what boys? Then he said, "Where did this Big Burp come from?"

"I read about it."

317

"Don't try to pretend, especially with a high-powered scientist, that you know anything about science. You're out of your league."

"I read about it in a science magazine."

"A science magazine! Popular science, like that Astronomer from Cornell—what's his name—

"—Carl Sagan."

"Sagan," he said with disdain. "A popularizer. Not a real scientist. Only juried magazines— journals—have any credibility. And this idea about a comet starting fires all over the world, and wiping out the dinosaurs? I'm sorry, Marilyn: Jenkins doesn't think much about your arm-chair play-scientist theories. Fires all over the world! Doesn't that sound ludicrous to you?"

I shrugged.

Then he stared ahead, onto the road which had flattened out, and which was leading us back to our rental. Snowflakes accumulated at a rapid rate on the road, making driving treacherous, and I was glad that we left when we did.

When it was our turn for dinner, I threw shovelfuls of snow over the brown and yellow depressions in the snow. I hung Gordon's rag rug on a clothesline that I had strung up between the house and the artist's shed where she kept her bigger projects, and relegated Gordon to the car during the dinner hour.

Unhappy to be confined to a cold, metal box, he chewed a seatbelt strap nearly in half.

The Jenkinses, especially the Dr., would not have appreciated a stealth dog lick as he attempted to eat my pizza—homemade pizza, whose whole wheat crust appealed to the organic side of Julia.

The crust could have risen more. It *was* soggy, but only near the center. Brent did not have an easy time cutting through it, vindicating my conclusions about his dexterity with a chain saw. The tomato sauce was a little sweet (it wasn't organic), and the cheese, not freshly grated, and I knew this, and I could have been more cognizant of the details, but I had been reading Stegner's Crossing to Safety, a novel I could not pull myself away from.

There was a salad with greens, but the greens were bitter and tough. How had that happened? Dr Jenkins wouldn't even try the salad; Julia, on the other hand, proclaimed beet greens healthy, although very unusual as a salad. She said she'd try it sometime at her house. Dessert was chocolate-chip cookies, and I tried culling the burnt ones (reading while cooking is always a mistake!), but Brent absconded with the acceptable ones before I noticed their disappearance.

"You could have made some effort," Brent told me after they left, watching me clean the kitchen.

That comment I was unprepared for: I had undertaken extra shopping expeditions, labored over the pizza, and stripped the cheese into thin manageable lines with a dull knife—without a cheese grater, which of course, the artist lacked. She certainly led the simple life.

"And those cockamamie science ideas. You should read something else. Why don't you take up accounting?"

"I don't feel well today," Lenny, the chief FMI technician, said. It was the Monday after the beet salad dinner with the Jenkinses, and I was trying to procure information about a machine from Lenny, who did not easily surrender information. He had to be bribed; the best bribe, other than alcohol, was dried fruit. I put a small bag of dried banana slices next to his keyboard. He was propped before his favorite machine, the Flow Condensate, his slender fingers off the keyboard for once, looking deflated, like a spaceship commander who just lost a companion on a remote planet. There were games on all his machines, but today, even the games were silent.

"Sorry," I said. I now initiated hellos and conversation at FMI, and it still always surprised me when I got a response. Friendly constituted effort, and with a high turnover rate, who had that kind of effort to be cavalier with?

"It's my own damn fault. I drank too much."

"Drink water," I said. Then I saw the tattoo again, *Boo*, on the underside of his wrist, a wrist that was surprisingly smaller than mine. "Is that a dog?"

"That's my dog. Boo. I loved my dog."

Loved. Then Lenny, greaser of leather-and-chains fame, who dyed his stringy hair jet black before it became the fashion, began to narrate the Tragedy of Boo. Boo had been at the SPCA for two weeks, and was on the short list for euthanasia for repeated antisocial behavior. A roamer and a biter, Boo was a dog who did not like himself. He acted out in the wider social sphere. Why was he so unhappy? So scared? Boo, a handsome mixed breed, enthusiastic and smart as they come, had everything going for him. But he felt unloved. Under-utilized. Unnecessary. Having been in that position himself, Lenny understood. Lenny paid the 50 bucks—money he didn't have—for shots and neutering, and he trained Boo, and got him so that he wasn't scared of himself anymore. He took Boo everywhere with him. You couldn't ask for a better dog.

Boo's job was to guard the house. Lenny lived out in the woods among the skunks, the raccoons, the coyotes and bears.

One day when Lenny was planting his tomatoes, Boo started barking frantically: a black bear had come up so close to Lenny that he could see his yellow fangs.

One look at the bear's dead brown eyes convinced Lenny that he was going to die, but just as suddenly, Boo appeared between them, giving Lenny the opportunity to get his shotgun. Lenny sacred away the bear, but in the meantime, the bear had taken a few swipes at Boo. Lenny ripped off his shirt, swaddled the bleeding Boo and took him to a vet. It was touch-and-go, but the vet was able to save the dog. Lenny had to take out a loan to pay the vet. Boo was tender after the attack, but Lenny nursed him, and Boo protected the house with even more dedication.

That same year, a movie magnate from California bought200 acres adjacent to Lenny's land and built a 6,000-square-foot house. There was a pool and a basketball court for the magnate's teenage boys, who were nothing but trouble.

They held loud beer-drinking parties in the woods and almost burnt the woods down. They teased Boo, who limped as a result of the bear confrontation. Then someone fed him chocolate, which Boo loved.

"A dog eats enough chocolate, and he can die," Lenny said.

How did Lenny know they had fed Boo chocolate? Kids like that brag, and Lenny knew his neighbors.

"Damn yuppies and their damn kids," Lenny said. "All they care about is money."

Then I told Lenny about Gordon: how I found him when Brent and I lived in Houston: undernourished, his black fur matted, never combed. I was running in Herman Park when a car sideswiped Gordon. He followed me home, to my apartment in Montrose, near the Houston Art Museum.

Every day after that, Lenny and I traded dog stories.

In December, I attended two Christmas parties. One was with the university's science department, held in the Andersen House which overlooked the lake. I wore my wool skirt and the maroon turtle neck with the undersleeve balls.

There was lots of rich food and wine, and I ate and drank to my heart's content. After a few drinks, I wandered around blissfully, eavesdropping on conversations. No one cared. And I knew no one except Julia Jenkins, who was lecturing to a bevy of women about how you can eat healthfully during the holidays. She winked a hello to me.

As I was deciding what type of fudge to eat next — fudge with nuts, fudge with cherries, black fudge or white fudge — a female twosome appeared, and after exchanging comments about the elaborate confections, they asked what I did in my spare time.

"I read," I said.

"How interesting," one of the twosome said. "Have you read The Bridges of Madison County?"

I shook my head no. "What's it about?"

"A woman who finds true love."

The other woman giggled.

"True love: what does that mean?" I said. By then I'd had three glasses of wine, and I would say anything that came to my mind, and I wanted to talk. I had doubts about true love, although I understood there were many types of love. There was love that faded after a few months or years; for instance, once you discovered that your soul mate went out of his way to hold the door for others, but wouldn't call you when he was going to be late, as if to teach you a lesson. A lesson about what? As I read Oates, Hoffman, Auster, Steinbeck, Stegner, I went on adventures with their protagonists and consequently refined my definition of love, how love could be like the moon –an old cliché' - waxing and waning — to love as being an intensity of attention, an intensity that did not waver even when life became difficult, in fact, the intensity increased when life became more difficult.

The two women looked at me as I described my theory. They both wore expensive breast-enhancing sweaters of the appropriate holiday colors and diamond earrings reminiscent of the stars in the sky that night we visited the Jenkinses. They were in their mid-thirties, at that age when perhaps you cease to examine definition of major concepts that drive your life. That was how I interpreted their stares as I extemporized on love.

"If you're married," one said, "you know what love is."

"Love means everything," the other said.

"Work," I said, trying to push them to specify. "Love requires work."

"Well..."

I went on: "Love is companionship." I closed my eyes for a moment and brought back the memory of my morning run with Gordon, and how much fun he'd had jumping through the snow, rolling in it, and biting it and looking at me as if to say *Now it's your turn!* It had been his first experience with snow, and he'd been utterly thrilled.

"Maybe you'd like to join our book group?" one of them said. "We meet every other Tuesday at someone's house." She delicately took a bite of the fudge. "That person provides dessert. We always have such lovely desserts."

"Sure," I said. Starting on the fourth glass of wine, as I was, I'd agree to anything! "Do you ever read science?" I asked them.

The two women looked at me, the golden and red pins on their sweaters glittering.

"Science is solid. Factual. Not as open to interpretation as, say, love is. It has definite boundaries. Often black and white boundaries." I was gearing up for an explanation of the Big Burp, and I felt it very important to explain it to someone this night:

right here and now. It had become suddenly essential to my identity. A funny thing about identity: sometimes you want to hide it, and sometimes, you need desperately to reveal it.

"Do we, Tess?" the woman said to her friend. "Read much science?"

"It's really not part of our repertoire. We leave that to the boys."

The two girls giggled, then Tess said: "Go ahead. Tell us about your Big Burp."

So I started with methane, not gaseous methane, but solid methane—slow moving molecules—molecules at temperatures beneath the freezing point, frozen in soils beneath the oceans, and how when ocean waters heat up, the sediments would release the methane, which would appear in the ocean waters as a gigantic burp of gas. Bigger than you could ever imagine.

"That sounds cold," Tess said, shivering, then laughing with her pal.

"Cold?" I said. "There's no such thing as cold, I mean, no scientist has ever gotten any material beneath absolute zero which is minus 273.15 Kelvin. What it is, is vibration of atoms and—"

"How interesting," they both said at the same time. Then with stiff smiles, they wandered off purposely, flowing but stiff.

I picked up a *Scientific American* on a table and sat down and started reading about the Moon's origin: captured or ablated? If captured, then when? To many scientists this was a big problem that required a solution and whoever solved it would be honored by every astronomer and every planetary scientist alive. He—

or she! — would become a celebrity.

As the night wore on, I looked up once or twice, and saw Tess and her friend exchanging presents with the other "girls." These presents were wrapped tightly in shiny wrapping paper with matching bows, a feat I was not capable of. I was keeping a mental list of my limitations: clothes, conversation, now presents. Poise! I had no poise. And attention to detail, because in small calligraphic script at the invitation's bottom, there had been a reminder about a Secret Santa. I was *supposed* to bring a present. But what would I have brought? A few women glanced in my direction, apparently deeming the ratty-haired, plaid-skirted woman-child insignificant, and so I was left alone with the *Scientific American*, and the question of moon ablation or capture, when I heard a familiar voice.

"You need to look like you're having fun."

I looked up to the man who was collecting plates littered with green strawberry tops and crumbs: it was Lenny, Boo's father, dressed in creased black jeans and a green T-shirt that said "Carter's Caterers" discreetly across the front. His black hair had been washed, and it was pulled neatly back into a pony tail.

"What are you doing here?" I said.

"Making a few extra bucks. My brother-in-law is part owner of Carter's. And you?"

I indicated Brent, but I didn't mention he was a post-doc. "The suit coat with the rubber pads." He was chatting with Dr. Jenkins and some other post-docs. How did they find so much to talk about? After five minutes I ran out of conversation, and talking about trivial things exhausted me. I never knew what to say.

"It's a party, Marilyn."

"I know."

"You need to look like you're having fun."

"I am."

"Marilyn, if you make them feel guilty, you'll pay for it later. Take an **hors** d'oeuvre."

I did.

That night, Julia took a photograph of everyone, and sent us all a copy, a Christmas present. When I looked at it, everyone was smiling. Even me. I had decided that she was a liar.

On the way home, Brent asked me what I was angry about.

"What makes you think I was angry?"

"You looked angry, the whole night you looked angry."

I denied it of course. What was there to be angry about?

"You didn't even say hello to Julia."

"She was busy. I tried."

He didn't answer, because he didn't believe me.

FMI had a Christmas party too. It was held in the cramped break room amid the towering junk food machines.

There weren't enough orange plastic chairs to go around, but no one complained: we felt lucky to get an extra half hour for lunch: paid half-hour. The party was potluck, so everyone brought something, clearly their best dishes which required effort and expense, and so there was shrimp and shrimp cocktail, chicken wings, scalloped potatoes, potato salad, fried potatoes, meat platters, mayonnaise and mustard stuffed in sliced green peppers, little sausages in a sweet sauce in a crock pot, fried cheese and macaroni-and- cheese. Dessert was homemade cookies and cakes. There was enough food for 60 people although there were only 25 of us. Dr. Mena was present and for once, he said nothing. In fact, there was very little talk except, "Gee, it's great to have a day off!" And "What are you doing for Christmas?"

Later during the luncheon, Lenny told me he was getting another dog. "I've been too long without a pal," he said.

Brent and I weren't invited to any more parties, because, I assumed —as with FMI—we had reached the limit of one party a year. This made my life easier: other than the wool plaid skirt/maroon turtleneck ensemble, I had no other party clothes. We did have the Jenkinses over once more, and perhaps remembering the insult of the unheated car, Gordon peed on Dr. Jenkins's blazer, which the doctor removed because it was so hot in the farmhouse. I had stoked up the stove, being careful, as the artist had warned me, of stray sparks—but careful of nothing else. How could I have predicted that Gordon would have reacted so? Never had I seen Gordon so jubilant: subterfuge was his specialty. Brent got so angry about the jacket that I thought he'd bury Gordon alive in the arboretum, but as it turned out, Gordon accompanied us as we moved from college to college, and state to state, finally settling in St. Paul, Minnesota. There Brent got tenure. We put $5,000 down on a house and bought furniture that matched. I stopped shopping at the Salvation Army.

It was in Minnesota that Gordon stopped grinning. It was also in Minnesota that I realized I was afraid, and although I could not put a name to my fear, it was a fear that I had been living with much of my life, something deep, slow, and moving.

Old and arthritic, Gordon cried out in pain as he tried to climb the few steps outside to the house's front yard to relieve himself. He'd snarl if I tried picking him up. Gordon, snarling at me! I imagined bone scraping against bone, all ligaments deteriorated. So the kids and I — I had three by then — cooked up a half dozen eggs with hotdogs. We watched Gordon eat out of the pan, scarfing down the feast. Then my eldest, who was 10, and I managed to load old Gordon into the Subaru.

The drive along the country road was so cold that the car's heater couldn't keep us warm, and we shivered even in our thick winter coats. Gordon compensated by farting and burping. No one cared, in fact, we laughed.

When we arrived at the vet's, it was already dark outside. This was an after-hour visit. The vet called us into the examination room and tried giving Gordon a treat, which he refused. Gordon sat on the old tile floor, a floor he had sat on many times before while the vet inspected his mouth and floppy ears, and gave him his vaccinations. This time was different, and Gordon, being the ever-perceptive individual that he was, knew that. I put my arm around his soft neck. The vet got out a shaver, the same kind of shaver that I use to cut my son's hair. The vet shaved a small patch of fur off of Gordon's front right leg. Then she readied a needle, and as it went in, Gordon looked at me as he always did, with love and trust. There was no struggle. He did not even cry out. I held his soft head in my hands as his eyes slowly closed.

The full weight of Gordon laid in my arms.

The next morning I woke up in a deep gloom. I had intended to run, but I could not get out of bed; there was no reason to. How could I run without Gordon?

Running had been an essential part of my life for the past 15 years. On the far side of the bed, Brent snored smoothly, with great contentment. The red numbers on the clock beside our bed said five a.m.. Then it was six. Six-thirty. Dawn would arrive soon, yet here I was, still in bed, my soul darkening by the second. It's easy when you're already in a groove to dig in deeper. There was to be a dinner tonight for one of Brent's young post-docs and his woman partner, and I had not yet decided what to cook: the tried-and-true fettuccini and salad greens, or baked Haddock with rice and broccoli? I could not decide. I could not make a decision about anything.

But I knew that if I did not get out of bed, and get out soon, that my present life would kill me. I was already 97 percent dead, and I needed only a small nudge to go all the way.

At the crossroads of my life, I was. Which way would I go? Brent continued to snore. The tiny clock beside the bed ticked. Then I heard a dog bark—I don't know whose dog it was—but I jumped out of bed—suddenly: it was like jumping into the lake in late May when the water temperature is still close to ice.

The bed rocked, there was a pause in Brent's snoring, but then his steady rhythm resumed. I dressed quickly, layering on the socks and sweats because it was January. Outside it was minus 30. I ran alone, missing Gordon with every step that I took on the hard packed snow. But as I ran, it also occurred to me that many years—15 years—of making Brent happy was enough.

Two other things happened that week: I'd gotten the photo that Julia Jenkins had taken in her house many, many years ago. We had not corresponded, and I don't know why she decided to send me the photo when she did: I had thought she'd forgotten all about me, but maybe she was following Brent in the news: he was where he wanted to be.

Brent and I looked younger, poorer, and comically out-of-date, but clearly, Brent was an up-and-coming Doctor Nanotube: healthy, grinning with that stare that said: "I'm going somewhere. I know what I want in life." But why was this woman with the guy?—you would have asked, if you saw the photo. Equivocation was written all over my face, even in the way I stood. I had no idea where I was going except that I was going along, following in the deeply-entrenched path chosen for me. The moment Julia snapped the photo, I remembered very clearly that I did not know what to do with my mouth, and I ended up with a crooked half smile. Yet if you looked closely at my eyes, you would have seen something else.

That night I did cook the dinner for Brent's post-doc couple: whole wheat pizza with beet green salad.

The dinner brought back memories of that dinner 14 years ago with the Jenkinses, but there were differences: there was no Gordon, but there were kids, although mostly I thought of them as mine as Brent was always away: working in his lab, visiting other labs, giving papers at conferences in Germany or Japan.

He was where he wanted to be, and I knew then that things would never change with him.

The kids normally loved pizza, and didn't mind so much if the crust was not quite crisp, but they couldn't eat much. We all sat around a big table, not knowing what to say to one another, memories of Gordon dominating our thoughts. What would he be doing if he were here, with us now? Brent mentioned the passing of Gordon to the couple, and they offered condolences but admitted they had no dog, that a dog would interfere with their lifestyle.

That week I did something else I'd never done before: I

volunteered for an environmental board. At the first meeting I had to talk in front of people — something I was not used to doing, and it scared me, but I wasn't going to back out.

I had been asked to describe myself and my environmental principles, and my life suddenly took on a new trajectory because the people on the board, to my surprise, welcomed me, and not only that, but they welcomed my ideas: they actually listened to me, and because they did, I talked more. I started reading science again, and talking even more, and this created a momentum and I reached a point where I could not be contained because once the words started, there was no end. It took a few more years, but then my life started to change in many ways, good ways that I had not anticipated, and in ways that I had never imagined possible.

Now, almost 15 years later, my kids are grown, and Brent has a new wife. I have been on other boards, and I have had other dogs, but none like Gordon. I still run, although not as vigorously as when I was in my twenties; my favorite time is still the morning, early morning, that transition time as night turns to day, as the trees become visible, and when anything in life is possible.

Made in the USA
Lexington, KY
19 August 2014